Kyo

L'Arc Berg

Therese

Yomogi

"If there's such a thing as destiny,
then I believe it is mine to put a stop to your ambitions!"

# Table of Contents

## Prologue: The Waves of Another World

"Pwaoooooo!"

The inter-dimensional Ganesha Shadow roared and swung a weapon that looked like oversized Buddhist prayer beads at me.

"Heh!" I blocked the attack with my shield, then grabbed his prayer beads out of the air. His weapon immobilized, the monster raged and roared even louder than before.

"That was awesome! I guess that's why they call you the Shield Hero, eh Kiddo?" L'Arc grunted next to me while he fought another ganesha.

"Awesome? I'm the Shield Hero. If I couldn't block an attack like that, what good would I be?"

I didn't feel like I had to explain myself to him, but it was true. Since I came to that new world, my main role in battle was to use my high defense rating to block the attacks of enemies. I guess I was sort of an exception.

I should mention that I was currently in yet another world, one that lay on the other side of the dimensional rifts that accompanied the waves of destruction.

"Don't let your guard down! Pay attention, will you, Boy?"

"Hey Kiddo, you better stop calling me 'Boy'!"

"If you keep calling me 'Kiddo,' I'm going to keep calling you 'Boy'!" Just then I got an even better idea, based on what I knew about his background. "Maybe I should call you 'Nobunaga' instead?"

"Hey! How did you know that Kizuna used to call me that?!"

I guess it fit pretty well. I'd have to remember to compliment Kizuna on her nicknaming skills.

"Mr. Naofumi, maybe you should stop with all the nicknames."

"Ahaha!"

"Don't just laugh it off!"

"Then let me be more clear about it. Aren't I the one who named a king and princess 'Trash' and 'Bitch'?"

"You're worse than I thought, Kiddo."

"This is why you're so often misunderstood . . ."

"It's true though, isn't it?"

"But you should tell him the circumstances around it, or he won't understand."

"I know, Kiddo, well enough, to figure that they had it coming."

"You think you know everything!"

If he was going to understand something about me, I wished he'd start with something else. It was kind of depressing. Why did we have to talk about things like this?

We were enemies up until a short while ago, but now we

were on the same team and already acting like old friends.

But we were getting too comfortable, and I had to make sure we didn't forget the reason we were here in the first place. I'd better go over it all from the beginning.

My name is Naofumi Iwatani. I was a typical otaku, college student back in Japan. One day I went to the local library and found a book called *The Records of the Four Holy Weapons*. I started reading it, only to find myself actually summoned to the world it depicted, as one of the characters in the book: The Shield Hero.

The people that summoned me asked me to lend them my strength to help save the world.

And, well, a whole lot of stuff happened after that.

"L'Arc, you understand Mr. Naofumi so well!"

"I know all sorts of people, so right from the get-go I could tell that he wasn't a bad guy."

"I'm the worst kind of guy!"

"Oh yeah, you think you're really tough, don't ya?"

"Shut up!"

What was WITH this guy?

By the way, the guy that was pretending to know all about me was L'Arc. That was short for L'Arc Berg. I still didn't know his last name.

He was an experienced adventurer in his late twenties. Generally, he was a pretty charming guy. He knew how to get people on his side. Sometimes he was a little childish, but that was probably just part of his charm.

When we first met he was wearing a set of light armor, but when we met up again, in this new world, he was dressed— I don't know why—like a member of the Shinsengumi. The style suited him, but I wondered which one was his usual look.

After all, Glass wore a kimono, and Kizuna wore a haori over a lolita-style dress.

He probably chose the clothes based on their effects. Maybe the Shinsengumi clothes he had picked up while sneaking around in this world were actually better than the light armor.

Why did I care so much about his clothes anyway? Alright, enough of that. Moving on.

"Just hurry up and kill the thing, will you? I'm tired of holding it down."

I'd kept my grip on the inter-dimensional Ganesha Shadow the entire time we'd been talking. It was one of the larger monsters in the area. It might have been a boss, but I wasn't sure yet. Its attacks were intense, but nothing we couldn't handle. The reason I was able to withstand its attacks so easily was related to the legendary shield I'd held since the moment I was summoned to the new world.

I couldn't take the shield off. It was like a curse. But I could absorb all sorts of items and materials into it, and doing so unlocked different versions of the shield. And those new versions all came with new abilities.

I became stronger by unlocking those abilities.

All of that was well and fine, but it came with a significant drawback: I wasn't able to deal any damage on my own. So, I needed party members that could handle all the offensive duties in battle.

"Mr. Naofumi! I'm going in!"

"Then I leave it to you."

"Okay!"

The girl that just rushed forward to attack the monster I was restraining was Raphtalia, a demi-human girl that used to be a slave. Demi-humans looked like humans, except they tended to have animal-like features, too. Raphtalia was a raccoon-type demi-human, and she had ears and a tail that looked like a raccoon, or maybe a tanuki.

She was also my most trusted companion. She was sort of like a daughter to me.

At the moment she was dressed in a miko outfit, and it looked great on her. L'Arc had encouraged her to wear it. She looked so good in it, in fact, that I hoped she would keep wearing it after all the business in this world was behind us.

"Hya! Instant Blade: Mist!"

Raphtalia flashed by the inter-dimensional Ganesha Shadow, her katana cutting deep into its flesh as she passed.

That was all it took to defeat the monster. It split into two pieces and disappeared.

"Alright! On to the next one! This wave's monsters seem stronger than normal!"

"I agree! They seem stronger than the monsters in our world, too."

Raphtalia was holding a special katana. Perhaps it was part of her mysterious destiny, but she had been chosen to wield the katana of the vassal weapons in the world on the other side of the wave's dimensional rifts.

I'll explain it all later, but it meant that she had become far more powerful than an ordinary person could ever hope to become.

"Watch out, master! Another monster is coming!" Filo called down from the sky above us.

She was a young monster-girl, and she loved to pull carriages. She used to also be a large, ostrich-like monster called a filolial. She had the ability to transform into a young girl with angel wings on her back, and she fought alongside me—or rather, under my leadership.

She was actually extremely powerful on the battlefield. Anyone deceived by her appearance would quickly come to regret it.

But, after we came to this other world, her monster form had changed. She was no longer a filolial, and that meant that her fighting style had changed too. In this world she was a humming fairy, a type of monster that turned into dramatically different things as it matured.

There was one point in particular that was very different between filolials and humming fairies—filolials can't fly, but humming fairies can. So now that Filo could fly, she had taken to the skies to observe the movements of the battle.

Of course the wave's monsters were throwing things at Filo and trying to hit her with magic, but she was very quick and had no trouble dodging whatever they threw at her.

"Let's do this!"

"Feh . . ."

That was Rishia. She was running towards me with a horde of monsters in tow. That must have been what Filo was trying to warn me about. I thought Rishia went to join Glass and Kizuna.

Her full name was Rishia Ivyred, and she was a human girl. She came from a ruined noble family back in Melromarc. She used to be on the Bow Hero's team. The Bow Hero was one of my fellow heroes, Itsuki Kawasumi. Then one day she did something in a wave battle that enraged him. Out of spite, he kicked her out of his party. That's when I found her, in trouble. So, I put her in my party.

She was very timid, but she came from a good background and had received a good education. Had this been a game, I'd say she was the sort of character whose status points had all been assigned to a stat that I couldn't see yet.

"Air Strike Shield!"

I used a skill that caused a shield to appear in mid-air, blocking the attacks of the monsters that were bearing down on Rishia as she ran.

Skills were a special kind of technique that only heroes like myself could use.

"Rishia! Are you alright?!"

"Feh? Y . . . Yes!"

"I thought you were with Kizuna! What happened?!"

"Kizuna and Glass are on the verge of being overrun by monsters, so they asked me to come get you!"

"Oh. Well, they are on the front lines, so I guess they need some help."

I'd sent Rishia to fight with them, because I thought it would be good experience for her. I guess she'd been in a little over her head.

As for what I'd been up to? My team had been focused on evacuating anyone caught in the monsters' path.

The wave had arrived close to a village, so we were very busy trying to save as many people as we could. Come to think of it, the waves always seemed to occur near villages. But, then again, I'd only fought in three waves so far. That probably wasn't enough to start drawing conclusions.

Anyway, the other group of teammates on the front lines, at the moment, was led by Kizuna Kazayama, who was one of the four holy heroes of this world—another world separate from the one that had summoned me.

She was called the Hunting Hero, which wasn't one of the four heroes back in the world that had summoned me. She fought with a wide variety of tools and weapons, all of which were loosely related to hunting or fishing in some way. She could use a wide variety of weapons, but she was also subject to a strict limitation: she was only able to fight against monsters and animals. She was useless in a battle against other people. Like myself, she probably also had some way to deal damage to people when she really had to, but it wouldn't be easy. It wasn't something she could just make happen whenever she wanted.

She appeared to be a young girl who wore her hair pinned up on the side, and she wore a haori over a gothic, lolita-style dress. But she said that she was eighteen years old.

I met her just after we came to this new world. We chased our enemy, Kyo, through a dimensional rift, only to fall into his trap and find ourselves imprisoned in a never-ending labyrinth.

With Kizuna's cooperation, we were eventually able to escape. After getting out of the labyrinth, we also found a way to sneak out of the enemy country that had imprisoned both of us in the labyrinth to begin with. Lots of things happened along the way.

It turned out that soul-healing water, a medicine that replenishes spent SP, didn't exist in this world. So, we made some and sold it for a high price. We used the money to buy earth crystals, which were an ore that actually gave experience points to people from the world that summoned me. Finally, we ended up fighting and defeating an obnoxious guy that was trying to kill Raphtalia. He was trying to kill her because he didn't like that the katana of the vassal weapons had chosen her over him.

Something about that guy had really reminded me of Kyo. He acted a lot like him. I guess this new world was full of jerks like that. No matter what world I found myself in, there was always trouble to deal with.

"Hey L'Arc, think Kizuna is having trouble? Is she asking for help because she can't attack?"

"Hm . . . Good question. To be honest, I don't really know."

The enemy had the word "shadow" attached to their names, which made me think that they would still be considered monsters. But who knew if Kizuna's weapons would agree with my judgement?

As for myself, it didn't matter if I was attacking a person or a monster, because none of my attacks did any damage to begin with. I thought that I might be able to get around the issue by using a tool, so I once tried throwing a bomb at an enemy. It just bounced off of them and rolled harmlessly to the ground. And yet, I was able to use weed killer to kill a plant-type monster once, so the rules were sometimes confusing.

Kizuna had a similar problem. Her ability to deal damage to an enemy depended on whether or not it was considered a person or a monster, and sometimes that line was hard to distinguish.

"Let's go then, quickly, L'Arc!"

"Right, I'm worried about Kizuna, too. Therese, let's finish this!"

That was Therese Alexanderite who was fighting side by side with L'Arc. She was a crystal-person, a Jewel. Jewels were a type of human that only existed in this new world on the other side of the wave's dimensional rifts, which I'm going to start calling "Kizuna's world" for the sake of brevity.

Jewels were a race of people that were born with a gemstone that served as a kind of magical core. They were skilled with magic, and were known for their dexterity. They were also known for being very sensitive, and based on the way that Therese had reacted to the bangle I made her, I agreed.

She had been hiding out with L'Arc, so she was wearing hakama, too.

"Great power in these stones, hear my plea and show yourself. My name is Therese Alexanderite, and I am your friend. Give me the strength to annihilate them!"

"Shining Stones: Ruby Flame!"

"Fusion Technique! Ruby Disc!"

A spinning wheel of ruby flame shot from L'Arc's scythe and slammed into the monsters that were chasing Rishia.

Skills could often be combined with the skills of other party members to make combo skills. I'd used them a few times with Raphtalia and Filo.

"Come on, Kiddo! Let's go!"

"You make all the decisions now, do you? Fine, let's go!"

"Although if Kizuna and Glass are fighting together, I'm pretty sure they'll be just fine."

I should tell you about Glass next. She looked like a ghost, wore a kimono, and fought with folding fans. Her hair was jet black, and her skin was so white it was nearly transparent . . . it actually might have been a bit transparent.

Her fans were one of the vassal weapons.

Kizuna was close friends with Glass, and she was really upset when she found out that Glass had been trying to kill me. Glass was very cold and sharp—she looked like she could kill you just by looking at you. But, she was different around Kizuna. She relaxed, she smiled.

Because of Kizuna's mediation, Glass and I now fought together.

L'Arc and I ran to help Kizuna and Glass.

Monsters poured from the dimensional rifts in the wave. This time they looked like monsters straight out of Indian mythology. Wasn't Ganesha basically an elephant-human hybrid?

There were also inter-dimensional ifrits, which looked like fire spirits. I saw some other monsters called inter-dimensonal nagaraja.

There were a lot of human-like monsters, too. They didn't seem to understand language, so I figured they were probably monsters, not people—even accounting for the wide variety of human-like people in these other worlds. They were pretty powerful.

Most of the monsters were powerful, actually. This wave was quite a bit more difficult than any of the other waves I'd fought in.

Over the past few days of training I'd managed to get to level 75, and I had powered up my shields considerably, but the enemy still had attacks that nearly broke through my defenses. I still hadn't recovered the sort of abilities I'd had in the last world, the world that had summoned me. It was a bit like playing an away game.

L'Arc had said the same thing.

"You don't think someone with a vassal weapon came with this wave, do you? Like Glass did?"

"That's not funny, Kiddo!"

"I wasn't joking!"

We went on yelling back and forth as we held off the monsters. Eventually, the dimensional rifts closed.

High in the sky above our heads, an enormous ship hovered and was engaged in battle with flying monsters that looked like garudas. The battle was fierce.

A lot of people had joined us in our fight against the wave.

"Looks like it's pretty much over."

"There were tons of monsters this time. I guess it just took some time to get rid of them all."

"Kiddo, you really had me worried there for a minute."

"Well, it's what you were doing. Don't forget that."

"I haven't forgotten, but it isn't something to make light of."

He'd crossed over to another world to kill its heroes, but now he was afraid to even think of the same thing happening to him.

"Hey!" Kizuna shouted, running over to us. Glass was right behind her.

"You asked for help, but it doesn't look like you needed it."

"Yeah, well, I asked Rishia to get you, and a bunch of the monsters followed her when she left. We ended up handling the leftovers ourselves."

I was impressed that Rishia had done as well as she had, especially considering how weak she was. Her stats never seemed to match her level, but at least she'd managed to stay alive this whole time.

"We were going to help her, but we had too many monsters to deal with ourselves. Besides, Rishia took off screaming and running."

"Yeah, yeah."

I could picture it easily enough. What monster wouldn't be drawn to that pathetic "fehhhh" of hers?"

"Rafu!"

"Feh?!"

The little creature sitting on Rishia's shoulder was Raph-chan. Raph-chan was my shikigami; we made her out of Raphtalia's hair. She was cute, a small little creature that looked something like a mix between a tanuki and a raccoon.

She looked like Raphtalia—if Raphtalia were turned into an animal.

She was a happy, energetic little creature. For some reason, she was currently riding on Rishia's back.

"Did you protect Rishia?"

"Rafu!" she barked and nodded.

Raph-chan was able to use the same illusion magic as Raphtalia.

When Raph-chan cast illusion magic on monsters, they weren't able to land any attacks on Rishia.

"Good work, Raph-chan."

"Rafu!"

"Pen!" chirped Chris. Chris was a penguin, and was Kizuna

and Glass's shikigami. It really looked exactly like a penguin. Chris has been around for longer than Raph-chan.

"You too, Chris. Thanks for protecting Rishia," said Kizuna.

"You did an excellent job," added Glass.

Raph-chan was the one who had really helped though—I made a point of rubbing her head in a way that everyone could see.

"Mr. Naofumi, what are you acting so competitive for? We have more important things to discuss," Raphtalia said, grabbing my shoulder. Raphtalia didn't seem to be very fond of Raph-chan.

"Kizuna, were you able to fight most of those monsters?"

"Most of them. I was a little concerned about the ones named after gods, but as it turns out, they were all just normal monsters."

Ganesha, ifrits, the snake-like nagas, the half-snake-half-human nagarajas . . . there were plenty of different monsters.

"What was the boss monster like?"

"It was an inter-dimensional girimekhala, but there was a mode-change halfway through and it became an airavata."

The boss was an elephant? How boring! I only knew what it was because I was such an otaku.

"Let's absorb as many materials as we can, then head back to the castle."

Kizuna called to Ethnobalt, who was waiting in the sky above us. He was from Kizuna's world, and used the ship of the vassal weapons. When he came to battle, he usually hung back and offered support from a distance.

Apparently he didn't like fighting.

He was a young boy that dressed like a wizard . . . or at least that's how he appeared at first glance. His true form was a monster, like Filo. I knew that he was some kind of rabbit, but I didn't know any more than that.

He was a skilled fortune teller, and he was the one that created Raph-chan for me. Judging from how useful Raph-chan had proven in the hunt for Raphtalia, Ethnobalt's abilities were the real deal.

"But seriously—Why do I have to come all the way to this world and fight in *your* waves?"

"You're asking that *now*?"

"Hey, I didn't come here because I wanted to fight in more waves. I'm just helping out on the side, while I've got the time."

"Yeah I know. And thank you for fighting on behalf of our world."

"Yeah, yeah . . . Let's head back and get ready for the next step. "

What did people in this world think the waves were? They happened all over the world, so it was hard to come up with one explanation that fit everything. Waves . . .

Back in the last world, the one that summoned me, I'd thought of them as a natural disaster. Now I knew that wasn't quite right. I'd finally learned what they really were, and I'd never have known if I hadn't crossed over to Kizuna's world.

The waves were, supposedly, a phenomenon that happened when worlds fused together. I say "supposedly" because this was all just something I'd heard. I didn't have proof one way or the other. In Kizuna's world there were records of fusions that had happened in the distant past.

If the worlds fused any more than they already had, they would be destroyed . . . or so they said. According to the legend, the way to save your world from destruction was to cross over to another world during a wave event and kill the four holy heroes (the people who hold the holy weapons) of the other world. If you did that, then their world would be destroyed and the life of your own world would be extended.

That was why Glass had crossed over into our world and tried to kill me . . . or so she said.

When Kizuna learned what had happen she was livid. She resolved to find another way to save her world.

Furthermore, back in the other world there was a monster called the Spirit Tortoise, and it sacrificed people and used their souls to produce a magic barrier that would prevent waves from happening.

As you might have guessed, there were monsters in Kizuna's world that could do the same thing.

Some of them had already been dealt with, like the White

Tiger, but there were four holy beasts here. I'd also heard them called the Four Symbols.

There was a so-called genius scientist here, who I liked to call Trash #2, and he had found a way to make replicas of the defeated White Tiger, turning those copies into weapons of war.

"We can't spend all our time thinking about the waves. There's a limit to how much time we can stay here."

"I know that! I'm doing all I can to help you," Kizuna said.

We had our own mission to accomplish. We had to punish Kyo for what he'd done to our world, for what he'd done to Ost. We had to bring the Spirit Tortoise's energy back to our world.

There was no time to waste.

# Chapter One: Otherworldly Techniques

"Alright then . . ."

I went back to what I had been doing before the wave came.

L'Arc was a king . . . or *boy*, and had a castle. I worked in a small workshop in the surrounding town for a few days. The culture there was interesting, a kind of a reflection of L'Arc himself. It was a near perfect mix of east and west.

People wore Japanese-style kimonos, but with Western sets of armor over them. No one thought it was strange. The neighboring countries were very Japan-like, and I'd heard that the eastern influence came in over the borders.

I was borrowing Romina the blacksmith's workshop to craft some accessories. Romina had made everyone's equipment.

It was a good place to work. I could quickly respond to questions or requests that Romina had, and I could get to the castle easily if anything important came up. Going to Kizuna's house every night was a little annoying because of the trek to the next town, so I was pretty content to borrow the workshop for a few days.

Raphtalia, Rishia, and Filo were all at the castle, training with L'Arc.

Raph-chan and Therese were both fascinated by my accessory crafting, so they stayed behind to watch me work. They were always interrupting me with stupid questions, so I did all that I could to ignore them. I couldn't help but feel like we were getting a bit too comfortable, but it was all we could do at the moment..

"So let's make a plan . . ." Kizuna said, walking in with Glass. She leaned on the counter and showed Romina the materials she'd gotten from the wave monsters, then asked for new equipment to be made.

They looked like they wanted to talk to me about strategy when they finished placing their equipment orders.

"Hey, there's something I wanted to ask you about."

"What?"

"If the waves occur so frequently, how do you deal with them all?"

"You should ask Glass about that."

"Indeed, we are very careful about such things."

"So? What do you do?"

"Romina, do you have one of those things here?"

"Yes. I get a lot of orders for them," Romina said, producing a necklace from behind the counter. There was a large gemstone hanging from it.

There were a number of different designs from what I could tell, but they all incorporated a large gemstone.

Was it a crystal? The stone shone with a faint light.

"This is a special tool that instantly transports its user to the site of a wave occurrence."

"Hey, that's pretty impressive."

The people in Kizuna's world had apparently done quite a bit of research into the different functions of the heroes' weapons. They invented ways to mimic the drop item functionality of them, which was impossible in the world that I came from. It required a special machine and the use of the dragon hourglass, but the technology was still very impressive.

"Yeah. The Jewels were the first people to make them."

"Hm . . . And?"

"So our friends all have these, and they are posted around the world to battle the waves whenever and wherever they occur."

"You certainly seem to know a lot of good people."

Kizuna had been summoned to this world before the waves started coming, and after going on a number of adventures, she ended up being thrown into an inescapable labyrinth. Before that she had met quite a lot of people.

"The ones I know of are on sale in the marketplace. They sell them to normal adventurers who want to battle in the waves."

"Just for the good of the world? There are so many noble people around here!"

Too bad there wasn't anyone like that in the world that I'd come from. Some adventurers had actually volunteered to help during the wave on the Cal Mira islands, but we never would have won that battle had it not been for the heroes.

"A lot of people show up to battle in the waves. Turns out they are mostly after the rare materials they can get from the monsters."

"Ah . . . Yeah, I guess that makes sense."

If they had the opportunity to get their hands on rare items and technologies, then a lot of people would probably show up—even if they had to put themselves at considerable risk. That must have been why some of the adventurers I'd met seemed to be used to handling themselves on the battlefield.

"I'm kind of jealous."

Deep knowledge of the waves was very uncommon in the world that had summoned me, and perhaps because of that, it was very rare to get any help from anyone when the waves came. Granted, a few adventurers here and there would get caught up in a wave if it happened to occur where they were, but they didn't help out very much when it came time to battle.

There were times when the waves would end even if the heroes didn't come to battle, but now I wondered if that was because someone in the other world was closing the dimensional rifts from their side.

Theoretically, there was a way to confirm my suspicion, but I couldn't think of a way to talk to whoever was on the other side of the rifts. There was also no way to know what sort of person we'd end up running into. What if they just attacked us? It was probably better to just leave them alone.

Back to the topic at hand—if there was an item that would automatically allow its user to participate in a wave battle, I wanted to get my hands on it. I figured it would prove useful once we finished up in this world and went back to the one that had summoned me.

Not only would it make my job as a hero easier, but I could probably make money if I found a way to mass produce it.

"I'd really like one of those."

Kizuna and Romina nodded as if they understood exactly what I was thinking.

"Naofumi, you love that kind of thing, don't you?"

"Alto makes that same face."

They had figured that I wanted to sell the necklaces back in the previous world. I must have really gotten a reputation as a penny-pincher.

"I'm just not sure that anyone back in my world is serious about fighting the waves. Not even the seven star heroes or the four holy heroes."

The other heroes, aside from myself, showed up in that world already knowing how things worked there. They used it to get ahead—but then they accused me of cheating when they realized my leveling and strength had outpaced them. They acted like everything was a game, even the waves. They weren't serious about anything at all.

Besides, when the second wave came, they were barely able to survive the fight with the boss. Any wave that came now would be much more powerful than that, so I wasn't sure how much I could count on them. A lot of the waves were left to Fitoria, the legendary filolial, to deal with. She was apparently very busy running around the world taking care of waves wherever they popped up.

I wonder how they were holding up without me.

I'd heard there were other heroes called the seven star heroes, but I'd never even met them. I didn't know who they were, but it was best to prepare for the worst. If these necklaces would help me do that, then I wanted them.

"Oh, I almost forgot! I figured something out after speaking with Glass."

"What?"

"She says that since I participated in the wave battle this time, the next wave will take longer to come to this area."

"Oh yeah?"

Kizuna mentioned something about that before—she'd

said that there was a reason the four holy heroes needed to battle against the waves.

There was a legend in her world that said the lifespan of the world itself could be extended if the four holy heroes of another world were killed. But even though Kizuna was a holy hero, she wasn't able to do any damage to human opponents, which meant that she had practically nothing to gain from participating in the wave battles.

She could either change the way she was registered in the party, or . . . at the very worst, she could avoid the waves by making sure she was in an inescapable labyrinth when they came. At least one of these inconsistencies was cleared up now. If the four holy heroes helped battle the waves, it would increase the time until the next wave came . . . at least according to Glass.

That was certainly a good hypothesis. We'd just have to try it a few more times to confirm that it was true.

"If there are a lot of adventurers helping battle the waves when they come, are they pretty easy to deal with in this world?"

Just then a person ducked into the workshop and blurted out, "Not exactly."

I turned to see who it was, and found myself looking at a person with blond hair, a man I think. His hair was pulled into a ponytail that hung over one of his shoulders. He reminded me a bit of Motoyasu Kitamura, only he didn't look Japanese and seemed a lot more relaxed, nicer.

Maybe he was some kind of new and improved spear hero of this world?

Motoyasu only thought of women. They were all he talked about. This guy didn't seem to have that obnoxious tendency. Was he an acquaintance of Kizuna? Kizuna was pretty attractive herself, but apparently so were all of her friends.

Judging from the way he dressed, I guessed he might be a merchant of some kind. His clothes were plain, but high quality.

"Alto!" Kizuna said, rushing over to hug the man.

So his name was "Alto." I wasn't sure if that was his real name or if it was a nickname.

"I heard from the guild that you were back. I walked away from a negotiation to come see you!"

"It's been so long! How have you been?"

"There's no point in asking that of a merchant."

He was vague. That was how merchants were. They never let on to how much they were making, I guess. If they did, it was like a get-rich scheme or something. But, I always held that if you were doing well, just show people, and that's how you attract more customers.

"Well, well. I heard a rumor that a holy hero from another world was here and also a savvy businessman. Guess it was true after all!"

He looked over at me and I met his gaze. Sparks were flying!

I suddenly realized that I could trust him as a businessman, but I probably couldn't trust him as a person. He looked like the kind of person that would betray you when the timing suited him. But wherever profit was involved, he could be trusted to act in its best interest.

I suddenly realized that I'd heard his name before.

"His name is Altorese. We call him Alto for short. He's a friend of mine. We used to run a shop together."

"I deal in anything there's a market for. Lately information has been fetching the highest price."

I'd been worried that he was going to be like the slave trader back in Melromarc, but he seemed like the sort of guy I could at least see eye to eye with. That is, if he was the sort of person that he seemed to be.

"This is a holy hero of another world, the Shield Hero. His name is Naofumi Iwatani."

He seemed a little soft-spoken, actually. That kind of reminded me of Itsuki. I wondered what he was really like—on the inside. If he was the merchant that everyone made him out to be, he probably wouldn't have an obsession with championing justice everywhere he went.

If he understood money, then at least we'd have that much in common.

"Why do you look so relieved?"

"You're the first person to ever look relieved at meeting Alto."

Glass and Kizuna were apparently perplexed by my reaction, they cocked their heads in confusion. What was so strange?

"He seems like an alright guy. He doesn't seem like some of the nasty merchants back where I come from."

"You really think so? Alto can be pretty ruthless when it comes to business."

"It we aren't judging from appearances, then maybe I'm wrong. But, let me show you how merchants look where I'm from."

I narrowed my eyes and glared at him, challenging him. Depending on the person, some people probably even saw light flashing in my eyes when I did that.

Alto looked almost worried! He immediately turned away.

He was good, sure—but it didn't look like he'd learned how to put on an act so that other people wouldn't be able to figure out how you really felt. And yet, if his timidity was actually an act, he'd really be impressive.

"So what was this? I thought waves would be easier with adventurers helping out, but you didn't seem to agree."

"Oh yeah, that's right. There are a lot of people willing to show you how brave they are, but aren't really strong enough to do anything."

"Yeah, I figured as much. Adventurers usually can't be as powerful as people with vassal weapons or the legendary heroes."

"But that's not what I meant. I mean there's the country . . . and other people too."

What was he talking about? There wasn't enough information to even guess. Even Kizuna looked confused. Luckily, Glass looked like she knew what was going on.

I was starting to figure it out too. Glass and Kizuna and the others were serious about fighting the waves, but what about that Trash #2 guy we recently defeated, Kyo, the holder of the book vassal weapon, and others like them? They certainly didn't seem to care about anything but themselves.

"The vassal weapons holders in enemy lands don't care about the waves, do they?"

"Exactly—good instincts. Actually most people don't seem to care, aside from the four holy heroes and the holders of vassal weapons that have aligned with them."

"You mean there are holders of holy weapons besides me?!"

"Yes, they were summoned quite a while ago."

Glass looked more pale than normal. Something must have gone wrong. If there were problems with the other heroes, I had plenty of sympathy. Just the idea of trying to convince the other stupid heroes of all this when I got back to the world I'd come from was exhausting.

"I've met them, just one time. However . . ."

"What were they like?"

"They weren't very serious about helping fight the wave. They made all kinds of excuses, something about 'upping' or 'dates.'"

"They probably meant 'update.' It's a word people use for patches to online games. If they're Japanese people, like me, then that's probably what it meant. It all sounds a bit familiar . . . do all these worlds work the same way?"

"I was about to ask the same thing, Naofumi."

I suddenly felt a great deal of sympathy for Glass.

Kizuna was the only hero in this world that had her act together. In a way, I was probably pretty lucky to have met her.

"What's with you guys, you look like you're agreeing on something?"

"Do you understand that word too, Kizuna?"

"'Update?' Yeah, it's a very game-like way of thinking, even though this is all a matter of life and death."

"Yeah, but considering all the stats and power-ups, I can understand why people might think all of this is a game."

Oftentimes the world really did seem like a game, but that didn't mean I could treat the battles like one. If I did, the consequences would be dire. If you weren't serious about mastering your skills and stats, then you would lose.

"The heroes back in my world are the same way." They probably actually thought they were in a game. The way that they went to attack the Spirit Tortoise without waiting for me made it clear that they didn't take their responsibilities seriously.

"In the end they refused to do their duty, claiming they didn't want to be controlled, and ran off to do their own thing. I don't know where they are now."

"You didn't try to force them?" I asked Glass.

"They were from a country with whom we have poor diplomatic relations. Any attempt to force their hand would have caused a crisis, so there was nothing we could do."

"I have a good idea where they are, but that doesn't mean I can just head on over and interfere in their business. It wouldn't be wise to get in a fight with the four holy heroes," Alto whined, waving his hands.

Every world I went to seemed to have the same kind of problems. People came to new worlds and treated them like games. In some ways, the world that had summoned me might have been better. At least the queen of Melromarc was a skilled negotiator and diplomat. Thinking back on what she'd accomplished, I was even more impressed now than I had been then. Not only did she get all of the four holy heroes on her side, but she managed to avoid international conflict at the same time.

"From the way you describe them, Naofumi, it sounds like the heroes in your world need to learn to work together. You can't let them die."

"Yeah. We all have our problems to deal with."

Fitoria was the one who had first explained the gravity of the situation to me. I had since explained it all to Kizuna. From what I could tell, the same rules were in effect in Kizuna's world too, so it was safe to assume that we were dealing with the same threats.

For the time being I was busy in Kizuna's world, so the plan was on hold, but when I got back to Melromarc, I still had to find a way to get the four holy heroes to join forces. It would be hard. Those three were stupid beyond belief—stupid enough to get captured by Kyo in the first place.

"The other problem with the vassal weapons holders is that they are always in competition with each other to command the rest of the fighting forces."

Ah . . . yeah, that would be a problem. Even if there were a lot of adventurers that volunteered to fight, even if it was so they could get their hands on rare materials, they would still need to be organized and led by someone. If the heroes and holders of the vassal weapons weren't serious about their battle strategy then they wouldn't be much help anyway.

And if they didn't share what they knew about powering up with each other, then they wouldn't be very powerful either

. . . although Kyo had certainly managed to get strong.

Maybe he was just very highly leveled, so he could get around the power up methods, or maybe he powered up in some other way. Whatever he'd done, he was powerful enough that Glass and L'Arc weren't able to defeat him.

"For now, Kizuna's friends have gone off to all corners of the world, and they are recruiting and training adventurers there. Other countries think that they are already dealing with the waves sufficiently, and therefore, aren't very worried about them."

So the leaders of other counties, most of the holders of the vassal weapons, and most of the holy heroes, were treating the waves as if they weren't a significant problem.

"But the monsters are getting stronger and they are giving more experience when defeated," Kizuna said.

"The countries just see that as a chance to gain more military power, they see profit in it for them. As far as they are concerned, all this talk of the end of the world is nothing but a fairy-tale," Alto explained.

"So anyway," Kizuna clipped. "Can I ask why you ran over to see me, Alto?"

"You don't think I just wanted to see your face?"

"I doubt it. That doesn't sound like the Alto I know."

So she didn't totally trust him. I could understand why. I didn't trust the slave trader either.

"To tell you the truth, I heard a rumor that there was an adventurer selling something called 'soul-healing water' in a nearby country. I couldn't suppress my fascination with this supposed item, so I came to see if I couldn't find out more about it."

Word travelled fast.

So he heard that someone was selling soul-healing water, figured out who it must have been, and came to meet us. If he were up against someone else, he might have had a chance— but against me? If he thought he was going to get knowledge, tools, or ingredients from me, he had another thing coming.

"So is it safe to assume that the person selling this soul-healing water was none other than Naofumi?"

"Yeah, but that doesn't mean I'm going to give you any— or teach you how to make it."

I learned how to make it from a book, so I was confident in my methodology. I was sure I could find the necessary tools and ingredients here if I needed them too. Still, I normally had my shield make it for me, so it had been a long time since I'd tried to make any from scratch.

"I guess I'm on my own then! It's been a while since someone has been so upfront with me."

"I enjoy negotiation. I'd teach you if you were willing to provide me with something of equal value."

"Naofumi, you better be careful. Alto would do anything for money."

"Maybe so, but you two seem to be friendly enough."

"There's still value in my relationship with Kizuna. It would cost me more to betray her."

His response was surprisingly frank.

I was most comfortable around guys like him. I wanted to see how much control I could exercise over him. I wanted him in the palm of my hand.

Hey look at that—Alto looked like he had goosebumps. I could tell his intuition was sharp.

"Besides, if you're the sort of guy that would do anything for money, I'd be doing myself a real disservice by teaching you how to make soul-healing water."

Soul-healing water, by the way, was a medicine that had an incredible effect on Spirit people like Glass—it rapidly and massively raised all of their stats. A Spirit's stats were all tied to their energy level, which was like other humans' levels, except that it always fluctuated.

Soul-healing water had a different effect on heroes and holders of vassal weapons—it restored our SP. But when used on a Spirit, it restored their energy levels.

If medicine like that was released to the public and made common throughout the world, the Spirit people would become immeasurably powerful. It would probably lead to war. I wasn't going to just hand out such important information, not without getting something equally valuable in return.

I looked over at Kizuna and tried to communicate all my thoughts with a glance. She must have understood, because she nodded.

"I guess you're right. I bet I can get it out of L'Arc or Glass."

"They won't tell you!"

"Even though it would lead to a renaissance of skill development? We could make even more concentrated soul-healing water."

"We still won't tell you."

What did he think he was trying to do anyway? I guess that was all he could do.

"Glass, you might want to get stronger, but don't you dare tell him anything."

Glass nodded. I'd have to keep an eye on her. I hadn't known her for very long, and I'd always found her insufferably serious.

"Alto, do you think you could sell a bottle of soul-healing water for four and a half kinhan? Naofumi was able to do it, with a little bit of trickery, of course."

"You think I can't?"

"You shouldn't challenge a real capitalist that way. If he says he can't, then he'll lose face."

Kizuna liked to be involved with sales too, but she wasn't an actual merchant, and there were things about it that she didn't understand.

A real capitalist would use whatever tricks they had at their disposal to raise their profits. They'd tell their customers that they could do things they couldn't really do—they'd do anything to affect the way that they were perceived. He had no choice but to answer a question like that in the affirmative.

"If you really want to see who's best, we should get Romina to make us something and then start a price war over it."

"Don't you dare! This is MY workshop!" Romina snapped.

She was a blacksmith, after all. She probably knew all about how troublesome merchants could be. If I really got into bargaining, I could seriously drop the price of a product.

The old guy back at the weapon shop had realized long ago that he'd have to work for very low wages on any projects I requested.

"Okay, okay. I actually had another reason for coming over. Kizuna, I heard that you stopped the development of tools that could be used to identify heroes from other worlds. Do you really hope to protect the world without such things?" Alto asked Kizuna. His tone was slowly growing more reproachful.

They were trying to make a tool that could positively identify heroes? If they had actually managed to make it, the other three heroes back in my world would have been killed a long time ago.

"That's right. I think it's terrible. I'm going to find another way around it."

"I understand why you feel that way, but you're the only hero around that seems to care about anything at all. At this rate, our world is as good as destroyed. How do you plan to save it?"

"I'm not going to complain about how unfair the whole system sounds to me, but at the very least, I think it's worth investigating other options."

"I see. You haven't changed a bit, Kizuna."

"You look like you've got something to add."

"And you're as perceptive as ever. I do—it's the reason I came to see you," Alto said, pulling out a number of books and showing them to us. They seemed to contain the same information, as if they'd been copied from one another.

"I found this in the ancient labyrinth library."

I looked at the book he was indicating. It included occasional illustrations, and many of them appeared to depict the waves. One of them showed two worlds intersecting, and the people at the intersection were bathed in the light of the legendary and vassal weapons.

There were also strange creatures in the picture, like genies, angels, and a monster that looked like a filolial.

There was a person that seemed to be made of light too. They were shining so brightly that I couldn't make out their faces, but I could see that their hands were outstretched toward the world.

I had no idea what to make of it. It seemed to depict two worlds at war, but then, at a certain point, the heroes on either side appeared to be shaking hands instead of fighting. It likely depicted exactly what Kizuna was searching for.

"The illustration is very old, and it undoubtedly contains coded information that will require time and effort to uncover. I've brought this as a present for you and your friends."

"Oh!"

"You have some impressive friends, don't you?"

"I just found this book recently. Had Kizuna not returned when she did, I probably would have put it in storage."

"If we can figure out what it means, it will probably be really useful."

"I hope so. So? What did you want to do about the war?"

"I'd like to avoid it if possible, but I also don't plan on bowing down. It seems likely now."

That's right, we were currently in the middle of preparations to go to war with the country that Kyo belonged to.

Kizuna and L'Arc implored the country to turn him over, but they refused to comply. And it turns out that Kyo's country had also managed to absorb several neighboring lands while my friends and I were split up. I heard they captured the country that Trash #2 was from and the country of the holder of the mirror of the vassal weapons just at about the time we escaped.

Diplomacy had failed, and the current situation was tense. We had no choice but to prepare for war, and so we did. It felt like war might break out at any moment.

We thought about a sneaking across the border with a small party to take Kyo out in secret, but the border was very secure and it was unlikely that we'd get through it.

We didn't know exactly where Kyo was either. So even if we did manage to sneak in, we'd have to find him without being found ourselves, which would be difficult. That left us with open war as our best option, so we were preparing for it.

If only we knew where Kyo was! We could have ended this so quickly!

"Naofumi-san! It's rude to give these precious things anything less than your full attention!"

"Rafu?!"

Therese had started to voice her opinions on my accessory making. I wished she wouldn't shout like that. She was scaring Raph-chan.

"Oh shut up already! Why don't you go see L'Arc or something?"

"I can't do that. I simply must observe the way you create these miracles with your hands!"

That's right, Therese was standing over my shoulder and watching me work.

"Naofumi, how's the work going?" Kizuna asked. They all had a look of unrestrained greed as they looked at the accessories I made.

What was with these people? Is that the real reason they wanted to meet and talk? Were they just after my crafting secrets? "As long as we are leaving the magic-imbuing process up to a specialist, then I'm making good progress."

I had intended to make a sheath for Raphtalia's katana and a cover for the gemstone in my shield. No one had any problems asking me to make things for them. Kizuna wanted a lure, Glass wanted decorations for her fans, and L'Arc wanted a plume. Who did they think I was, their servant?

I did what I could with the gemstones we had, and I'd managed to produce some attractive pieces, though I wasn't sure what kind of effects to expect from them.

You see, they say that if an accessory is fitted to a hero's weapon that it will cause special effects. Kizuna and I powered up our weapons in different ways, but we both seemed to have this in common.

Conceptually it was similar to wearing armor that granted the user special effects. It wasn't the same as the power-up methods we used to actually change the stats and abilities of our weapons.

The plan for the moment was that I would attempt to make the accessories, but they'd be passed on to an imbuing specialist for imbuing. Then, we would see what kind of effects the accessories granted when they came back from the specialist.

"I just finished making Raphtalia's. I wonder if Rishia would be able to read that book? I'm done here for now, so maybe I'll take it over to her and see what she can figure out."

"It was fascinating to see—the way you made that sheath, I mean."

"I guess."

Romina, one of Kizuna's friends, had helped me make the sheath for Raphtalia's katana.

I used a rare ore to form the sheath itself, and then inlayed the area where the blade enters the sheath with gemstones. I have to admit that it looked pretty cool.

I thought about adding a symbol to the center of the sheath, something to indicate ownership, but I wasn't sure what would be appropriate. My best idea was to use Raph-chan's face as a symbol, but I could see Raphtalia getting angry about that. I decided against it and left it plain.

I'd let Romina handle the lacquering.

All in all it came out great. As a set with the katana vassal weapon, it was great. But the sheath could hold its own in a beauty contest.

When that was done, I'd gone on to make a small cap that would fit over the gemstone in the center of my shield. I based it on a similar object that the old man at the weapon shop back in Melromarc had made for me. I didn't know what sort of effect to expect from it, but I was excited to see what would happen.

"Hey Kizuna. Here's the lure you wanted. Take it to the imbuing specialist if you want something else added to it.

"Oh!"

I'd made her a shiny, flashy—honestly quite gaudy— fishing lure.

"Is it a minnow? A popper? A crankbait?"

"How should I know? I just made, you know . . . whatever."

"How fun! An original! I can't wait to try it out!"

I passed Glass the decoration that I'd made for her fans. It was the sort of charm that hangs from a string near the fan's handle. In this case, it was a circular jewel that the string passed through.

Oh jeez, she was smiling. She looked excited! Ugh! Couldn't she just pretend not to be interested for my sake?

"You can go with Kizuna to have it imbued."

"Understood."

"It was wonderful watching you work!" Therese gasped, clasping her hands together in a fit of ecstasy.

That woman was starting to really creep me out. I don't know what L'Arc saw in her.

"You really are a skilled accessory maker. I was surprised, to tell you the truth. Working with gemstones is quite difficult."

"Yeah, well . . . I had a particularly obnoxious teacher back in the other world."

It was a long time ago, but I'd learned these skills from a professional accessory maker.

Honestly, I didn't think it was very difficult. And I had skills from my shield that would improve the overall quality of anything that I made, so it wasn't stressful work.

But, I guess I did a good job, because everyone seemed really impressed.

"Kizuna, you could do it too, if you tried. You have one of the legendary weapons, so you should have access to skills that would make it easier."

"I guess so . . . But I like having other people make them! It makes it feel more. . . . special!"

"Don't go thinking this is a present! You'd better learn to do it yourself! Where are you going to get your accessories once I go back to the world I came from?"

"Kizuna, please try to make Naofumi something that he would find useful," Therese said. Why did she think I needed her support?

When Kizuna noticed how intensely Therese was staring at her, she turned her eyes away and let out a deep breath. She'd been a bit excited too, but seeing Therese's excessive passion must have snapped her back to reality.

"You all seem to be having so much fun. It's a joy just to watch!" Alto chimed in, laughing.

Looking back on it, I guess it had actually been a pretty good day. These would be fond memories soon. But, all this socializing was something I'd rather see in an anime or manga.

"Alright, I'm going to bring this over to Raphtalia. Romina, how's that tool I ordered coming?"

"I'm still analyzing it. It should be ready before the battle."

"I'm interested to see what happens, but I'm not expecting much. Okay then, I'm heading over to the castle."

I took the sheath in hand and left for the castle where Raphtalia and the others were busy training.

## Chapter Two: Quick Draw

A little while later, Alto said that he had something he wanted to discuss with L'Arc, so he left us and went off on his own.

"How's progress?"

We went to the castle courtyard where . . . okay, so they were doing the same thing that we'd done back in Melromarc—training.

We were in a completely new world, but we were still training as hard as ever. There was no time to rest. When Rishia had the time, she joined Raphtalia and the others.

"It's been going very well, I think."

"Sounds like you're pretty confident."

"I am."

After Raphtalia was chosen by the katana of the vassal weapons, she was forced to flee from her pursuers with L'Arc and Glass. They had seen to her training during that time. During that same period, I spent all of my time making money and raising my levels. I hadn't done any real training to speak of. I hope she hadn't gotten good enough to embarrass me.

"I was just showing Rishia all that I've learned about how to control energy."

Yeah, I was pretty sure she'd pulled ahead of me.

"I just want to make sure we're on the same page. You're talking about the same thing that the old Hengen Muso lady was talking about, right?"

"Yes. Should I have avoided the topic?"

"That's not what I meant."

"Anyway, Rishia and Filo were . . ."

"Feh?!"

When I turned and looked at Rishia, she jumped as if I had startled her. Her eyes darted anxiously around the courtyard. Had I said anything that deserved a reaction like that? Maybe she was just afraid of me. Whatever the reason, I don't think I'd ever seen her calm and relaxed.

"How's Filo?"

"Excellent question, Mr. Naofumi. Filo seems to have completely mastered energy control."

"What do you mean?" I asked. Raphtalia glanced over at Filo.

"Filo."

"Whaaat?"

"Show us how you control that power that Fitoria taught you about."

"I don't wanna! I'm tired . . ."

Filo seemed to have lost a good deal of her previously impressive stamina when we crossed over to this new world.

Now she tired very quickly.

She lost some stamina, but now she could fly. It wasn't a bad trade, but she focused mainly on magic during battle nowadays.

"Just show us a little. Mr. Naofumi will be really impressed!"

"Okay!"

Filo snapped to attention and started to focus her power.

I wanted to see it, but I never agreed to be impressed or say anything nice. Oh well.

After Fitoria taught Filo how to fight, she became very quick on her feet. Her attacks were sharper too.

"Whew. I'm too tired, so I have to get some power first."

She started gathering magic power around herself. It looked like the technique she'd used during our battle with the Spirit Tortoise's heart.

"Glass also knew of a technique that uses energy in a similar way, so we shared our ideas with each other," Raphtalia explained.

"Yes, the technique reminded me of my training in prana, a technique we use to gather, increase, and store our energy."

The techniques sounded similar. But, I wasn't sure to what extent the technique would line up with the energy theory the old lady had taught us. I guess we would find out.

"And yet, I have never seen such things performed so effectively. Therefore, I also have much to learn on this topic, and so, I have been training with Ms. Raphtalia for the last few days," Glass informed me.

If that meant that Glass was going to get even more powerful than she already was, I almost felt like I didn't want to teach her anything. She even said that after training with Raphtalia she had developed the ability to actually see energy. She was a force to be reckoned with. She watched Filo and analyzed her technique.

"This young girl has incredible potential."

"So she's using the same kind of energy?"

I'd had Filo assist Rishia with her training for a while now, but now that I think back on it, I'd never had Filo train with the old lady. Actually, I think the old lady had said that Filo didn't need training.

I was starting to understand why she'd said that.

"It's likely that we use the same kind of energy, though there may be some differences. With more training, I believe we can all improve."

"Sounds good to me. Hear that, Filo?"

"Yup!"

I shot another glance at Rishia and said, "Raphtalia, Glass, how's Rishia doing?"

"Not all that well, honestly."

I should have assumed as much. From what I could tell she was making a concerted effort, but the training didn't seem to be having much effect.

"The old lady says that she has potential—that a great strength slumbers within her. I've seen her." I turned to Rishia, "I've seen glimpses of it myself. I'm still expecting a lot from you."

"Feh . . ."

I wish Glass would teach her something.

"She has . . . talent? Really?" Glass looked her over with disbelief. "She can use energy? To my eyes, she seems to have less prana than normal."

"So you're saying she has no ability?"

"Mr. Naofumi, can't you phrase that a bit more kindly?"

Rishia had plenty of use outside of battle. And besides, I'd seen her fight as if her abilities were suddenly awakened. I wasn't ready to give up on her just yet.

"That's not what I mean, it's just difficult to explain. As far as ability, or potential, is concerned, I think you're correct that she may have a propensity."

"I'm getting confused."

"Me too," Kizuna said. "What do you mean?"

Glass scratched her chin and tried to explain. "It's confusing for me too, but I've seen flashes of brilliance in her as well. Short flashes that quickly vanish."

"Hm . . ."

"To be more specific, it's a bit like what Filo was just doing, where she supplements her own prana with prana from her surroundings. As far as I understand it, she . . ."

Glass went on blabbing for a while. She used a lot of specialized vocabulary I'd never heard before, so most of it went right over my head.

The gist of it seemed to be that Rishia had far less prana than most people do, but that she had an exceptional gift for gathering and absorbing prana from her surroundings. That made sense to me, because of what had happened when she used a bottle of life-force water on herself back in Melromarc. She'd grown incredibly powerful and lost control over herself.

Glass had seen Rishia's battle ability skyrocket during the fight with Kyo. Her theory was that this phenomenon occurred as Rishia became more emotional, and then she was able to better control her power.

"So she gets stronger the more effort she makes?"

"In a sense, yes."

"You could have just said that. I didn't need to hear the whole speech."

"Don't say that," Kizuna said. "That's mean."

I wondered if Kizuna saw Glass's face scrunch up when she defended her.

Anyway, if Glass agreed that Rishia had some kind of unrealized potential, then it must have been true. I still expected her to prove herself useful with her bookish knowledge.

"I'm almost jealous," Ethnobalt said, entering the conversation.

What now? Why did he have to throw in his two cents?

Ethnobalt was always relegated to supporting the rest of us in battle. Even though he possessed a vassal weapon, he didn't seem to be all that powerful—maybe that's why he was jealous.

He had only muttered softly to himself, but Kizuna and Glass seemed to deflate upon hearing him.

"Why? What's wrong?"

"Oh right," Kizuna said. "You don't know why Ethnobalt has to avoid the front lines, do you, Naofumi?"

"No."

When I thought about it, I realized he did always support the group from a distance, and he hadn't come with us when we went searching for Glass and the others.

I'd just assumed that he was the intellectual, magic-using type, and that he used the ship vassal weapon to get around. But, maybe it was more complicated than that. Because I don't think he had really done anything during the wave battle either.

I thought maybe he was just taking it easy, but that didn't seem to be the case.

The vassal weapons typically conferred a duty in battle on those that held them. I'm not sure I'd ever really seen Ethnobalt fight. He always went out of his way to avoid battle, and no one ever asked him about it. There must have been an explanation for all of this.

Maybe the ship vassal weapon had limitations, like my

shield, or Kizuna's hunting tools.

"Members of my race generally do not gain power when their levels increase."

What?

I stared at him in silence. Then I looked over at Rishia, but no one was paying any attention.

"That's right. Back when I first got here, Ethnobalt used to go on adventures with me just like anyone else. He gained plenty of levels too, but . . ."

"I was shocked by how quickly Kizuna's stats outpaced my own. It didn't matter how many levels I gained, my stats only grew by insignificant amounts. The power difference between us grew and grew."

"Can you make up for it by powering up your weapon?"

"A little bit. But it isn't enough, not even close."

He must have survived by status bonuses granted when new abilities are unlocked. But it wasn't enough—he wasn't strong enough to battle in this world. Admittedly, the monsters, people, and waves in this world were powerful by Melromarc standards. Little status bonuses could only take him so far.

"I have learned a large variety of magic spells, but my power didn't grow with my knowledge, and it got to the point where I was clearly holding everyone back."

He was saying that he wasn't even good at supporting others in battle.

No doubt about it, he reminded me of Rishia.

"Everyone tried to protect me. If I was on the front lines, I would likely end up getting killed. It fell to others to protect me. But I'm a holder of a vassal weapon! I didn't want to hold the others back."

That's why he was jealous. He wanted to protect others, not to be protected by them.

"That all sounds well and fine, but I don't think your actions are as impressive as your intentions."

"Mr. Naofumi, can't you say something nicer than that?"

But it was true.

He wasn't like me. I didn't want to battle at all, but I was forced to protect other people. He had a choice in this. He could attack monsters and people if he wanted. He just hadn't found a way to make it work.

He had the ship vassal weapon, after all. When we used it to fly through the sky, I noticed that it was equipped with cannons. If he could fire all those cannons at once, then he could probably do plenty of damage if he wanted to. Unless the cannon damage was dependent on his stats, which I suppose was actually a possibility.

But if he was convinced that everything came down to his stats, then he should stop asking for sympathy and being so dependent on them!

"Take a look at Rishia! Her stats are so low it's not even

funny! And you have the ship vassal weapon! What are you whining about?"

"Fehhh?!" Rishia yelped.

"Naofumi, isn't that a little rude? Not just to Ethnobalt, but to Rishia?"

"No, I don't think so. I'm talking about their motivation, about their effort."

I waved Kizuna over and whispered Rishia's stats in her ear, starting with the best ones.

Rishia had technically become my slave to gain the benefits of my slave maturation adjustment skill. That's why I knew what her stats were. The more stats I listed, the more color drained from Kizuna's face.

"No way! They're really that low?"

"Yeah, normally. Aside from the battle with Kyo, that's what her stats are like."

"Wh . . . What do you mean?" Glass asked Kizuna, bewildered.

Then Glass dropped to her knees before Rishia and bowed until her head was on the floor.

"Forgive me. I hadn't realized that you were so unfit for battle. I should never have put you in danger by bringing you into the battle against the wave."

"Fehh?!"

"I don't think you need to bow to her . . ."

Kizuna turned on me next, "Naofumi! We've brought Rishia into battle without a second thought, but knowing what I know now, we never should have done that! We put her in real danger!" she shouted angrily. Was it really that bad?

When you really think about it, wasn't their reaction worse than anything I had done? Raphtalia looked troubled, like she wasn't sure how to respond.

"Well, Rishia has always said that she wanted to get stronger, so isn't it okay if she joins us in battle? I don't see a problem with it."

"Raphtalia, there is a difference between bravery and recklessness! With stats like that, Rishia's going to get herself killed!"

What was going on? The conversation was clearly derailed. All I'd wanted to say to Ethnobalt was that he had no right to be jealous of Rishia, if he wasn't going to make a real effort. Why was everyone mad at me?

"I see what you are driving at. I lack the level of decisiveness, or courage, that Ms. Rishia has. Is that it?" Ethnobalt said after realizing how devoted to battle Rishia was, in spite of her stats and abilities.

"There's no way to know when talent will show itself, when your true strength will be revealed. You think you can wait for levels to do it for you? You can't slack off and hope that everything will just change for you some day."

He held a vassal weapon, after all.

I understand how discouraging it can be when you don't seem to be making any progress. But, if Ethnobalt had enough free time to sit around lamenting how weak he was in comparison to others, then he should devote that time to training and self-improvement. That's what Rishia did.

"If you're satisfied with playing a back-up role, then that's fine. But if you want to be stronger, then you have to put in the work. There's more to power than stats, you know? If you think there's nothing you can do, you're just wrong."

"Mr. Naofumi . . . "

"You sound so cool, Naofumi. You talk a big game, especially considering that you're subject to the same sort of limitations in battle that I am," Kizuna said.

"Shut up."

I'd attack if I could, I really would. But I was cursed with this stupid shield, so being an offensive fighter wasn't an option—but I wasn't giving up.

If Ethnobalt's weapon allowed him to attack, then there was still hope for him.

And everyone kept saying that Rishia had potential. I believed it too, considering what she'd done in the battle with Kyo. She'd prove herself eventually, and she'd get there because she never gave up trying.

It's better to regret trying and failing than to regret not trying at all.

As far as I was concerned, Ethnobalt didn't have the right to complain until he had really made an effort.

"I understand. Very well then, Glass, may I participate in these training exercises?"

"Are . . . Are you sure?"

"Yes. I want to protect you all, so I must work as hard as I can to get to that point, just like Ms. Rishia."

"We can do it!" Rishia chirped. They were really hitting it off.

Glass looked over at them and smiled, "I'm a tough teacher!"

Glass appeared to be filled with fresh determination. She looked tougher, taller than normal. "We'll start by training the body! Let's get going!"

"Okay!"

"Understood!"

The three of them took off running. Then Ethnobalt and Rishia tripped and fell.

They had a lot in common, those two. They were both so clumsy.

"Now then, Mr. Naofumi. Why did you come to see us today?"

"That's right, I'd nearly forgotten."

I got so wrapped up in talking about Rishia's stats and strengths that I'd neglected the reason I came. I pulled out the katana sheath I'd made and gave it to Raphtalia.

"Thank you very much!" She smiled warmly. That was the face I'd come to see.

I had put a cheap sword into the sheath for the time being, but with the actual katana in it, the design was a perfect match. It made the katana look even more beautiful. When she slid the blade in, it sealed with a satisfying *clack*.

When the blade slipped all the way in, I thought I saw the sheath's gemstone flash.

I turned to Kizuna, "You said that special effects can be triggered when vassal weapons, or one of the four holy weapons, are equipped with accessories, right?"

"Yeah, but I don't know what sort of effects they are."

"I asked for the accessories to be imbued with effects that would increase Raphtalia's agility, so she can move around the battlefield easier."

That's what I asked the official imbuing specialists to do. When the accessories came back, I checked them over, and from what I could tell, they appeared to have been imbued with the effects I requested.

I guess there was a chance that they had snuck something troublesome in there, but successfully imbuing a vassal weapon at all was difficult enough already, so I highly doubt they could have pulled that off.

"I wonder if it worked?" Raphtalia asked.

"Doesn't it look like the sheath's gemstone is shining?"

"Yeah. It actually looks like it's slowly filling with light."

"Hmm . . . I wonder what will happen when it's full?"

"I guess we'll just have to wait and see."

"I don't even know what the sheath would do, never mind the shining gemstone."

"Me neither."

"Maybe you should try to draw the katana and see what happens?" Kizuna asked.

She had a point. An effect might trigger when certain conditions are met. The accessory I got from the old guy at the weapon shop in Melromarc had been like that. Its effect might have triggered because I'd been blocking so many attacks at once. Something had triggered it, and it made a defensive barrier like the shooting star shield skill I have. It might have even been better than shooting star shield, because it had actually damaged enemies that touched it.

I hoped that the accessories I'd made would function the same way. Anyway . . . I was getting distracted. Back to the topic at hand.

"Good idea. Raphtalia, try drawing the sword."

"Alright."

She slid the blade out of the sheath, and the light drained out of the gemstone.

"The light went out."

"Maybe you can't draw the sword until the light is fully charged?"

"That might be it," Raphtalia said, reinserting the sword. We waited until the gemstone was filled with light.

"Maybe you have to fight with the sword still in the sheath? Should I pull the blade out some?"

"Then what's the point of the sheath?"

"That is a problem. We'll need to try using it in all sorts of ways."

"It takes a while for the gemstone to charge up, doesn't it?"

"Maybe you should carry another, secondary sword to use while this one is charging."

"I'm pretty sure that Glass's fan can split into two separate fans. She dances with them, but it's similar to fighting with two swords."

"So you think if she learns a technique or a skill, she'll be able to use more than one?"

"Maybe."

"Um . . . Could you please stop staring at my sword and analyzing me?" Raphtalia muttered uncomfortably.

It wasn't my fault that her accessory was finished first. We had to figure out how they worked somehow.

"It's so shiny and pretty!"

"Raful!"

Filo turned into her humming falcon form and perched on my shoulder while I inspected the katana sheath.

It was turning into a pretty weird scene.

Anyway, it felt like three minutes or so had passed by the time the gemstone was fully charged. A bright light flashed, and there was a sound like dropping coins into a piggy bank. The meaning was unmistakable.

"Great. Raphtalia, try drawing the katana again."

"Alright."

She held the sheath in her left hand, and used her right hand to slowly draw the blade.

Hm? Was I seeing double? It looked like there were two Raphtalias standing in front of me.

Kizuna cocked her head and blinked. She must have been seeing the same thing that I was.

It's hard to explain what it looked like. If I tried really hard I could follow her with my eyes, but it was like she was moving faster than her body could keep up with. It looked just like Filo's haikuikku attack, actually. Like she was moving so fast she was a flickering blur.

I was impressed that Kizuna and I were able to keep track of her.

Never mind Therese, who had been standing off to the side silently and watching with stars in her eyes.

A few seconds went by and then Raphtalia's speed returned to normal.

"Huh? Mr. Naofumi?"

"What happened?"

"When I unsheathed the katana you all started moving in slow motion."

"I bet. You started moving so fast that I could hardly tell where you were. It was like Filo's haikuikku move."

"If you attacked us at that speed, I don't think I'd be able to block it."

"Yeah, me neither."

I'd have to be really lucky to block an attack that fast.

"It appears that if you keep the katana sheathed until the gemstone is charged, it will activate haikuikku upon drawing the blade."

"That's pretty amazing. You can slay monsters the moment you draw your sword! That's so cool!"

"I've seen you kill monsters with one swipe of that tuna knife, so you must know what you're talking about. I agree that it's pretty cool."

I had to mention that, because even if Raphtalia could fell monsters with one swipe, Kizuna could do the same thing. That much hadn't changed. Actually, Kizuna's attack was probably better, because Raphtalia's skill only activated the first time she drew her sword. If she missed her chance the first time, she'd have to wait another three minutes or so without attacking to get another shot.

She could probably go after enemies with her bare hands in the meantime, but she wouldn't be able to use her sword to fight, because then it wouldn't charge the gemstone. Some of that could probably be mitigated with support magic, but it wouldn't be wise to plan our battle strategy around those initial attacks of hers.

Anyway, the move had limitations, but I was certainly glad to have it.

"Again, I really wish you would stop inspecting me like that . . ."

"If she could learn to fight with two swords, like that technique that Glass uses, then maybe she could fight with one while the other one charges."

"It could be limited to this one weapon though."

"Maybe. It's still pretty good."

"Are you listening to me?"

"Oh, right—sorry. When Kizuna and I get talking, it's hard to stop."

Raphtalia looked irritated by our nonstop commentary.

Maybe she was . . . jealous?

I was sort of a father figure to her, so maybe she didn't like that I was talking with another woman so much. Maybe she felt like she was going to lose her parent.

"I feel weird with you looking at me like that!"

"Alright already. Anyway, that ability is sure to come in

handy when we are out hunting monsters."

"Good point. We can probably end a lot of battles before they ever begin."

Getting the first attack in was always an advantage.

Filo could move quickly too, but it was obvious when she was charging up for the attack, and that made the enemy extra cautious. But Raphtalia's katana would retain the element of surprise, so the enemy would fall before they knew what hit them.

With any luck, this new attack would prove very useful.

"I wonder if there is a way that the stone can retain its charge. It's a shame to lose all that progress just because you had to draw the sword."

"I'll ask the imbuing specialist about it. They'll know more about those subtle particulars."

"Good point. Let's see what we can find out."

Raphtalia frowned, "Enough already! Now you're already trying to alter my weapon without asking me? What about your accessory, Mr. Naofumi?"

"It isn't ready yet."

I'd worked on it with a firm idea of how I wanted it to come out, but I wasn't very confident that I was going to be successful.

"What about yours, Kizuna?"

"Thanks for asking! Check it out! Ta-da!" Kizuna smiled

and pulled out the tacky lure that I'd made for her.

When she saw what it looked like, Raphtalia shot me a disappointed look.

"That's what she wanted."

"I'm going to bring it by the imbuing specialist to see what they can do, and then, I'll use it to go fishing tonight!"

"You really enjoy fishing, don't you Kizuna," Raphtalia said.

"Of course I do! It's my favorite pastime."

It didn't seem like anything to be proud of to me. That reminds me, a day or two ago Glass was whining about something related. When we got back to Kizuna's house, we found the walls covered with gyotaku fish prints.

There were so many of them that it was hard to believe that Kizuna had really caught them all.

Some of them were strange looking creatures—I wasn't even sure if they should be counted as fish.

"I'll ask Ethnobalt to take me fishing on his boat!"

"We'll be leaving in the morning, so don't stay out too late."

"Yeah, yeah!"

She'd probably be out until well past midnight.

"We're going somewhere in the morning?"

"Yeah, we're going through some monster hunting exercises with L'Arc. Try to take it easy tonight, will you?"

"Very well."

I felt good about how the sheath had come out. Raphtalia would definitely benefit from that new attack.

"Hey! Rishiaaa!" I shouted to her as she ran. I'd completely forgotten something important.

"What is it?"

"This book is supposed to say something about the waves."

Rishia started flipping through the book that I handed to her.

"I thought that you might be able to get some information out of it, since you're so good with languages. Would you take a look at it for me?"

"Why me?!"

"Because you're good with books and studying."

"I like to read, but I don't know if I'll be able to understand it all."

Humility was a good thing, but Rishia was starting to get on my nerves. She was naturally gifted when it came to books and studying, so it was kind of sad that she wanted to be an athletic warrior.

"Take it as an order, and do your best to see what you can get out of it. The more we figure out, the more weight we can take off of Itsuki's shoulders."

The book might detail the wave's secrets. Rishia wasn't

usually much help at all, but this could be a great opportunity for her to contribute.

"I'll see what I can do!" Rishia stuffed the book into her bag and ran off.

"Naofumi, what shall we do about today's magic practice?" Therese asked. She'd been quiet this whole time, probably privately freaking out over accessories or something.

I forgot to mention that Therese was giving me lessons in magic use when I wasn't busy crafting accessories.

I learned a new technique from Ost when I got the Spirit Tortoise Heart Shield. It was called the Way of the Dragon Vein. It seemed to be a new way to use magic, but I didn't understand it very well.

At the time she had walked me through a sort of magical puzzle, but now I couldn't even figure out how to access it. It was supposed to be a type of magic that let me borrow power from something outside of myself.

I didn't have any ideas, and I'd seen Therese do something similar once, so one day I just asked her. She said that she was familiar with a different system, and that her techniques might work for me too. So she started to teach me how to use magic.

I'd learned a lot from her over the last few days, but honestly it was pretty difficult. A lot of it went over my head.

"Let's do it. I want to learn that support magic too."

Thanks to Ost's help, I'd been able to cast a very powerful

support magic spell called "All Liberation Aura." It substantially raised everyone's stats.

We were going to need it to survive what was coming. Besides, I had a responsibility to Ost. I had to learn to command the power she'd entrusted to me. There was no time to relax or slack off.

So, in return for her help with magic training, I agreed to let Therese watch me when I worked on crafting accessories. This agreement had been in place for a few days now.

To learn from Therese, we needed gemstones to work with, so I was crafting those too. Therese was a Jewel, and so she didn't actually need to use the gemstones I made. I needed them so I could borrow their power during our training.

"Then let's start our training for the day, shall we?"

"Sure."

I stood in the castle courtyard with a gemstone in one hand, and our training session began.

"Do your best, Mr. Naofumi! I'll be training with Glass!" Raphtalia shouted.

"Thanks, good luck, Raphtalia. I want to learn how to use energy too, so I'll join your training session later."

I had to focus on magic first.

I needed to find a way to fight against enemies that were able to use a terrible technique called "defense rating attacks." But more than anything else, I wanted to learn how to use the power that Ost had given me.

## Chapter Three: Lure

The next morning, right when we were about to leave to meet up with L'Arc, Kizuna showed up with heavy bags under her eyes. I was so annoyed I couldn't think of anything to say.

The night before, she had gone out to the ocean with the new lure I'd made for her. She must have stayed out really late with it.

"This lure is amazing! I just attached it to my fishing line and threw it in and the fish lined up to bite it! I catch something every time I cast it. I love it! Can we put off this trip until tomorrow?"

Was she insane?

Her pupils were wide and dilated, and she looked like she was about to run off and go fishing again. She looked like something out of a horror movie.

Glass looked like she understood what was going on, so she tried to calm Kizuna down a bit.

"Kizuna, you're a little worn out, aren't you? Why don't we take a little break?"

"I don't want to! If I take this lure to another place, I can catch even bigger fish! Don't you want to eat something good? Don't you? If you do, you better let me go!"

"Kizuna! That's enough! Enough! Please calm down. You need to rest."

"But . . ."

She was stuck between her duty and her love of fishing and the scales seemed to hang evenly.

I didn't see what she was so obsessed with. Her eyes were freaking me out. I wished she'd stop looking at me.

"Fine. Alright. But you have to let me go fishing when we get back."

"Very well," Glass said, and Kizuna sat down with a humph.

She was already worn out by all the battles and training. Then she went fishing all night on top of that. She must have been exhausted.

How much fun can fishing really be?

"That lure must be cursed."

"You're the one that made it."

"Are you trying to kill our Kizuna?!"

"This is *my* fault now?"

Kizuna was the one that was obsessed with the lure. It wasn't my fault.

"Hey Alto, are you coming too?"

"Yeah, just to see what sort of materials I can get my hands on. I don't enjoy fighting very much."

He was a merchant, after all. He was competitive on a

different battlefield. I assumed that he was coming along to see if he could find any interesting drop items.

"I'm coming along for the drops. I'm trying to buy some special powders, the sort that have ability names."

"What's that?"

"You know, like strength powder and magic powder."

I'd never heard of anything like that, but the concept was intriguing. I felt the itch to start collecting and categorizing.

"They're mostly used to make various medicines. Medicines made with those powders fetch a good price because they have fantastic ability-enhancing properties."

"Hm . . ." I'd run into the concept before in older RPGs.

Heroes like myself didn't need to depend on such things, because every material we found unlocked more weapons and abilities.

A trickle of water becomes a river—as insignificant as they may seem, adventurers that had reached their level cap would probably chase after materials like that, as they'd be the only way to continue raising their stats.

That explained something that had been bothering me. There were a lot of adventurers in this world that were very powerful, even without holding a legendary or vassal weapon. These powders must have had something to do with it.

"I'd rather use them than sell them."

"They become less effective the more you use them, so

most people sell them once the efficiency starts to drop off."

I could understand that. That would explain how Trash #2's friends had been able to break through my shooting star shield barrier. They looked like weak underlings, so I'd been surprised by how powerful they actually were.

Ethnobalt spoke next, directing us toward his ship, "Then shall we get going? Perhaps Kizuna could use our travel time to get some rest."

I hadn't realized that we were going to be traveling by his strange ship. I guess it made sense—ease of travel was probably the best part of having the ship vassal weapon. The ship was like a knock-off of my portal skills, and it worked by traveling over these things call "dragon veins," which were currents of some kind. We'd used it once before, and it had been very fast.

We were moving very fast now, fast enough to ignore them, but I couldn't help but notice how many monsters there were flying around up in the sky.

I guess flying monsters weren't particularly rare, but I was surprised to see so many.

"There are quite a lot of them up here today. It's crowded."

"Oh yeah?"

"Yes. I think I'll take a short detour."

If we had to be in a mid-air battle aboard the ship, people with ranged attacks would fare better than anyone else.

Too bad our resident monster-hunting hero was busy taking a nap.

"I'm so glad to get away from all that boring diplomacy! Time for some action!" L'Arc shouted. I ignored him. If you ask me, he wasn't the kind of guy who should be put in a position of authority over anyone.

We were flying through the air on Ethnobalt's ship to go to an area with strong monsters. Ethnobalt may not be much use in battle, but his vassal weapon sure was convenient.

"Hey Ethnobalt, you're a monster, aren't you? What's your species called?"

Was he a demi-human, like Raphtalia? He was a giant, talking rabbit, after all.

"In L'Arc's country we are known as library rabbits."

"There's only one place they live naturally, and that's in the labyrinth libraries," L'Arc explained.

"I wonder if they are like the beast men in the world that I was summoned to."

If they weren't so different, then the definitions of human and monster were in need of an update.

"We'll be passing my hometown shortly. Shall we stop by and have a look?" Ethnobalt said, turning the ship around into a wide detour that brought us up to a large, shrine-like building. A tall rabbit was walking nearby, and Ethnobalt called him over to us.

The rabbit came over and bowed to us before sniffing at the air in silence with its little nose.

"So that's a library rabbit?"

"But when you're in rabbit form, you must be twice as tall as this guy."

Was Ethnobalt some kind of boss version?

"Yes, well. Do your best," Ethnobalt said to the other rabbit, who just kept sniffing in response. Couldn't the stupid thing talk?

Filo interjected. "He said, 'Yes, our great chief.'"

Why did Filo understand him?

If they spoke in monster language, then I guess it was safe to categorize them as monsters? I mean, were they really talking? It just looked like sniffing to me. I guess the rabbit was more intelligent than it appeared.

"We are on our way to training grounds. I wish to become strong enough to help protect the world."

Many more rabbits came hopping over and they started clapping, though their paws didn't make very much noise.

It was a surreal sight to behold.

"Ethnobalt is the leader of this tribe. His people are fond of him, which is a sign of a good leader," L'Arc said. He was a king himself. But I'd keep calling him Boy.

Kizuna had managed to surround herself with people in positions of authority.

Had I managed the same thing back in Melromarc? The only friend I had in a position of power was Melty. She was the princess, so if the queen were to die, then she would become monarch of Melromarc, just like L'Arc. Heh—when that happened, I would go on calling her Princess. I could see it now: her face turning bright red with anger. She'd probably stomp her feet and yell at me.

Anyway, ever since I met him, I felt that Ethnobalt had something in common with Fitoria—even if he was much weaker. I decided to act on my hunch and ask him directly.

"How old are you, Ethnobalt?"

"Me? I'm turning fifteen this year."

Hm . . . that wasn't what I was I expecting. I didn't know how old Fitoria was, but she's been alive since there were other heroes, so probably generations old.

So how could Ethnobalt be so young? Wasn't he supposed to be the monster version of a hero?

"What are library rabbits like? How do they live?"

"Why do you care?"

"It's not important, but I'm wondering if they're anything like these filolials back in the world I came from. Filo here is one of them, and . . ." I explained all I knew about the filolials to Glass and L'Arc.

"Ah, do you mean the giant monster that appeared to assist us during the battle with the Spirit Tortoise? That thing was the same type of monster as Filo?"

"Yes. Apparently they gain unique abilities when they're raised by heroes. That's why Filo is such a strong fighter, but I don't know if that's how things work in this world."

Ethnobalt pulled out a book and began flipping through it.

"There are tales of a legendary library rabbit . . . yes, here." He showed us an illustration of a library rabbit wearing robes much like the clothes that Ethnobalt was wearing.

"They say that all library rabbits are descended from this individual, and that this legendary ancestor was killed in an ancient battle."

So, this legendary rabbit had been killed. It looked very intellectual in the illustration.

"I was named after this legendary library rabbit. But, I am not yet worthy of the name. There is so much I do not know, but I hope to become like him in time."

"Hm . . ."

Kizuna finally woke up.

"Wow! I guess all of worlds have these sorts of things in common."

"I don't know if I'd go that far. But Ethnobalt, you say you want to get stronger . . ."

He held a vassal weapon. I wonder if that would prevent me from putting a monster spell on him and putting him under my control. There were ofuda in this world that lent people control over monsters. I think they were called "control ofuda."

"Kizuna, why don't you trying raising him with a control ofuda? It might change the way that he levels."

Ethnobalt frowned, "Then I would have even less to show for myself."

"Deal with it."

Filo could grow to be stronger than Fitoria. So, you never know how things will end up.

"It's long been said that the library rabbits are not suited for battle."

Was that some kind of racial characteristic? Like a whole race, a whole species, of Rishia clones? How sad would that be?

"If they mature differently, based on whether or not they are under the control of a hero, then they are probably like the filolials back in my world."

"I suppose we could try it," Kizuna agreed.

"I . . . I will do what I must!" Ethnobalt replied.

Did he think that was impressive? As far as I could see, you couldn't afford to slack off if you held a vassal weapon. He had a responsibility to the weapon.

"For now, just do all that you can in battle, and don't push it too far. We'll take care of the rest."

"Alright."

We finished talking and took off again. When we arrived at our destination, we found ourselves surrounded by angry monsters. They bared their fangs and attacked.

"Whoa!" I quickly used Shooting Star Shield to protect us.

"Ha!" Raphtalia drew her sword from the fully charged sheath and flew through the crowd of monsters, faster than the eye could see.

A few monsters fell to the ground defeated, but then even more appeared, drawn by all the sudden commotion.

"Hya!" Glass shouted, slapping open her fan and swiping at an approaching monster.

A bolt of light shot from it and slammed into the charging beast.

"What was . . ." Glass muttered, looking at me and then at the fan in her hand.

"Was that a skill?"

"Something like that, but I didn't do anything to make it happen. And it didn't use any of my energy reserves."

"I wonder if it's an effect from the accessory that Naofumi made for your fan?"

"It must be. I've never seen an accessory with such a noticeable effect. The craftsmanship must be truly excellent," Glass said, smiling. It was always exciting to get your hands on a new weapon.

She continued swiping left and right with her fan, sending out shockwaves through the waves of approaching monsters.

"Now it's my turn to show off!" L'Arc shouted, swinging his scythe. The blade glowed with energy and sliced a nearby monster in two. "Nice! My scythe is even stronger than it was! That accessory you made is really something!"

I didn't mind all the compliments. I even enjoyed them. But it did feel strange to think about how much I had done for these people, especially considering that we might end up having to fight them at the end of all this.

They had all grown so powerful. I was honestly shocked at how effective my accessories were.

But then, as L'Arc continued to swing his scythe, the accessory began to smoke.

"L'Arc, it looks like it will break if you keep on using it without giving it a rest. Better keep an eye on it."

"Good idea. It must be the sort of thing that I should save. Only use it when I really need it."

"I think so. But man, just look at all these monsters."

Monsters had swarmed at us in endlessly since the moment we entered the labyrinth.

And because Kizuna and I were in the same place, we weren't getting any experience points out of it. Holders of the vassal weapons were subject to the same issue, so Glass and the others weren't gaining experience either. Only Rishia, Filo, and Therese were actually leveling in these battles.

"It's quite strange," Ethnobalt said, covering Rishia and the others from the back line.

"I've been here before, and even I think it's weird!" I shouted.

L'Arc looked at the approaching hordes of monsters with confusion. He didn't understand what was going on either.

The monsters weren't so powerful that we couldn't handle them, but their numbers were unbelievable. We'd eventually get worn down by the sheer number of them, if we didn't come up with a plan. Otherwise, we'd have to find a way to escape.

"Ha!"

Kizuna switched between fighting with her knife for close battles and her fishing rod for ranged attacks. She had access to other tools besides those two things, so I don't know why she didn't use them more.

The lure I'd made for her hung from her weapon, no matter what form it took. I remembered her freaking out about the lure. What had she said? "This lure is amazing! I just attached it to my fishing line and threw it in and the fish lined up to bite it! I catch something every time I cast it. I love it! Can we put off this trip until tomorrow?"

"Kizuna, try removing that lure for a minute!"

"Huh? Okay!" she said, taking the lure off of her weapon.

The moment she did, the waves of monsters stopped coming.

"I thought so."

"What does it mean?"

"I think that lure is attracting the monsters."

I had a skill that did the same thing. It was called Hate Reaction. It looked like Kizuna's lure did that as long as she had it attached to her weapon.

"Looks like that thing I made had a really negative effect. I'll get rid of it for you later."

"No. You. Won't!" Kizuna barked, clutching the lure like a string of pearls. "Do you have any idea how many fish I can catch with this thing? Who cares if it attracts monsters too?"

"Well, I guess as long as you choose when to use it there's no problem."

"Yes there is! Kizuna, give me that lure!" Glass shouted, holding out her hand expectantly.

Kizuna simply shook her head.

I understood why Glass felt the way she did, but she was overreacting a bit. Maybe there was something I didn't know about.

"Kizuna. Listen to us. Give the accessory to Glass," L'Arc said calmly. Everyone, including Therese and Ethnobalt, reacted the same way. They must have been aware of a risk that I wasn't.

"Rafu?"

"What's all this about?" Raphtalia and Rafu both looked as confused as I was.

I looked around and saw that Filo and Rishia were confused too.

"Kiddo, Kizuna's a great girl, but she's got some issues when it comes to fishing. She even tried to fish off of the ghost ship we were on that day," L'Arc sighed heavily. "Of course we stopped her."

"You mean she thinks about fishing even in the middle of battle?"

"Absolutely."

"I do not!" Kizuna shouted.

"Then will you give me that lure?"

"I . . . Um . . ."

"Let her have it. We'll just keep an eye on her."

"You can't. You'll see. She'll try fishing for mice the second she gets a break."

Fishing for mice? Would she really do that? Even if she knew it would attract other monsters? Kizuna had never seemed like a careless person to me.

Ethnobalt nodded, as if he'd suddenly realized something, "That was why there were so many flying monsters today. We almost collided with some in the air."

I remembered that he had mentioned there were more monsters than usual.

"Good point. Maybe you should hand it over to Glass. When you want to use it, Glass will let you," I told her.

"But then I might miss my chance to catch the big one! What if Glass isn't around when I need it?!"

"What do I care? Get over it already. I'm sure you can work this out amongst yourselves."

"Mr. Naofumi, don't give up so easily. We have to convince her."

"I have a dream! I want to catch a fish bigger than anyone has ever seen!"

"Then go catch a whale!"

I regretted saying that. I didn't want her leaving a wave battle to go fishing.

"Kiddo, you get her from the right, I'll take her from the left. Glass and Raphtalia—you two make sure she doesn't get away."

"Fine."

Everyone sprang to it immediately, and soon we had Kizuna surrounded.

"What are you doing? Leave me alone!"

She could resist if she wanted, but we were going to get that lure from her if we had to kill her to do it.

She could play with her lure after we defeated Kyo and went back to our world.

"Noooo! You stole it from me! My favorite accessory!"

Kizuna whined. Her childish screams echoed in our ears.

She finally sounded her age.

"Alright then . . ." I turned to survey the area, ignoring Kizuna's pouting and begging.

The monsters were tough, but nothing that we couldn't handle.

We'd come out to this place to check the effects of the new accessories. All of them were more impressive than I had expected, and we weren't having any trouble with the monsters. That wasn't surprising, considering that most of our party was made up of people with vassal weapons, and the others were holy heroes from an assortment of worlds.

"There are monsters coming. Let's do this."

"Yes!"

"Right on! Let's get some nice materials from them and see what Naofumi can make for us next!"

"Ask L'Arc or Romina to do it!" I snapped at Kizuna.

As for the battle itself, it wasn't even worth describing. We won easily.

We pressed on, and the monsters we encountered slowly grew stronger.

We hadn't yet met any that were strong enough to break through my defenses, though we had met a few that could get through the Shooting Star Shield.

Kizuna, L'Arc, and Glass were starting to get tired.

"Let's take a break," I said, and everyone agreed.

"It'll be dark soon. Should we build a fire?"

"We'll take turns keeping watch."

"Sounds good, then I'll . . ." Kizuna started.

"No fishing."

"I wasn't going to say that!"

We sat down to rest, taking turns keeping watch.

There would have been a time, long ago, when I'd found the idea of camping romantic. Now, the reality was less so. Someone had to stay awake and keep an eye out, and the whole thing was pretty exhausting. Still, I was used to it by now, and it wasn't a problem.

I had some free time, so I decided to see what I could craft from the materials I had stored in the shield. Kizuna and the others spent their time doing the same thing.

Filo and Rafu snuggled up next to me and went to sleep.

Raphtalia took the time to practice with her sword. She was really invested in that new weapon. And as for Rishia, she hunched over a book and started to study. She was either trying to figure out how to read the writing in this world, or she already could and was just reading the book. Probably the latter. She was pretty amazing when it came to studying—keep it up!

Once I indicated what I wanted the shield to craft, I ended

up with nothing to do. I was a little too wound up to sleep. I had time on my hands, so I decided to use it.

"Raph-chan."

"Rafu?"

Raph-chan had been sleeping nearby, so I picked her up and set her on my knees. I called up the menu for the shikigami power-ups, and started looking through the list of materials I could use to power-up her abilities.

Shikigami didn't have levels like other people and monsters did. Instead, their stats and abilities could be adjusted directly by using various objects and materials. It was a bit like adjusting the bioplant specifications, and it seemed like there was a lot to learn. It was even possible to adjust the shininess of her fur!

It was deeper than that too. There wasn't just a single number to play with, but many. The stiffness, softness, fluffiness, sleekness, length, and other things could all be adjusted.

So, whenever I found myself with some free time on my hands, I'd take to fiddling with Raph-chan's power-ups.

At the moment, I had gotten her to the point where she could use illusion magic to back us up in battle. Eventually, I hoped that she'd be able to take over some of Raphtalia's role as my right hand in battle.

"Rafu!"

I was sitting there patting Raph-chan and mulling over the possibilities when I realized something large was nearby. I turned to see what it was and found Ethnobalt sitting behind me.

He was in his rabbit form, and was just large enough to make a perfect backrest.

"What?"

"Nothing. I just . . . this is the easiest place to relax."

"Huh?"

"Naofumi, you're so popular with monsters," Kizuna smiled.

I had no idea what they were talking about.

"Mr. Naofumi is a very good caregiver. I am where I am today due to his kindness," Raphtalia said. She probably thought she was saying something nice, but it didn't make me happy.

I couldn't shake the feeling that they were making fun of me.

"Master! Master is mine! Mine!"

"I don't think so Filo. No one owns me—certainly not you."

"Rafu?"

"Pen!"

"Filo and Chris sure have hit it off. They're like old friends now," Kizuna said.

I looked to see what she meant, only to discover myself surrounded by Filo, Raph-chan, Chris, and Ethnobalt.

Glass nodded, "Naofumi may be from another world, but he is the Shield Hero, is he not? Monsters must realize that he is not their enemy, but that he is here to protect them."

"Yeah, and Naofumi's side is probably the safest place to be."

"I guess that could be it. But damn! It's so hot with these things all around me!" I stood up and moved, carrying Raph-chan with me.

The minute I sat down, Filo, Chris, and Ethnobalt followed me and plopped down around me again. It was a little better than the last arrangement, but not by much. I could hardly understand humans, much less all these monsters. I guess that made sense in a way—they wanted to sleep somewhere they knew they would be protected. It was a natural instinct.

"I don't have time to play with these things," I said, flipping Raph-chan onto her back and rubbing her fluffy belly to see how her fur looked.

"That's probably the least convincing thing you've ever said."

"How so?"

"Rafuuuu . . ."

"Mr. Naofumi, don't pet Raph-chan too much."

"How come?"

Whenever I paid a lot of attention to Raph-chan, Raphtalia looked a little irritated.

"Well, Raph-chan was made from my hair, and . . . well, I feel a little embarrassed when you pet her like that."

"Oh come on. You're just a little kid yourself. I'll pet Raph-chan if I want to."

Raphtalia puffed out her cheeks, unimpressed with my answer, and went back to practicing with her sword. She looked like she was swinging it harder than she had been.

"That's just like you, Naofumi . . ."

"Rafu!" Raph-chan raised her hand and shook her head.

Had I said something wrong?

Raphtalia was like my daughter, and Raph-chan reminded me of her, so of course I cared about Raph-chan too. I don't understand what's so weird about that.

"What's that supposed to mean?"

"Oh nothing. You should get some rest, don't you think? L'Arc is already snoring over there."

She was right. L'Arc was passed out and snoring. It was so loud I was afraid it would attract monsters.

Just when I started to wonder about it, Therese walked over and placed a blanket over him, then cast a spell that silenced his snoring. It didn't bother me really, but something about it felt wrong.

Glass had been talking just a minute ago, but now she was asleep next to Kizuna.

"There's still plenty of time. Raphtalia and I will keep watch, so why don't you get some sleep?"

"Alright already."

Ever since I was betrayed by Bitch, I had trouble getting in a deep sleep. I'd have to take the opportunity to rest while I had it.

I laid down to rest, thinking that the trip had turned into a training camp.

We finished our training around noon of the following day, and returned to the castle.

Filo leveled up a fair amount on our trip, so I should explain what happened there. When we crossed over into this world, Filo turned into a humming fairy, and humming fairies change into different forms as they level.

Perhaps because she was originally a filolial, Filo was able to change into any of her humming fairy forms at will.

"Master! Do you think I look more like how I used to look now?"

"Yeah, much closer."

We were back in the castle courtyard, and Filo was changing into different forms to show off.

I was starting to hope that Raph-chan would be able to change forms, just like Filo could. If she was just a little bigger, she would be perfect for cuddling with when I sleep.

Or if she got even bigger, I could lay down on her belly to sleep. I'd seen something like that in an anime once.

Sure, I could do that with Ethnobalt or Filo, but I'd rather snuggle with Raph-chan.

Ok, that was a bit of a digression.

Filo had currently taken the form of something Kizuna called a humming big owl, which looked exactly like you would expect from the name. She was the same size as she used to be when in her filolial queen form. She looked pretty similar, except for the area around her waist.

She could also turn into a humming emperor penguin, complete with a crest of feathers on her head. Kizuna's shikigami, Chris, was also a penguin, and he looked over at Filo with jealousy.

"And you know what? I can sing really good now!" Filo yelled. Then she puffed up her throat and started to sing.

It almost sounded like there was back-up music. It made for an energized performance.

I couldn't figure out how she was making so many different sounds at once, but it sounded like someone was playing a koto along with her song.

This world's traditional music sounded pretty Japanese to me.

The country that Kizuna had established herself in was mostly Western-styled, but the clothing people wore looked like a fusion between Japanese and western elements.

We were in a bar once and I saw a musician playing a shamisen—it looked strange, to say the least. It wasn't all bad though—I was certainly pleased with Raphtalia's new miko outfit.

"Rafu!" Raph-chan jumped up and started dancing along with Filo's song.

"Oh wow. Nice!" I shouted, disinterested, and went back to the magic practice I'd been doing. Filo had said it was a fun song that gave you energy. And I did sort of feel like my magic power replenished faster than usual. Raphtalia's training went really well too.

Was it an effect of Filo's song?

"I'm about ready to head home for the day."

"Okay!"

So we spent our days preparing for the coming battle. But then, that night, when we were all asleep, something happened. Thinking back on it now, I'm surprised that we hadn't been more on guard, especially considering how long it had been since Kyo had tried anything.

We paid for our lack of caution.

## Chapter Four: Like a Charging Wild Boar

I woke up suddenly to the sound of explosions. The ground was shaking.

"What is that?!"

"Rafu?!"

"What's going on?"

"Feh! Master Itsuki?!"

We were sleeping at Kizuna's house in the neighboring town. We jumped out of bed and tried to get our bearings. I ran to the window to look outside. We were on the third floor, and there was a rush of noise coming from downstairs.

"I don't know what's happening, but it doesn't sound good. Be careful."

Everyone nodded.

We left the room and made for the first floor, where we found Kizuna, Glass, and Chris. Their weapons were drawn and they were facing the entrance.

Aside from those three, we were the only ones in the house.

L'Arc and Therese were at the castle, and Ethnobalt was working at the library.

I was currently using a shield I'd received after the battle with Trash #2, the White Tiger Clone Shield. I had finally reached a level that unlocked it, but I was surprised by how weak it was. The Spirit Tortoise Heart Shield had a higher defense rating, but I hadn't been able to unlock that shield since crossing over to this world.

> **White Tiger Clone Shield (awakened)**
> **abilities locked: equip bonus: skill: Chain Shield**
> **equip effect: agility up (medium), impact absorption (low), parry (low)**

The abilities and effects were not very exciting. I suppose that's all I could expect, since the enemy had only been a clone of the original White Tiger. The agility boost would be useful, but there was an issue with impact absorption and parry. If I were to be positive about it, I'd say that they might end up proving useful against defense rating attacks, like the kind that Glass and L'Arc used.

If only I could have gotten my hands on some of the real materials, things might have been different. But according to Romina, there were hardly any more left in the world, because so many different people and countries had used them. L'Arc managed the national storehouse, and there was practically none left.

But they had promised to find some for me before the final battle came.

L'Arc figured that my level wouldn't be high enough to access whatever shield the materials unlocked for a while yet, and I couldn't argue with his logic.

Anyway, this shield didn't have any counter effects, so I didn't really want to use it. Still, it could cover the gap between shields until I got to a level where I could access the Spirit Tortoise Heart Shield.

I hadn't used the Shield of Wrath in a very long time, so I figured I could always switch to that if I needed it. But then again, it had a powerful effect on Filo too, and because she had changed so much when we crossed between the worlds, I was a bit worried about how that shield would affect her now.

Fitoria's feather had kept her from losing her mind, but I didn't think it would work in this world.

So that's why I was using this shield. Even though it didn't have the best effects, I could at least depend on it for its defense rating.

Oh, and Chain Shield seemed to be a different version of Change Shield.

When I used Air Strike Shield, then Second Shield, and so on, I could use Chain Shield to link them all together in a chain. It was pretty useful because I could move them all at the same time. If I could figure out how to work with it, it would probably be a good skill to have in my arsenal, but as things stood now I wasn't really sure how to use it.

"So you've got new friends. But they won't save you now!" someone shouted. Whoever it was, Kizuna and Glass were facing her in the entrance, which, by the way, had been completely destroyed.

A woman in a hakama stood in the rubble.

Her hair was pulled back into a ponytail. She stood about as tall as Glass.

She had a nice face . . . you know, I feel like I've been saying this a whole lot lately. But anyway, she was beautiful.

"What the hell is going on? Kizuna, is she a friend of yours?"

I hadn't seen her in any of Kizuna's group pictures. Maybe she'd been sick that day?

She didn't look like she'd just stopped by to pay her respects.

"Does she look like a friend?"

"We were about to turn in when she started banging on the door and causing a fuss."

"You have no idea who she is?"

"Judging from her entrance, I don't think she likes us."

"Good point."

Back in the world I came from, there were a lot of people who hated me, so many I couldn't count them if I tried. I seriously doubt I'd recognize them all if they showed up on my doorstep.

"Who are you!?" Kizuna demanded of the attacker.

I wasn't expecting an honest answer.

"My name is Yomogi Emarl! I come on behalf of Kyo to punish those who hold vassal and holy weapons!"

". . ."

Huh. So she just told us the truth. It was all a bit confusing.

Kizuna didn't flinch or let her guard down for a second, but she looked annoyed at the foolishness of her opponent.

I mean, I'm glad she was so forthcoming with the introduction, but how stupid can you be? Was she really an assassin that Kyo sent?

"I will defeat you! Come at me!" Yomogi shouted, drawing a strange looking sword and dashing across the room at us.

"I thought you wanted us to come to you? What the hell?"

This girl was seriously confusing.

"Hya!"

She was fast though! She was so fast that, had it not been for my recent training and level growth, I probably wouldn't have been able to react in time.

I reflexively shot across the room, jumped before Kizuna and Glass, and got my shield up just in time to block her blade, which slammed into the shield. It shook in my hands.

"Ugh . . ."

She wasn't powerful enough to cut through my defenses, but it took all I had to keep my footing.

I wasn't sure if the White Tiger Clone Shield was going to be enough to make it through this fight.

"Thunder Sword!"

A crackling attack of lightning shot from her blade.

"I don't think so!" Raphtalia shouted, drawing her katana from its fully charged sheath. Her speed attack activated, but . . .

"Your footing is all wrong!" Yomogi clipped, jumping back a step and parrying Raphtalia's attack with her blade.

She'd been able to see where Raphtalia was going. Even though she had been in her haikuikku mode. Even though Kizuna and I had trouble seeing it.

"Raphtalia! Back down!" Glass shouted, opening her fan, "Circle Dance Attack Formation: Flower Wind!"

Glass spun on her heels and swiped at Yomogi with her fan. A flower made of pure light shot from the fan, and my accessory's effect activated at the same time, sending out three of them. She'd used that skill before.

We were fighting in Kizuna's house, which sort of made me want to hold back. You didn't want to put years of work into making a house only to bust it up in a battle.

"Ugh!"

Yomogi had rushed to attack Raphtalia, but she had to pivot to dodge Glass's attack.

"So, you're all going to team up on me, are you? It's just as Kyo said, you're evil!"

"Are you kidding? You broke into our house in the middle of the night."

"Ha?!" Yomogi glared at me. She was sweating. "That's right! I had to give priority to my mission, so I chose the cowardly way!"

Huh? Was she joking? Was she an idiot?

She was genuinely confusing.

And yet, she could follow Raphtalia's attack, dodge Glass's attack, move really quickly, and her attacks were powerful.

That sword of hers was piquing my interest. Something about it was strange. The design reminded me of my Spirit Tortoise Heart Shield.

The shape of it was strange too. The gems in the hilt, the shape of the guard . . . Many things about it reminded me of Ren's sword. And she seemed to be able to use skills too.

"But even if you team up against me, it won't save you! I don't care how many of you I have to face—I WILL emerge victorious!"

"You think you stand a chance against all of us together?" I laughed, sounding like a cheap pirate. Oh well.

"Naofumi, that's what people say before they lose."

"Shut up, Kizuna. You're no good against a human opponent anyway. Back off and leave this one to the adults."

"How dare you!"

Kizuna wasn't able to fight against other humans, and

I was pretty sure this Yomogi character was a human. She didn't look like a Grass person, and she didn't look like a Spirit person either.

"I'll show you!" Yomogi barked, rushing at me with her sword.

I was the only guy in the group, and I was standing at the front, so it was only natural that she came at me first.

"Whoa! Air Strike Shield!"

The shield appeared in the air and Yomogi's sword clanged against it.

"You're up to something! But it's not going to work!"

She'd rushed at me, but now she had decided to be cautious, and she started to back up.

I'd seen this kind of thing before. I wonder what Kyo had told her about the Shield Hero.

"Second Shield."

Right before she could jump away, I sent out another shield, and it appeared in midair just behind her knees.

"Huh?!"

"Dritte Shield."

Yomogi could hardly stay on her feet, so just to finish her off, I sent a third shield flying at her, and it appeared in the air by her chest. She had to twist herself into an unnatural position to avoid the shields. She wouldn't be able to hold it for long, unless she was a professional contortionist or something.

Her knees were bent back over the shield behind her, and she couldn't stand up to avoid it, because of the shield in front of her. She was stuck.

"You coward!"

She hadn't fallen yet, but it seemed to take all of her energy to avoid collapsing.

"I'm impressed you're still standing up."

"L'Arc told me about when you did that to him. He said it was really hard to fight back,' Glass said.

"That's the Shield Hero for you," added Kizuna.

"I appreciate the commentary, but will you please contribute to the fight now?!"

"Here I go!"

"Me tooo!"

"Feh . . . Should I help too?"

Raphtalia dashed forward to take advantage of Yomogi's instability, while Filo started to chant an incantation.

Rishia was fumbling with an ofuda and getting ready to throw it.

I was reaching for Yomogi's sword, just to make sure, but I wasn't going to make it in time. So there was only one thing to do.

"Chain Shield!"

A chain appeared and linked the shields all together.

Because of their position, Yomogi found herself entangled

in the chain. Then the shields began to spin and rotate around her.

"Ugh . . ."

It was a good combo. Perfect, really. I'd wrap her up and try to wring information about Kyo out of her.

"Ha!"

Yomogi thrust her sword into the ground. With an eruption of sparks the chain shattered, and all the shields vanished.

That was a mighty fine sword she had. If only a certain Sword Hero I knew was half as good with his sword . . .

. . . Not that this was the time or place to bring that up.

"You're pretty good. But I'm not going to lose!" Yomogi shouted.

But Raphtalia was already flying at her. Kizuna used her Bait Lure attack—it would double the effect of the following attack.

"Instant Blade: Mist!"

With any luck, this should end the battle.

Raphtalia, with blinding speed, swung her sword across, right at Yomogi, ending the . . .

"Take this! Dragon Point Technique!"

Yomogi vanished in a flash, leaving behind an afterimage before appearing on the other side of Raphtalia's attack, her sword drawn.

"Wha . . ."

Their swords clashed and showered the ground with sparks.

"Not yet!"

"Ugh!"

Yomogi parried Raphtalia's katana to the side and thrust forward at the opening.

Not on my watch!

"Shooting Star Shield!"

The barrier appeared instantly. Yomogi's sword clattered against it, protecting Raphtalia and repelling Yomogi. Filo rushed to counterattack.

"Zweite Wind Cutter!"

Filo flapped her arms and blade after blade of wind shot at Yomogi, who used her sword to defend herself from each one.

"Wow! Master! This lady is tough!"

"I know. Stay focused!"

"A strange attack indeed! Truly a style from another world!"

"Ha! I could say the same thing!"

"Naofumi, don't you think there's something odd about her sword?" Kizuna shouted.

I took another hard look at it.

There was a gemstone set in the handle, but now it looked more like an eyeball.

It was swiveling and turning in its socket. What was that thing?

"More! More power! Kyo made this weapon, and I am worthy to wield it!"

The blade flashed red and seemed to sizzle with heat before crescent moons shot from its tip and flew at me.

"Ugh . . ." Even with the Shooting Star Shield barrier in place, I wasn't sure if I'd be able to block it.

I readied my shield just as the barrier shattered all around me. The sickles of light kept coming, and they slammed into my shield. Hard.

"Argh!"

I pressed forward with all my might and deflected the attack, sending it soaring off to the right.

It ripped right through the wall of the house and flew off into the sky.

I'd just been mocking the parrying ability of this shield, and now it had saved my life. Oh the irony!

"I'm amazed you survived that. Congratulations. But I will not allow myself to lose to villains like you!"

Was she going to use the same attack again?

Then I noticed something strange. A piece of the shattered barrier was still floating in the air. The barrier itself had shattered, but one of the pieces was still there, hovering in the air. Why? Did it have something to do with my new accessory? Is that all it did?

I didn't have time to wonder too long, because the floating piece of the barrier suddenly accelerated and shot towards Yomogi.

"What?!"

Yomogi snapped to attention and used her sword to block the incoming barrier piece. She was able to stop it, but she left herself wide open.

I guess the accessory made it so that my shattered barrier would turn itself into a flying attack.

"First the strange attacks. Now it's an attack that turns your defensive barrier into an offensive missile. You certainly are a strange one."

There had to be a good way to put this new ability to use.

The best things about Shooting Star Shield were its short cool down time and its efficient SP use. And now it would turn itself into an attack after it broke—which was all the more useful, because my current shield didn't have any counter abilities. I liked the sound of that!

But this battle was starting to stress me out. I was worried about Filo, but at the same time, I was also ready to use the Shield of Wrath to burn this girl to ash.

"Glass, if you don't get into gear and end this thing, I'll end it for you. But, I might take the house out with me."

"Mr. Naofumi, you don't mean . . ."

"That's exactly what I mean. I don't know what it will do

to Filo though, so we better keep an eye on her."

"I'll do my best!" Filo chirped.

"Don't do it!" Glass shouted, understanding what I meant, "Would you destroy the house that Kizuna and I built?!"

"If that's what it takes to end this fight! Our attacks aren't bothering her one bit!"

Hadn't they been watching? She'd blocked every attack we'd thrown at her.

If Rishia didn't watch out, she was going to get herself killed. And this girl might have had attacks that even I couldn't block. To top it all off, Kizuna wasn't any use in a battle against another human.

If the battle went on any longer, we'd probably draw the attention of the authorities, and maybe the castle would send backup.

Everyone was in the middle of scaling up for battle anyway. To jump into a situation like this wasn't very smart.

Whatever happened, we were going to need an attack powerful enough to get rid of this stupid idiot.

Or . . .

"Raphtalia, can you use Illusion Sword?"

"I should be able to, but I'm sure she'll notice."

Raphtalia had about as much attack power as Filo had had in the previous world.

She'd been using a lot of skills, but none of them had

been strong enough to end the match. Had she lost the ability to use those attacks she used to know?"

"What about Ying-Yang Sword, or Directional Blade of Heaven? Can you still use those?"

"Yes, I can."

"Good. I'll buy us some time. You slice this girl up."

"Ah . . . Very well," Raphtalia said, turning her blade horizontal and charging her magic power.

"An opening!" Yomogi yelled, thrusting.

"That's not an opening, that's charging up for an attack. I'll be taking over until she's ready."

"Then I'll just have to take care of you first!"

"Heh, what's a weakling like you going to do?" I said condescendingly, trying to get her riled up.

Yomogi's face turned bright red and she tightened her grip on her sword and said, "What did you say?!"

Yes. It was working. As long as she was paying more attention to me than to Raphtalia, my plan would work. I wasn't relying entirely on Raphtalia's attack. Filo and Glass and Kizuna all had attacks too.

I just had to make sure that this crazy woman's attacks didn't reach any of my teammates. I'd have to provoke her. I needed all her attention on me.

That's when I came up with it. I laughed condescendingly and looked at Yomogi.

"What's so funny?"

"Huh? Oh nothing. I was just thinking about how stupid Kyo looked. It made me laugh, that's all."

"How dare you!"

"How is that gloomy guy? He sure talked himself up, but if he sent you to take us out, he must be too scared to come himself. How did he ask you to come after us? 'I'm too scared. Hewp mweeeee pweeeease?' Ahahaha!"

"You bastard!"

It worked! Her face went red with anger, and she glared at me spitefully. In that moment, she wanted nothing more than to come after me.

"Naofumi, you sure are good at that sort of thing."

"Yes, Kizuna, but it is also helpful," Raphtalia offered.

"Yeah, I know."

I wanted to yell, "Enough with the chit-chat already!" But I didn't get a chance to before Yomogi thrust her sword at me and I blocked it with my shield. For a moment, we were locked in place, my shield against her sword, neither of us overpowering the other.

I suddenly realized that I had never tried to change my shield in a situation like that. It was as good a time as ever to try it. I decided to switch to a shield with a counter effect, so I chose a shield that I'd unlocked from the boss monster that Kizuna had fought during the last wave battle: the Demon Elephant Shield.

Of course, I had already leveled it up. Glass and the others had helped me gather the materials I needed to level it up, so the process had gone quickly.

**Demon Elephant Shield C**
**abilities locked: equip bonus: defense 30: shadow defense up while mounted: rickshaw skill up 4: abilities increase while carrying (medium): special effect: Demon Elephant Tusk (critical)**

My filolial series had an ability adjustment while mounted (high) effect, so in order not to overlap that shield, this shield offered a defense boost instead.

I didn't know anything about the other effects. Was I supposed to pull a rickshaw? I don't think so! It might have meant that anyone I carried would get an ability boost, but I wasn't going to carry anyone, so I guess I'll never find out.

Was I supposed to carry Raphtalia on my shoulders in a battle? Ha!

I was distracted, imagining the absurdity for a second, but I quickly snapped back to the battle at hand, and I had just changed to a new shield.

The new shield appeared instantly in the place of the old one, and as Yomogi's sword clattered against it, the counter effect Demon Elephant Tusk (critical) activated.

"What?!"

The elephant tusk relief on the exterior of the shield began to glow. It then fired a sphere of black light at Yomogi.

"Ugh! But . . . You haven't got me yet."

She'd been too close to dodge the attack, maybe because her sword was locked up against my shield. The effect activated a couple more times. The dark spheres of light slammed into her with satisfying power and sound.

"Ugh . . ."

Yomogi tried to thrust at me again, but she failed and was forced to jump back to get some distance. She was breathing hard, holding the shoulder that had been hit by the spheres of light. Had I managed to do some real damage?

"That was some trick. You managed to hurt me."

It looked like the Demon Elephant Tusk (critical) made critical hits from time to time.

"Hey Master! I think I can do something!"

"Raful!"

Raph-chan and Filo, in her humming falcon form, hopped up onto my shoulders and started chanting incantations.

"Imma do it! Raph-chan, do it with me!"

"Raful!"

They chanted so quickly! What were they doing?

I didn't have time to wonder. They combined their powers for a new spell.

"Joint Magic! Pinwheel!"

When Filo and Raph-chan cast their spell all the lights around us started flashing on and off, and then the room was plunged into darkness. The light was so blinding I had trouble adjusting my eyes.

Then four blades made of wind, like throwing stars, shot at Yomogi from all directions.

"Fascinating! I've never heard of such an attack!" Yomogi shouted.

Was she enjoying herself?

"Glass! Hope you're ready to help us out here!"

"Yes I am!" she shouted, opening her fan and dancing in the darkness, once again triggering Circle Dance Attack Formation: Flower Wind. Yomogi could hardly keep up. She was forced further back.

"You think you've got me, is that it?!" Yomogi yelled, thrusting her blade into the ground. Was she going to use that attack again?

No, she had other plans.

The eyeball-like decoration on the hilt of her sword opened its eyelid and shot a beam of light at us. I rushed forward to block the beam before it could hit anyone.

"Ready?"

"Yes, I'm ready!" Raphtalia shouted, jumping out from the shadows and slashing horizontally with her katana.

She looked really cool when she did it, appearing from the darkness behind Yomogi and brandishing her sword like that.

"Directional Blade of Heaven!"

Ying-yang patterned circles appeared around her. The swirling black and white pattern grew increasingly intricate and complex, then the spheres split in two. I hadn't realized there were so many intricate details before. Had the attack changed? Or was this some kind of effect of the vassal weapon?

"Ya!"

Did she miss?

No—Yomogi used her sword to block the attack, filling the air around her with showers of sparks.

"Ugh . . . I'm not giving up so easily! If I give up now, I'll never be able to face Kyo again!"

"Ew! Why would you even want to?"

"I'll not have you insult Kyo!"

"Mr. Naofumi!"

Yomogi had been about to go after Raphtalia in retaliation, but my new insult had upset her so much that she turned to me instead, slicing at me with her sword. Of course, I blocked it with my shield, but something about her attacks felt different than last time.

"Hey, that sword of yours . . ."

The eyeball-like gemstone looked different than before. The eye was wide open. It looked wicked. I'm not saying that

I had the abilities of a master craftsman, but something was definitely wrong. I felt like something terrible was coming, that we'd all be in serious trouble if we didn't get rid of that sword as soon as possible.

"Your sword is going crazy! Get rid of it!"

"What? You suggest there are faults with Kyo's masterful creation?"

I felt it when the blade was locked against my shield. It felt like a heartbeat. Was I imagining it? What was worse was it seemed to be speeding up. Faster and faster. It was like it was counting down to an explosion.

"I'm telling you—let that sword go!"

I didn't care what happened to Yomogi, I just didn't want to get caught up in an explosion.

"How stupid do you think I am? Put down my weapon when faced with enemies?!"

She was determined. She whipped around to dash at Raphtalia, ready to strike a killing blow. But then . . .

An ofuda flew across the room and hit her hand. Yomogi and I both looked down at it, then scanned the room to see where it had come from.

"Oh, I didn't miss!"

Yes—Way to go Rishia! She sure was a good shot!

"What?!"

The ofuda stuck to her hand and burst into flames, forcing her to drop the sword.

Yomogi yelped, but it was too late. I ran to kick it across the room, but I was too late.

Something like a vine shot from the sword and wrapped itself around Yomogi's arm.

"What the!" she shouted in shock, terrified, as if she hadn't realized how strange her weapon had been until that very moment.

"Ughhhhh."

The vine wrapped tighter around her wrist. It seemed to be sucking something out of her. Was it . . . Blood? It must have been stealing her magic power too, and maybe even poisoning her as it did.

Yomogi glanced at me with bloodshot eyes, then hoisted the sword high over her head. "My body! It's moving on its own!"

I raised my shield to block the attack, but she brought the blade down with so much power that the impact sent me sliding backwards.

Luckily, I was able to keep my footing, but if I hadn't been lucky, she'd be slamming me into the ground by now.

The glowing light in the hilt of her sword was growing stronger.

"Drop it! Drop the sword!"

Realizing the danger, she used her free hand to try and pry her fingers from the handle. But the vines shot out and gripped her even tighter.

"Ugh . . ."

I didn't like the look of this. It looked like it might explode at any minute.

I readied my shield to protect everyone from the coming blast. I thought about Yomogi too, but I couldn't see a way to save her from what was coming. The only thing I could do was to protect my friends and try to limit the damage.

"Bait Lure!"

Kizuna hit the glowing sword with her lure and said, "Don't give up yet!" as she turned her weapon into the tuna knife and prepared to attack.

"Blood Flower Strike!"

That was Kizuna's favorite attack. It didn't work against human opponents, but it was devastating for a monster. She sent the attack flying at the sword.

It was a powerful attack, but it wasn't enough to destroy the sword, which was tougher than I had thought. Yomogi herself was unharmed, but the vines wrapped around her arm had been destroyed by Kizuna's attack. She quickly dropped the sword.

"Yes! Good one!" I shouted, grabbing the sword where it lay.

It must have decided that I was its new target, because it shot more of its vine-like appendages at me.

Heh . . . I wasn't dumb enough to fall for that. I wasn't like

Yomogi. I wouldn't let myself be taken over by some kind of monster sword!

"Aaarrrggh!" I drew back and threw the sword with all my might. I sent it right out through the hole in the wall.

"I'll follow up!" Glass shouted, sending another of her Circle Dance Attack Formation: Flower Wind attacks hurdling after the sword.

Her attack hit the sword while it was still in the air, and it went careening off into the sky.

That was a good hit. Did her attack have a homing ability?

Finally, the sword exploded in the air.

"I'm glad we got rid of it. It would have been bad if that thing had exploded in here."

"I cannot believe that Kyo's masterful invention would malfunction like this . . ." Yomogi muttered holding her wounded arm and wincing in pain.

"Well you don't have a weapon anymore, so what are you thinking of doing now? It looks like that thing managed to sap a lot of your strength before we got rid of it."

Did she think we were just going to let her run away?

"Before you think of running, I should let you know that we have the Hunting Hero with us, who is better at hunting than anyone. If you want to run, then go ahead. It will be hunting time."

"You make me sound so evil when you put it that way," Kizuna said.

"Don't worry about it, Kizuna. He just enjoys threatening people," Glass said.

I could go without her commentary, but she wasn't exactly wrong either.

"Ahh . . . well, let's leave that up to Mr. Naofumi, shall we?"

"Rafu."

"That was some explosion. Oh look! The light is coming back to Master.

The light from the explosions fell like snow, slowly falling back toward me. What did it mean?

"So what's next?"

We had better start by punishing this crazy person who came to kill us in the middle of the night. We could tie her up and torture her for information. She looked like she would just tell us the truth regardless though.

"Ugh . . . Kill me!" Yomogi shouted, raising her hands in the air.

"Fine, we'll let that greasy old man take care of you. Raphtalia, wasn't there a monster that looked like a pig demi-human around here? I think his name was Oak?"

"I'll survive whatever torture you can think of!" she barked.

"Heh. Don't go thinking that you'll come out of this in one piece."

"How do you ever think of these things?"

"Naofumi, you get all this from your otaku days, don't you? Particularly from the 'adult' stuff," Kizuna gave me the side eye. But, wasn't that obvious?

Besides, it actually sounded like something Eclair would have said, like something she'd say to a prisoner.

"Anyway, your name is Yomogi, right? Well Yomogi, we're going to tie you up now."

And so we succeeded in capturing Kyo's midnight assassin alive.

## Chapter Five: Together, With Conditions

"Let's head to the castle for now."

"Let's lock her up, so we have guards watching her."

I had a feeling her stats were high enough to break out of a jail cell if she wasn't watched. In the last world, they would reset your level when you were thrown in jail. From what I could tell, that wasn't the case in this world.

"We can torture her for information after we get to the castle."

"You're really stuck on that, aren't you? But I guess you're right."

"Well, we have a war to win here, don't we? This girl came after us wielding an invention created by the very enemy we are trying to defeat. This is our best chance to find out what we are up against, isn't it?"

"I'll bite my own tongue off before I say anything to you!" Yomogi shouted, and tried to bite through her tongue.

"Zweite Heal." I immediately touched her face and healed her.

"You'd prevent me from hurting myself? You bastard!"

"Can we gag her for now?"

"But I—maghfm!" I stuffed a ball of cloth into her mouth

to keep her from trying to bite her tongue again. Then I realized it had been a dirty dust cloth. The torture was starting early. Oh well.

Yomogi squirmed uncomfortably.

"Good thing we have healing spells," Kizuna said. She hadn't noticed that I used a dirty cloth. Raphtalia and Glass noticed though, and they both were just about to mention it . . .

"Alright."

Just then reinforcements from the castle arrived.

"Ms. Kizuna! Ms. Glass! The hero from another world! Master L'Arc has sent us to request your assistance!"

"What happened?"

"Advance enemy troops are attacking the castle and they are surprisingly strong. L'Arc is unable to hold them off on his own!"

They must have been assassins Kyo sent. He was coming after all of us. He planned all these attacks out in advance. He must have been serious about trying to kill us. I looked over at Yomogi—she looked shocked. Ha!

She came charging after us like a wild boar—hadn't she known that Kyo had other plans in the works? Kyo had been right to keep it from her. She seemed like the sort of person to run her mouth. He was like a yakuza boss, probably treating his assassins as disposable.

"We better hurry!"

"Yeah . . . But something about this bothers me . . ."

Glass nodded along with me, "I know what you mean. We had best proceed with caution. Something tells me that Kyo has other plans we don't know about."

Kyo was smart. He would have thought long and hard about a plan to kill us. *Think!* What sort of attack would he expect to be effective against us?

If I were Kyo I'd try to use the technology available to me in the country that I had taken control over. This is the same man that invented things that took control of the Spirit Tortoise. His ambition was a forced to be reckoned with—no doubt his actual plans would outstrip whatever I came up with. I was just guessing, but I thought he'd try to do something to disrupt us, to keep us distracted and confused.

If there was one thing I'd learned since coming to this world, it was that the people here were always coming up with inventions to overcome their limitations.

"We're going to the castle no matter what, right?"

"Yeah."

"And we'd normally use Portal Shield, or Kizuna's return transcript skill, right?"

"Yeah."

I tried to use Portal Shield to teleport to the castle, only to find that something was interfering with it. The skill failed.

"Something is messing with my Portal Shield skill. Better assume that Kyo has a deeper plan than it seems."

"How are we going to get there in time!? We need to hurry!" Kizuna said, flustered.

Glass tried to calm her down, "Relax. How can we be sure that this isn't part of his plan?"

"We can't. But we can't dillydally either!"

"Kizuna, Glass. Calm down and think. All the countries that Kyo has allied with had vassal weapons, didn't they?"

Raphtalia had taken the katana vassal weapon from the country that owned it, which had robbed that country of its power. But, the country with the mirror vassal weapon had fallen under Kyo's control. Was he after the technology in those countries? If so . . .

"What if they are after the dragon hourglasses?"

"Huh?"

"Kizuna, I know you remember what we saw. That guy that was after Raphtalia—hadn't he invented some way to replicate the dragon hourglass's teleport ability? What if they are using that to attack us?"

I don't know how it worked, but they had found some way to replicate the Return Dragon Vein teleport ability. They might have been using it to attack the castle.

The hourglasses were placed in important spots in the national capitals. If they could use this new technology to send as many soldiers as they wanted straight into the heart of a city, then the possibility for destruction was immense. They wouldn't have to defend themselves on the journey here, so they could dedicate all of their resources to the attack itself.

Granted, I didn't know much about how wars worked when the soldiers had levels and status magic. But if they could teleport as many soldiers as they wanted past our defenses, then they'd eventually overpower us, no matter how high-leveled we were—the battle might already be over for all I knew.

This was all hypothetical at this point, but I couldn't deny the possibility that Kyo already had access to the technology that would make it all possible.

"Kizuna, what do you need to use Return Dragon Vein?"

"You need to have visited and registered the hourglass you want to warp to, and you need to be at an hourglass to use it."

"To replicate it you'd need special materials, and you'd need a certain amount of power to make it work."

"We thought of that. The security has been strengthened on that account."

Of course, Glass had thought of that. She wasn't stupid.

The hourglasses in other countries were all closed to the public. Guards would only allow holy heroes or vassal weapon holders to approach.

"If they've broken through the defenses and managed

to register the hourglass, we're in serious trouble . . . it might have already happened!"

"Jewel people have set up a special system to prevent any non-specified persons from teleporting in using the dragon hourglass."

So that's how they prevented us from using Return Transcript.

"Whatever the case, I'm guessing the attack on the castle is a diversion. Their real goal must be the hourglass. If L'Arc is busy fighting them off at the castle, the hourglass might not be watched as closely as it should be."

"Let's use Return Transcript to warp to the hourglass and check it out," Kizuna suggested.

"Good idea," I agreed. "What about her?"

I looked over at Yomogi, who was sitting quietly with an overjoyed look on her face.

"Are you coming with us? If you get lucky, you might even find a chance to escape!"

She didn't enjoy being toyed with. She leaned forward and struggled against her ropes.

"We don't want her biting through her tongue before we can get information out of her."

"True. But, in order to include her in the teleport, I have to invite her into our party. What a pain. Why don't we just leave her with the soldiers here?"

"I guess so."

But, I sent her a party invitation anyway, just for the heck of it.

Huh? She accepted?

Well, I certainly wasn't going to bring her with us, so I immediately kicked her out of the party. Then she whined through her gag and started kicking and squirming.

"What's going on over there?"

"Nothing? I sent her an invite and she accepted, so I went ahead and kicked her out of the party."

"If you want to keep her around, we could just bring her with us."

"Are you serious? She just tried to kill us. You saw that right? Why would we bring her with us?"

"I know that, but . . ."

"Mugh! Mugguh!"

"I wonder what she's trying to say. What should we do?"

I guess it was worth hearing her out. She couldn't speak through that dirty old rag.

If she tried to bite through her tongue, or to cast a spell, I could always just jam it back in.

I pulled out the rag, and immediately, she stuck her tongue out at me and glared with spite.

"What? If you've got something to say then you better spit it out now."

"What's going on?!"

"Who knows? It sure sounds like you're not the only assassin that Kyo sent out tonight."

"That can't be! I was the only one involved with this!"

"I guess he doesn't trust you to get the job done. Either that, or he used you as a distraction."

That sword she'd had would have exploded and taken her out with it. That might have been his plan from the beginning.

"Let me find out what's going on!"

"Ha! Do you understand the situation you're in?"

She tried to kill us in the middle of the night, and now she thought I'd just take her with us so she could satisfy her curiosity?

And yet, she seemed to say everything on her mind, which was a sort of honesty. She was serious too.

"Kyo wouldn't do that! I know he sometimes has contradictory ideas, but he saves a lot of people! He's a good person!"

"We must not be talking about the same guy."

She really glorified Kyo in her head—kind of like what Raphtalia did when she thought about me. I wanted to be the sort of parent that she thought I was.

But Kyo wasn't like that. I remembered how angry he got when Rishia lectured him. I was pretty sure that he wasn't the sort of person that Yomogi seemed to think he was.

"What should we do, Mr. Naofumi?"

"Hm . . ."

"If she'll listen to us, then we might be able to give her a little freedom, no?"

"I guess. And if she tries anything, we'll just kill her."

"Ahh . . . Even though I lost the battle, I cannot believe I must suffer through this. I suppose I will have to endure this punishment."

Seriously, who did this girl think she was?

We didn't have to do anything at all for her. Didn't she understand that?

"She thinks that we're wrong about Kyo, and that he'll come rescue her before she's executed."

"You can read my mind?! I didn't realize you had such powers!"

My god she was simple. Even if I had that ability, I wouldn't have use it to read hers.

"Then let's make a deal. We'll take you with us, so you can find out what's going on. Then when you find out that things aren't as you wished, you tell us what you know. Deal?"

"Very well. I am a warrior, and I keep my promises."

She certainly was forthcoming. She didn't understand the predicament she was in at all, but she couldn't resist making promises and swearing to keep them.

"Kizuna, Glass, if she tries anything, don't hesitate to kill her. I'm not feeling merciful."

"I know."

"Your name's Yomogi, right? When you discover the truth, don't you dare try to escape from it. And don't think that you'll get away. If you do, we'll torture you for information."

"I wouldn't!"

She probably wouldn't. She was obsessed with honor—she lived in a fairytale.

If she decided to turn on us it could be trouble. If only I could have used the slave sealing magic from the last world!

"Mr. Naofumi! Please don't look at Rishia that way," Raphtalia scolded me.

How couldn't I? She was the only one I could still use the slave spell on.

"I bet you were thinking what a help the slave spell would be in this situation."

She read me like a book. But it really would have been helpful.

"Oh yeah, you said something about that before. So . . ." Kizuna said, running to grab a ofuda from the partially destroyed storeroom, "You can use this control ofuda. I never thought I'd use it, but here we are."

"Kizuna, would you really . . . ?"

"Don't we need it to ensure that Yomogi keeps her end of the bargain?"

Yomogi looked at the ofuda in Kizuna's hand and nodded.

"I understand. If that will help you to trust our agreement, I will submit to it."

Huh? That was convenient.

It must have been like the ofuda that had been stuck on Filo back where we found her.

"What is that thing?"

"It's an ofuda that uses magic to control people. They have a bad reputation. You've probably seen them before in . . . Chinese zombie movies?"

Ah . . . those zombies with the ofuda hanging down off of their face or hat. Right.

"The ofuda lends you control over their subconscious. If you're good, you can even make it so that they can only move when commanded to."

"Sounds pretty dangerous. What if someone used them to take control of us?"

"It's possible to resist the ofuda's power, and luckily, they don't work on holy heroes or holders of the vassal weapons. But, they can be very dangerous in the hands of a powerful user though."

These ofuda things might be better than the slave spell I was used to.

"What happens when someone tries to resist it?"

"They have to use all their energy to try and get it off. And while they are occupied, you have a chance to kill them."

Heh . . . that sounded like the perfect system.

So Yomogi would be under my control, just like a slave, but she could remove the ofuda if she really tried. But it would take time to do so, and I could always finish her off while she struggled with it.

"Let's set it up so that she can't get more than a certain distance away from us," Kizuna said, slapping the ofuda onto Yomogi's forehead.

I could see that a great deal of magical power was contained in it. It snapped and crackled with electricity, and slowly peeled off of her forehead. Then a magical pattern flickered and glowed on the ground around Yomogi's feet.

Glass and Kizuna were chanting an incantation, and the mandala-like pattern on the ground appeared to react to it. Finally, Kizuna wrote some characters on the ofuda with blood. Yomogi squirmed with discomfort.

"Now we just need to set the rules and . . . all done. It does draw attention to itself though, so we should try to avoid using it in public."

"Imagine if people used these things to control their armies."

"They are pretty tough, but they are weak against fire and water. They're not as all-powerful as you might hope."

"If this will convince you to take me with you, then I will not try to remove it. Now then, let's get going!"

I wasn't sure if I could trust the ofuda to operate as effectively as the spell I was used to. But then again, we were just using it as insurance against Yomogi's treachery.

"Let's go."

"Yeah, let's go," Kizuna said. She started to chant the return transcript incantation.

A moment later and we were all standing before the dragon hourglass.

There were a lot of guards milling about, but I didn't see any sign of a recent or impending attack. The guards around the hourglass had been instructed to remain cautious, so despite everything happening at the castle, they hadn't left their posts. They could be counted on for that much.

Back where I was from, you couldn't really count on guards to stand their ground. If a guard didn't actually guard anything, then what were they good for?

"Everything looks fine, right?"

"The enemy might be nearby, watching the guards for a chance to strike."

"Aren't you a little paranoid?"

"It's what I would do if I were in his situation. Someone should stay here to keep watch."

"I'm telling you, Kyo wouldn't do that! He's not a coward!" Yomogi shouted.

Glass and Kizuna crossed their arms and knit their brows in thought.

"You're right. We should leave someone here we can trust. Raphtalia, can you stay behind?" I asked Raphtalia.

"But I . . ."

She was strong enough to handle trouble if it showed up. I didn't want to leave her behind, but we could count on her."

" . . . I will stay behind and keep an eye on things."

"Glass?!"

Glass raised her hand to volunteer for the job, and Kizuna yelped with surprise.

We could trust Glass with the job and she was experienced enough to deal with whatever came up. Besides, she was from this world. It made more sense to leave it her hands.

"I believe Naofumi is correct. Kyo has made a fuss at the castle, but if he is truly in possession of technology of the sort you describe, then he may well come after the hourglass. We must ensure its safety."

"But . . ." Kizuna tried to protest.

Then I added, "If you discover that you need my assistance, tell the guards to fire three flares into the air."

Kizuna looked at the smoking castle in the distance and nodded, "Okay. Glass, we're leaving this to you."

"Chris, protect her while I'm gone."

"Pen!"

I found it hard to believe that the penguin was going to be much use, but he bowed deeply in response to Glass's charge and tottered over to stand by Kizuna.

"Alright, Naofumi. We're leaving Glass behind, so you better step up," Kizuna said.

"I know, and I will. Let's go!"

"Alright!" everyone shouted in unison.

With Raph-chan and Filo on my shoulders, I took off running. Everyone followed me.

I was worried that Rishia would trip and fall, but she managed to keep up.

We ran toward the smoking castle. The town we ran through on the way didn't seem damaged. But it did look like some looters, who had tried to take advantage of the chaos, had been caught and tied up though.

What was going on?

We ran through the castle gates to find L'Arc, Therese, and a number of soldiers fighting. But, what were they fighting? They were monsters, but they looked like humans, too. The battle was intense.

The castle grounds were filled with smoke, and there seemed to be battle happening everywhere at once.

"Hyaa!"

Therese cast support magic on L'Arc, and he shot a skill at the enemy.

But the monsters were quick on their feet, and they dodged his attack. Were these monsters faster than L'Arc? He had a vassal weapon!

One of them appeared behind him, trying to take advantage of an opening in his defenses. I quickly used a skill.

"Air Strike Shield!"

The shield materialized just in time to protect L'Arc from the monster's claws. The monster was caught off guard, which left it open for attack—a chance that L'Arc wasn't going to miss. He swung his scythe.

. . . But the monster dodged again!

"Kiddo! Kizuna!"

"We're so glad you're here!"

L'Arc and Therese smiled. They looked relieved.

"Shooting Star Shield!"

The barrier appeared and covered us all, protecting us from the monsters. When the barrier appeared, the enemy stopped attacking and stared straight at me.

"Hero from another world! How wonderful to see you!"

Huh? What? The enemy turned and stared at us with hate-filled eyes.

Were we their target?

I looked closer. It was pretty dark, so I hadn't gotten a very good look at the monsters yet. But they weren't exactly humans that were turned into monsters . . .

What?! Their faces were strange—half beast, half human. Their bodies also seemed to be split down the center in human and beast halves.

It looked like they'd been made of two different things stuck together. They were really ugly, to be honest.

The leader of the group looked like it was half white tiger. The other half was a woman with a ponytail. Her human eye was sharp and angular, and the other eye was a cat eye. She wore light armor, and it was torn in places, probably a result of the battle.

The human half of her face was actually pretty attractive.

The other enemy troops were similar, but some of them had feathers and bird-like features, others had tortoise shells on their backs. All of them appeared to be some kind of human-animal hybrid, their hands were like claws.

They were clearly not like the demi-humans back in the world I'd been summoned to. Something about them seemed . . . unnatural. The demi-humans I knew weren't like that.

Their human parts . . . their faces . . . I felt like I'd seen them before—but where?

"Hey . . ."

"Raphtalia, Rishia, and Kizuna were pointing at the enemy troops, speechless."

"What happened to you?!" Kizuna screamed. But damn it! I still couldn't figure out who they were.

"Raphtalia," I said, motioning for her to come over. I whispered in her ear, "Who are these people?"

"You mean you don't remember?!"

"You don't remember us?! How dare you!"

The enemy reacted to Raphtalia's comment and shouted in rage.

They rushed at me, their weapons brandished. One thrusted a naginata at me.

"Uh-oh!"

The barrier shattered, and the pieces floated in the air around us.

I blocked the naginata thrust with my shield and grabbed the handle. The other enemy troops howled with rage and came charging at me.

"Die! Everyone! Massacre them all!"

"That's right. They're the ones that came after me and accused me of stealing the katana of the vassal weapons," Raphtalia explained.

I finally remembered those faces. It was the gaggle of women that had been with Trash #2. They were so loud and raucous that I never did figure out what his name was.

The shards of the shattered barrier flew at Trash #2's friends.

The charging people weren't able to avoid the shards. Some of them blocked the shards and kept running. Others had shields like tortoise shells to block them.

L'Arc and Therese didn't miss their chance. He swung his scythe and she shot magical spells. Raphtalia drew her sword and shot across the battlefield.

It wasn't clear if Kizuna would be able to damage these half-human enemies, so she was staying back with Yomogi. I tried to keep Filo and Rishia from getting caught up in the fight.

"Go Chris!"

Kizuna picked up Chris and threw him!

Chris spun in circles and shot through the battle, just like Filo's Spiral Strike attack.

Chris blew right past the monsters, but a lot of their armor and clothing was torn in the process, and blood seeped through the cuts.

Heh . . . So that's how Kizuna was able to attack.

"Rafu?"

I looked at Raph-chan. Her eyes sparkled with understanding.

She wanted to try the same thing, but she wasn't strong enough yet. She'd have to stay on my shoulder for the time being.

"Master! I wanna try that!" Filo shouted.

She wasn't the best melee fighter these days. I thought she'd make a better support fighter. I was hoping she'd have some bird songs with some good effects.

"Not now!"

"But . . ."

"I want you to work with Raph-chan to support the rest of us with magic."

"Okay!"

With both of them on my shoulders, I continued to block and avoid the attacks of Trash #2's cohorts.

"Shield Prison!"

The wall of shields bought me some time. I looked over at Raphtalia who had locked swords with the leader.

"What happened to you? Why do you look like this?!"

"Isn't it amazing? After you killed our leader, we were left without direction, and our lands were taken over by another country. We thought it was the end for us, but then Kyo, the holder of the book of the vassal weapons, saved us."

"What?!"

"He doesn't want to rule over us, he wants to give us the opportunity to exact our revenge. He gave us this power so that we could kill you!"

"But . . ."

"Up until now we could never have won a battle against a vassal weapon, or against one of the holy heroes. So Kyo gave us this power, this power he took from the copies of the Four Symbols, the four holy beasts!"

"And that's why you look like this?!" Kizuna yelped.

A woman nodded.

"Kyo will return us to our previous forms once we defeat you! When we defeat you, all will be returned to how it should be, to how it was!"

"That's why you must . . ." they all shouted in unison, charging up for an inhuman attack, "Die!!!"

The tiger-lady was wrapped in howling winds, which flew into her weapon. She charged us.

The bird-lady's wings burst into flame. She flapped them hard, sending the flames roaring at us.

The tortoise-lady sent huge boulders to rain down on us from above.

The dragon-lady . . . didn't seem to be there.

"Air Strike Shield! Second Shield! Dritte Shield!"

I sent out the trio of shields and immediately followed them with Shooting Star Shield, blocking all of their attacks.

Then I focused for a minute and cast Zwiete Aura on everyone, starting with Raphtalia.

"No! Kyo would never do something so inhumane!" Yomogi shouted behind me. She reached out with her good hand and grabbed Kizuna's shoulder. "Hunting Hero, I have a request. Please allow me to fight with you. These fools that would speak ill of Kyo must be silenced!" She grabbed a sword that had fallen at her feet.

"If you try to attack us, you'll regret it."

"I will not do such a thing!"

Kizuna nodded, and Yomogi took off running. She jumped into battle, slashing at the woman that Raphtalia was fighting.

"Stay out of this!"

"Ha! You think I can't dodge your bumbling attacks?" Yomogi said, jumping back to avoid the woman's attack and then charging forward again with Raphtalia. "How dare you tell such lies about Kyo! He would never do such things!"

"You'd call me a liar?!" the beast-woman shouted. She looked confused by the accusation. "We can bring back our leader if we kill you! You sliced him in two! Kyo can bring back master!"

"He can bring back the dead?!"

"Since when did Kyo have that kind of power?"

That would be amazing, really. Was there a deeper taboo in all of creation? I guess you saw it in old RPGs from time to time. But if he could do that, why not send Trash #2 as his assassin?

There was something else, some other layer to his plan.

"The Kyo that you speak of is not the Kyo that I know!" Yomogi shouted and continued her assault. Raphtalia looked confused.

"You fool! You have yet to see my true power!" The beast side of the woman started to glow, then slowly expand, growing larger and larger. I didn't like the look of it.

I was doing all I could to stop the endless string of attacks coming from the other women. There were too many of them, and they were all pretty damn strong.

It was like the battle we had in the chamber of the Spirit Tortoise's core. The neo-guardians had been about this strong.

"Tsugumi! Take this!" one of the other women said and threw a spear to their leader, who was locked in battle with Yomogi and Raphtalia. One look at the spear and I could hardly believe my eyes.

"Can it be?!"

The spear looked just like the creepy weapon that Yomogi had been carrying when she tried to attack us back at the house, and now, it was in their leader's hand.

## Chapter Six: The Reformed

"Hyaaa!" The woman named Tsugumi raised the spear over her head and swung it in a circle. She didn't actually hit anyone with it, but the motion produced a shockwave powerful enough to send Raphtalia and Yomogi flying.

"Ugh . . ."

"Uh . . ."

Both of them took the brunt of the impact, and were bleeding all over.

This wasn't good. I'd tried to defend them, but I wasn't fast enough.

Judging from the battle we'd had with Yomogi, I assumed that the spear was making her attacks more powerful. Yomogi didn't seem as imposing now, without her special sword.

But now Tsugumi was faster and stronger than Raphtalia. Her abilities were on par with Eclair—maybe even better. She was probably as good as Raphtalia had been before she was chosen to wield the katana of the vassal weapons.

Yeah, she was pretty strong. Those that held a vassal weapon could improve the growth stats of their party members. I was guessing that these women had gotten a boost from Kyo.

They were strong, but that didn't mean that victory was certain—not yet.

Filo had always been my trump card, the back-up surprise when things got rough for Raphtalia.

Raphtalia had just gotten her hands on the katana recently, and she had already grown so powerful that she was almost as strong as Glass. If this woman was able to send her flying with a simple swipe of her spear, she must have been pretty powerful too.

Considering how easily she'd parried their attacks, we'd be in trouble if she hit us with a skill, or a technique, or whatever. I'd try to block it, but who knew if I'd be able to?

Regardless, there was another problem we had to face first.

"That weapon . . . Kyo must have made that." Yomogi muttered, her face pale.

Had she finally lost faith in him? Was she just afraid of the weapon? It was hard to say, but she was definitely unnerved.

"Calm down," Raphtalia said.

Yomogi snapped back to reality, and shook her head, "Where did you get that weapon?!"

"Don't you know? Kyo gave it to me as a way to ensure the departure of the holy heroes and your vassal weapon holding friends."

Yomogi shook her head in disbelief, "Lies! Even if that's

true, you must know how dangerous that weapon is! Kyo must have given it to you without realizing the danger it put you in!"

"Kiddo, what do you know about that weapon?" L'Arc asked, parrying one of the beast-woman's attacks.

It wasn't the time or place to sit down and give a lecture about the weapon, but if it worked like Yomogi's sword, we were all in serious trouble. We had to find a way to get rid of it without setting it off.

"That thing was probably made with energy he took from the Spirit Tortoise—it's a monster. It will give you unbelievable power when you wield it, but it has a mind of its own, and pretty soon it will go on a rampage and explode."

Whether the rampage and explosion were part of the design or a result of an experiment was hard to say. But I was sure of one thing: Kyo had taken the Spirit Tortoise familiars (mimic type) and found a way to turn them into weapons.

"There's still time! I had one of those weapons too, and it nearly killed me. You have to let it go!"

Tsugumi answered Yomogi's warning with an attack.

I immediately deployed Shooting Star Shield, and followed that with Air Strike Shield to protect her.

"Ha!"

"Ugh . . ."

The attack shattered the barrier and the Air Strike Shield, slamming into my shield with a burst of sparks. Then it broke the defense level of the shield and the armor I was wearing took a little damage. The power of that weapon was monstrous!

We had a real problem on our hands.

"Ha!"

"To prove that Kyo is right, you mustn't use that weapon! The Kyo that I know wouldn't want you to do this!"

Tsugumi was off her guard after I blocked her attack, so Yomogi and Raphtalia rushed to attack. But Tsugumi was too fast, and dodged at the last second.

"You'll die here tonight!"

Damn it . . .

"Second Shield!"

I quickly blocked the attack with Second Shield, maneuvered around her spear, and caught the handle between my arm and torso, pushing her back and off balance.

Luckily, I'd learned a thing or two about fighting a spear-wielding opponent when dealing with Motoyasu. I'd only imagined doing that move before, but it ended up working.

Spears are best for keeping the enemy at a distance, so if you got up close, the spear became a liability—you could only use the shaft.

To a degree . . . I was somehow able to restrain her.

"Not so fast!" she shouted.

Even the handle could be a weapon with the right amount of attack power. It really hurt.

"Therese!"

I didn't have time to cast spells, so I'd need to rely on Therese for support.

"Great power in these stones, hear my plea and show yourself. My name is Therese Alexanderite, and I am your friend. Give them the power of unshakeable protection!"

"Shining Stones: Hardened Protection!"

Therese's spell took effect, and I felt my defense rating rise.

The pain disappeared almost entirely. Therese's magic must have worked by multiplying my stats, so if my defense rating was already high, then her spell worked even better.

"Ah, so you're tougher now? You otherworldly hero! Kyo said that you were useless aside from defense, but you sure are annoying!"

I guess they'd been gossiping about me. I hope they'd heard about my counter effects.

Too bad she didn't just drop the spear and run away. I really would have preferred that.

"Master!"

"Rafu!"

Filo and Raph-chan jumped at Tsugumi.

"Hey, what are you—"

"How irritating!" Tsugumi shouted, swiping at them with her beast hand.

"Yikes!"

"Rafu!"

Before Tsugumi could slice at them with her claws they both disappeared in a puff of smoke. Where did they go?"

"That was close!"

Filo reappeared a short distance away, carrying Raph-chan.

"Rafuful!"

I guess they used Raph-chan's illusion magic to escape just in time.

"Be careful, you two. You're not strong enough for this yet."

"We're okay, master! We can dodge that lady's attacks!"

I guess Filo could use haikuikku if she needed to. She'd have to charge up her magic power, but she could also fight in that energy-conserving mode that Fitoria taught her.

But this wasn't the time. The enemy was too dangerous.

"Charge up!"

Both of them jumped onto my shoulders.

"We can get stronger if we ride on your shoulders for a bit!"

Ah, right. That must be what abilities increase while carrying (medium) did.

Hopefully it would come in handy.

"Tsugumi!"

The group of women all focused on me now, deciding I was the leader of the group.

"Better watch out, Kiddo, looks like they've got it out for you!"

"I guess so. I won't make it easy on them!"

"Indeed. We cannot afford the possibility of your loss, Naofumi. I have many gemstones that require your skilled attention," Therese exclaimed.

"What are you talking about?" I barked. I wasn't sure I liked the way Therese was thinking. L'Arc better rein her in.

Anyway, back to business.

"Feh . . ." Rishia whimpered, tossing an ofuda.

"Wh . . ."

"What?!"

It fluttered helplessly from her hands and hit one of the beast women, prompting a yelp of surprise. It might actually come in handy. It looked really weak and pathetic, so they would probably ignore it—only for it come back and bite them later.

Anyway, I still had a hold on Tsugumi's spear, but I didn't know how long I could keep it. With my boosted defense, I was hoping to twist her to the ground. But I didn't have much hope that it would work. Come to think of it, I don't think I had pulled it off since the Cal Mira islands.

Regardless, I was thinking it over when Tsugumi tightened her grip on the spear, and its point started to flash behind me. The point of the spear snapped and cracked behind me, and it started to feel like it was burning me.

I'd been through this before! When I was fighting the high priest!

He'd held a replica of the holy weapons. His attacks had burned just like this.

There was only one thing to do.

"Filo! Get out of here and prepare yourself!"

"Okay!"

"Rafu!"

Filo knew what I meant. She grabbed Raph-chan and flew off.

"Mr. Naofumi!"

"Kiddo, are you doing what I think you're doing?! Everyone get away!"

"What? What's happening?" Kizuna shouted as L'Arc pulled her away with him.

"Mr. Naofumi!"

"It'll be okay! Raphtalia, help protect Yomogi and Filo!"

I hadn't done this in a long time, but I didn't have any other way to survive this beast-woman's attacks.

As for unlocking the Spirit Tortoise Heart Shield, I may have finally been able to do it in this world, but the Shield of Wrath was still stronger.

I knew it was risky, but I had to protect everyone from the attack this lady was about to unleash, and I didn't have any other ideas.

I had to do it. I readied my shield and prepared to use the most forbidden power I had.

The Shield of Wrath—I'm forced to turn to you again.

I didn't want to do this!

"Wh . . . What?"

"What's the otherworldly hero up to now?" Yomogi shouted as L'Arc pulled her and Raphtalia out of harm's way.

"Kiddo just switched to a weapon that will hurt him, but it's strong enough to stop their attacks."

"Hurt him? But . . ."

"Has Kyo used it?"

The women regrouped and came rushing at us, seeing Kizuna and Raphtalia fleeing as an opportunity. They attacked in wave after wave.

"Arrrhhhh!"

"Take that! Piercing shot!"

I had my grip on the shaft of the spear, but the spear point pushed against my shield, unleashing a deadly skill. A burst of energy shot out of the spear. But I was able to hold it off.

Like trying to stick your finger in a faucet to stop the water, the energy beams burst out anyway. The light shot through the castle walls, and there was a crater left on the ground around us afterward. But that was the end of it.

"ARRHHHHH!" Tsugumi roared, getting ready to blast me away.

I had to fill her with despair. I had to make her think she had no hope for victory.

The spear started to glow, and the eyeball set in the handle opened and looked around in short, erratic jerks.

"Everyone! Focus your attack on him!"

"Right!" they all shouted together.

"Come at me then!"

If they attacked me, they weren't going to like what happened next.

I pulled on the spear and spun it around, grazing the rushing attackers.

"Ahhhh!"

"Ugh!"

It had barely touched them, but they took plenty of damage. Luckily for them, half of their bodies had been reformed with monster parts, so they were a bit singed, but they were fine. A little healing magic would heal them.

"You're damn persistent."

"All I have is a shield. I have to do what I can."

Locked neck and neck with her, I was still able to continue to hold off Tsugumi's energy attacks.

But, finally, the skill seemed to run out of steam. There was a deflating hiss, and smoke streamed from the tip of her spear.

"Give up already!"

I had to get this fight over with.

"No thanks!"

"Then you'll pay for it!"

I'd pay them back for all the pain they've caused—and more.

"Therese! Get a defense spell on us! Filo, you help! Get everyone you can on this! Protect everyone!"

"Alright!" Therese shouted. She called some other soldiers over and they all began to summon a protective barrier.

The flames might've been so powerful they would've turned everything to ash. But, I'd tried my best during the battle with Glass, and she had survived. So, I just wanted to make sure I didn't do any unnecessary damage. I used Air Strike Shield just in case.

"Ugh!"

The shield was starting to take over my mind. A deep hatred burned in my head, telling me to kill everyone.

But there were people I had to protect—wanted to protect.

Not only Raphtalia and Filo.

After the battle with the high priest, so many things had happened. There were more people on my side now—more people that needed my protection. The more I cared about, the less I could use this shield.

During the battle with the Spirit Tortoise, Ost had taken

the rage and hatred from the shield and made it into power, power that made the shield even stronger.

Yes . . . now my rage had a direction. I didn't just hate the whole world. It was focused on a single point . . .

To protect my friends, I had to control my rage.

Rage, hate, disgust, loathing, resentment, anger . . .

They weren't for everyone. I had to focus them on those in front of me.

"AAAAGHHHHH!"

Dark Curse Burning S activated, roaring forth from my shield.

"I thought he could only defend?!"

"Haven't you been paying attention? Of course I can counter attack!"

Black flames leapt from my shield, fanning out before me and rushing over the enemy.

"Ahhhhhh!"

"Arrrughgh!"

I had never felt such power in these detestable flames before. They were stronger than they had ever been, roaring in my ears as they burned everything before me.

"Whoa . . ."

"So that's . . . That's Naofumi's forbidden attack . . ."

"It's a bit different from yours, isn't it? Pretty dangerous. Glass needed soul-healing water to stand up to it."

"Enough chitchat! Fight!"

I felt the hatred wane, but I knew that it would come back. That's how the attack worked.

Just withstanding it was almost enough to drive me crazy. It was a battle I had to fight with myself. But I had friends now, Raphtalia, Filo, and the others. I had to protect them. It might sound a little cheesy, but if I wanted to protect my friends, I couldn't allow myself to be swallowed by the hate.

"Damn it! We're not giving up!"

Even after being hit with an attack like that, she still refused to drop the spear.

How was I supposed to stop someone so obsessed?

Trash #2 was a real creep, from what I knew about him. But if there were all these people that still felt strongly for him, I guess he must have done some good things in his life too. I guess if everything had gone how he wanted it to, his inventions might never have been used, and all these women wouldn't have ended up the way they did.

Besides, Glass did warn him at the end. Don't move, she said.

He's the one who ignored the warning, and that's why he died. Why did they insist on making all of this our fault?

Ah! The Shield of Wrath was taking over my mind again.

I had to stay on my toes. I couldn't afford to get lost in the hate.

"More power! More! Enough to destroy these fools!"

The burned enemies slowly rose to their feet.

As if to regenerate what they lost to the flames, the beast side of their bodies grew and spread.

Damn it! How much did I have to burn them to get them to stay down?

"Hyaaaaa!"

Not good! Just like what had happened with Yomogi, the spear was glowing with heat, and tentacle-like vines whipped out and wrapped around Tsugumi's arm.

But Tsugumi didn't seem to mind. Maybe it was because of her beast-half?

What was I supposed to do? Kizuna cut the vines last time, but . . .

"Blood Flower Strike!"

Kizuna was on her in a flash. She sliced through the vines and fell back to safety. But the vines grew back almost immediately and wrapped around Tsugumi's arm again.

Did she really not notice or care what was happening?

The power she emitted steadily grew stronger. I . . . can't hold it off much longer!

"This is the end!"

The tip of her spear suddenly shot . . . yes, shot stars!

There was no doubt in my mind. This weapon of hers was a copy of Motoyasu's spear.

This attack was probably Shooting Star Spear.

"Ahaha! That should end it! Die!"

She wrenched the spear free from my grip and pointed it at me, ready to shoot a beam, when . . .

There was an awful sound, like the tearing of flesh.

"Gyaaaaahhhh!"

The smile disappeared from her face as Tsugumi fell to the floor. She wriggled and writhed.

"Tsugumi?!"

"What's happening?!"

The other women ran over to Tsugumi where she lay on the ground.

"Ahhh! Ag . . . argh!"

She twitched violently as her eyes rolled back into her head.

Was it the spear that was doing this?

Before I even had the time to wonder, the women that were locked in battle with Raphtalia and L'Arc stopped fighting and began to groan. It was like their medicine had suddenly worn off.

"What the hell is going on?"

"You think WE did this?" The cursed flames had the special effect of delaying any restorative effects for a while—but that wouldn't have been enough to cause this.

"You don't think this has anything to do with those creepy animal bodies of yours?" Kizuna asked.

But there wasn't any time to waste on that.

"Kizuna, they aren't our biggest problem right now."

"You're right!"

The spear was still wrapped around Tsugumi's arm as she writhed on the ground. It was sucking all of her power, just like it had done with Yomogi. That meant that it was probably just about ready to explode.

Damn it! Did we even have time to throw it?

I was worried about that crystalline eyeball in the handle. It was shining brighter than Yomogi's sword had, which made me fear that the explosion was going to be bigger than last time.

"Kizuna! Wait!"

"What?!"

"Don't cut the vines yet. It might trigger the explosion."

I hadn't known what to look out for during the fight with Yomogi, but looking back on it now, the vines may have caused it.

"Maybe it won't explode as long as it is sucking energy out of her."

"Are you saying we should just leave her like this?"

She had a point. If she was twitching on the ground, then she was probably almost out of energy anyway. If we weren't going to be cruel, we'd have to get them to a safe place before we let the thing explode.

Kizuna and Raphtalia probably wouldn't like that plan. I wasn't too fond of it either, but we didn't have many options.

There wasn't enough time to have a discussion either way.

"Ahhhh!" they all shouted in pain. Then they crawled to their feet like beasts and began to howl and shout.

Falling on all fours, they started to walk and stalk around the battlefield like the animals they were based on.

"Damn. What the hell is going on with these people?!" L'Arc shouted as he worked with Raphtalia and Yomogi to control the raging beasts.

They didn't move with intelligence, or with a plan, but they were faster and harder to predict than before.

"Fehh . . ."

"Raful!"

Raph-chan puffed up her tail and cast a spell on the marauding beast women. They all turned to an empty area of the battlefield and rushed to attack it. Raph-chan must have fooled them with some kind of illusion magic. Judging from what I knew about games, illusion magic tended to work best against wild enemies. Of course, on the other hand, there were enemies that it didn't work against at all.

"Stop! Look at what is happening to Tsugumi! Abandon your revenge and do what you can to help her!"

But they weren't listening—or they had lost the ability to listen.

"You all better calm down. That might happen to you next. Better to save your strength."

Then they all seemed to calm down, as if they had lost the will to fight.

"That's it. The ones that are freaking out the most were the most belligerent ones."

". . ."

"Ahhh . . . Ah . . ."

Like a sponge being squeezed, Tsugumi shriveled up before our very eyes. Her cheeks sunk in over her bones, and she looked like a mummy.

It was probably happening because of a combination of two things. The irrational raging that came from her twisted animal side, and that creepy spear thing her hands. Speaking of the spear, I had no doubt that it would explode once it finished sucking the life out of her.

"I can't use portal."

But there is another way I can use portal.

The problem was that it only worked with party members, but even if I didn't set it to teleport myself, I could still open a portal to anywhere I'd been before. I had hoped that I could use it to do something about the spear and Tsumugi, but it didn't work if she wasn't already in my party.

And there was another problem. The beast half of her body was related to the White Tiger, which was having a jamming effect on my ability to use portal too.

There was no good way out.

But I had another idea.

"Cast support magic on her! Don't forget to replenish her magic and SP!"

"What are you thinking?!"

"We're going to bring her somewhere away from everyone and then run for it. If we don't, that weapon will kill us all when it explodes."

"But what about Tsugumi?!"

"We'll think of something as we buy ourselves some time."

But before I could finish my thought, a creepy laugh echoed over the battlefield. It came from the eyeball in the spear.

"You think . . . You can . . . get away?"

The voice cut in and out, but it clearly belonged to Kyo.

He didn't have to tell me. I knew we were out of time.

"Seems . . . failed . . . plenty to get rid of you . . . still . . . this is the . . . !"

There was a deafening clang, and the whole spear began to glow, just like what had happened with Yomogi.

"Kyo! It can't be! This was your plan all along?" Yomogi shouted, but Kyo's voice had already vanished. I guess he had cut it off from his side.

The spear was shining much brighter than Yomogi's sword had. It was definitely about to explode.

"Ha!" Kizuna shouted, dashing forward to cut through the vines.

I couldn't afford to stand back and watch.

I grabbed the spear and tried to throw it as high above our heads as I could. I knew that it was right about to explode.

We weren't going to make it. I felt like a soldier trying to throw back a grenade.

What should I do? What COULD I do?

Time seemed to slow down.

Everyone was going to die.

From what I could tell, the monster that took the form of the spear seemed to have died before it could explode. The same thing had happened with Yomogi back at the house. I felt—and I'm not sure why—like maybe I could absorb it into my shield.

Back at the house I had prioritized throwing the sword away, but I knew that there wasn't time for that now.

There was only one thing left to try. I let my shield absorb it. There was a little resistance at first, but then, as if the shield understood what was happening, it slid in easily the rest of the way.

"Mr. Naofumi?!"

"What?!"

"There's no time. I have no idea if it will work, but I've got to try!"

"It's crazy!"

"What other choice do I have? This shield sucked up the light from the last explosion, so maybe . . ."

Right—this spear thing had probably been made from the Spirit Tortoise's energy. The energy released in the blast was probably returning to the Spirit Tortoise Heart Shield.

A spear icon blinked in my vision. Was it trying to say that there was a foreign object in the shield? The icon was red and flashing.

What if it broke the shield itself? What would happen to me in that case?

I had no idea, but if it would lessen the damage to my surroundings, I had to do it.

"Shield Prison!"

"Mr. Naofumi!"

"Rafu!"

"Master!"

Raphtalia and the others were running over, so I enclosed myself in the shield prison to keep them away. If the shield exploded, it would help with the shockwave too.

"Kiddo . . ."

"Naofumi, you . . ."

"Naofumi . . ."

I heard them shouting through the wall of shields. Then I covered myself with my own shield to protect them from the blast.

I was still using the Shield of Wrath. It was the strongest shield I had, so hopefully it would be enough to stop the explosion!

The red spear icon blinked forebodingly.

The Spirit Tortoise Heart Shield icon appeared and began to glow with a faint light, as if it were sucking the energy away from the spear.

It happened a second later. There was a heavy thud deep within my body, and I felt something tear. The spear must have exploded.

"Ugh . . ."

A terrible, creeping feeling coursed through me, like poison was making its way through my veins. Damn. I thought I might die.

It wasn't like me at all, but I really might end up giving my life to save these people. I'd rather not die if I could!

Shield Prison normally didn't last very long, but it wasn't showing any signs of disappearing yet. What did it mean? Either the skill was lasting longer, or my sense of time was slowing down.

If the latter was the case, then it felt like a second had become a minute or more.

Goddammit! It hurt so much. How long did I have to bear it? I felt like I might lose my mind.

The pain was unlike anything I knew, unlike the burning flames of the Shield of Wrath. I grit my teeth against it and eventually, the spear began to glow and melt away.

Was it over?

"Ugh . . ."

I was so dizzy I thought I might fall over.

I felt like I'd been poisoned.

I was lightheaded and I was afraid I'd pass out any second.

There were still problems to deal with. There were still enemies outside of the prison. I couldn't afford to pass out here. Not yet.

Then I saw . . . a phantom? A hallucination?

Shimmering like a mirage, I thought I saw Ost come running over to help me stay on my feet.

She didn't say anything, but her eyes told me what she was thinking.

She was supporting me, keeping me awake, and giving me energy.

My feet found their place, and I rose to stand tall.

When I looked for her again, she was gone . . . or maybe she hadn't been there to begin with. Normally, I would have laughed at the very suggestion that someone had come back from the other side to help me. But this was no ordinary time.

I had to carry out the task she'd entrusted to me.

Which meant that I couldn't afford to lose here, now, to these people.

The Shield Prison finally vanished, and everyone came running over to me, their eyes wet with tears.

"Mr. Naofumi! Are you alright? What happened?"

"I'm fine. It was a little rough there, for a minute."

I'd thought I was going to die. I was still a bit exhausted, but at least I could stay on my feet.

"We still have work to do!" I shouted, and everyone immediately resumed their battle positions.

"Gaahhhhh!"

Tsugumi was back on her feet, freaking out and acting wild. She still looked like she might die at any moment.

"Stop it! Don't you see we've been tricked? Let's surrender, this is not our battle to fight!" one of the other beast women called. Tsugumi paid her no mind. She went on raging. She looked like she would kill anything that crossed her path.

"Please, we have no right to ask this of you, but please help us!"

I wanted to balk at the suggestion, but before I could Kizuna rushed forward and nodded.

"Fine. We know what it's like to be used and abandoned by Kyo. And we killed your friend. We have a responsibility here."

"He got what was coming to him, if you ask me."

Kizuna held a finger over her lips, as if to tell me to shut up.

Hey now, shouldn't THEY shut up?

"I realized this during the battle, but you know as the Hunting Hero I can't damage human opponents, right? Well I also can't damage demi-humans like Raphtalia. And yet, I can fight against them without any trouble at all."

"Yeah? Well, they're sort of just hobbled together, aren't they?"

"That's not what I mean. It's like . . . When you just did what you did to protect everyone, I got the chills from it. I kept thinking that I wanted to protect people the way that you do, that I want to save people. I wondered if there was anything I could do, you know? And then it was like I heard a voice. Like the answer was inside of me."

Kizuna looked like she was moved by her own speech. But man, she sure did take her time, didn't she? Get to it already? What happened? I didn't have time to listen to a whole oration here.

I wanted to say hurry up and get to the point, will you?

Kizuna drew her tuna knife and turned to face the raging Tsugumi.

"My name is Kizuna Kazayama. I am the Hunting Hero, one of the four holy heroes, and I cannot kill a human. On my honor as a hero, I will save you all!"

She quickly shot across the battlefield.

As soon as I understood what was happening, I cleared my head and cast a support spell on her.

"Zweite Aura!"

Soon she was up against the raging Tsugumi. She shouted.

"Break Down! Scale Removal!"

There was a flash, and a crushing sound, and innumerable blades arced through the air, slicing Tsugumi apart.

So many of Kizuna's skills emphasized her speed.

"Gah!"

Tsugumi went stiff as a board.

"To think I'd . . . If I move I'll . . . just like master . . ." she muttered.

A second later and all the fur fell from her beast side. The cuts must have gone deeper than that too, because the fur was followed by spurts of blood.

"Ahhhh!" everyone shouted. I ran over to check the corpse.

But . . .

"You don't need to worry about her. She's tougher than she looks."

I was sure she was dead, but she wasn't. I hoisted her up and showed her to everyone.

Half of her face was covered in lacerations, but she was breathing deeply and steadily.

"Zweite Heal," I cast the spell over her face.

As the spell took effect, her face looked more and more human. Like the beast side had been killed and vanquished.

The other women came running over, sighing with relief when they realized she was safe.

"It'll be a while before she's back on her feet."

There were still places where she had white tiger parts, but she wasn't acting strangely anymore.

It would take time to heal her completely, but it looked like she was going to be okay.

. . . And it's all thanks to our resident Hunting Hero, I guess.

She couldn't hunt humans, so her attack had only hurt the beast side of Tsugumi. It was like a surgical operation.

But "Scale Removal?" What was that, like cleaning a fish? Maybe she should be the cleaning hero, or the break down hero.

"So do you still feel like fighting?"

I looked over and locked eyes with each of the other women. They slowly sat down and announced: "We surrender. We've been used."

"You probably don't want to hear it, but you need to think about who you can trust."

After all I'd been through with Bitch, I knew what I was talking about.

"Anyway, at least you'll get out of this alive now."

". . ."

"Honestly I'd prefer to get rid of you here and now, but . . ."

The women looked shocked and terrified.

"But I guess the commander in these parts wants you all alive. I'm just an outsider here, so I don't have a say in it."

Besides, my arms were full with Tsugumi. I couldn't fight them off now if I wanted to.

Oh well, things could be worse.

"Naofumi . . ."

"Mr. Naofumi . . ."

Raphtalia gazed at me, her eyes filled with emotion.

What, did they really think I was going to kill everyone?

"Rafu . . ."

"I'm tiiiiired," Filo whined.

"Anyway, let's talk it through. This is no time to get in an argument," L'Arc said.

I guess they didn't want to fight anymore. They just sort of surrendered.

"Kizuna, take care of the others like you did with her."

"Sure thing!" she said, approaching the women.

Sigh. We would be going to war soon. We didn't need this crap to deal with now.

"Wait! What about Glass?!"

The women snapped to attention when Kizuna asked about Glass.

"That's right! Kyo's strategy had . . ."

Oh give me a break already. There's more?

"He was going to send troops to the dragon hourglass while we attacked the castle!"

I knew it. It was easy to predict his shallow strategy. He did whatever would bother us the most.

"It's just like you said, Naofumi."

"He's driving me nuts. You," I said, turning to the women. "Can you convince these people to stop the attack?"

They nodded.

"If you betray us, Glass and I will kill you!"

"Let's get going!"

"Yeah!" L'Arc shouted. "Troops! See to the injured, the repairs and reports! I'm leaving!"

"Yeah well, I guess this is your country after all. It's no fun to sit around and be attacked, is it? Let's go finish this thing!"

"Yes. Let us expose the truth to those who are deceived," Raphtalia said.

"Yes! Return Transcript!"

Kizuna used her skill and led us back to the dragon hourglass.

My surroundings instantly changed to the room that housed the hourglass, and from the room, I could hear the sounds of battle raging outside.

"Circle Dance Zero Formation: Reverse Snow Moon Flower!"

Through a doorway, I heard Glass shouting, and saw an explosion of snow-like flower petals. I saw the shapes of people falling.

There were people writhing on the ground. The square had become a battlefield.

Glass was drinking the bottle of soul-healing water I'd left her, and firing off skill after skill.

Kizuna was pretty damn powerful, but Glass could hold her own.

Her abilities had grown even sharper after discussing vassal weapon power-up methods with Raphtalia.

I was glad that Glass stayed behind. That was the right choice.

None of the enemy troops had gotten past her yet.

Kyo hadn't sent too many of them. He must not have been expecting us to guard it.

Actually, the main attack force at the caste, Trash #2's women, had been pretty sparse too.

The enemy seemed to have lost its will to fight upon my arrival. Either that or they knew they were already fighting a losing battle by the time we got there.

"All of you, calm down! The Hunting Hero is here to save those of you that have lost yourselves to madness! Stop the fighting now!"

"Kyo is just using us!" the women that had been fighting with us at the castle shouted. The other women fighters who were still engaged in battle turned and replied, "But! But what about—?"

I almost heard Trash #2's name, but there was a crash nearby that drowned it out. Was I ever going to get his name?

"You know what I'm talking about! Someone here is going to lose it! It happened to Tsugumi back at the castle! She had a weapon that nearly exploded and killed us all! We're just pawns in Kyo's game!"

"But . . . But . . ."

"If you want to keep fighting, then keep on fighting. Raphtalia, Kizuna, L'Arc, Glass—everyone. That's just how they are. We don't have time to entertain them. Take them alive, or don't. Try to keep the damages to a minimum."

"Roger that! We'll save the chat until we've taken care of these guys!" Kizuna shot off like a bullet, slicing through the wild beast half of the women. It was only one attack, but the seemingly immortal women fell to the ground. Those that remained conscious writhed in pain.

A few of them remained on their feet, desperate to continue the fight. Raphtalia took care of them in a flash.

Strength really does come with numbers, doesn't it? I wanted to get more people on my side.

"What are you after? What were you going to do to the dragon hourglass?"

The captured women turned to their leader, who held out a pendant. It looked like the sort of gemstone that adventurers in this world used to check for drop items.

"He said . . . He said that if we registered the dragon hourglass with this, then we would . . . win . . ."

"I figured it was something like that. He wanted to recreate Return Dragon Vein. Then he could have sent as many troops as he wanted into the center of the castle."

Speaking of strength in numbers, he could have sent his whole army over. Victory would be all but assured.

L'Arc, Glass, and Raphtalia might be some of the strongest fighters around, but there was a limit to what we could take on by ourselves.

"It was just an idea. I can't believe he really . . ."

"It's just like him. He even sent three separate attacks."

He sent Yomogi to attack us at Kizuna's house. Then he sent half of Trash #2's women to the castle, and the other half to the dragon hourglass to try and make sure that he could send even more troops over.

"Anyway, you're all lucky that Kizuna stopped you. You could have gone crazy at any minute. You can hate us for this if you want, but you should at least realize why your commander died."

I turned my back on them and continued, "We can probably get you healed with medicine, but I don't know if the people at the castle will want to help you. Maybe I can figure something out."

"Aren't you a charmer, Naofumi?" Kizuna said.

"That's what so great about Mr. Naofumi!"

"Rafu!"

"It's one of your best qualities, Kiddo."

"Shut up already!"

Finally, the night was over. A lot had happened—too much, for my tastes.

## Chapter Seven: Barbaroi Armor

I was stuck the next morning trying to figure out how to cure the women of whatever Kyo had done to them.

". . ."

Tsugumi wasn't looking good.

That spear had taken so much out of her, it was a miracle she could even stand up. Kizuna had sliced off her beast side. And we kept a consistent application of medicine to the wounds. The scars of her reformed body were slowly starting to heal.

It reminded me of the parasite-like way that the Spirit Tortoise familiars had infected people back in Melromarc.

Tsugumi was silent the whole time, apparently ashamed that we had saved her.

"I don't have to hear you say it. You know the truth, and you're never going to escape it."

"Mr. Naofumi . . ."

I didn't mind if she hated me.

"But think about this. I know he was your beloved commander, or whatever, but do you really think that he was right about everything he said? Don't you think that sounds like brainwashing?"

After all, these people chased Raphtalia. They tried to kill her. It was hard for me to believe that their relentless pursuit of Raphtalia was the only bad thing they'd ever done.

We'd only exchanged a few words. But, I was sure they had other plans.

"Shut up!"

"Guess I hit a nerve, huh?"

If I had died without managing to save Raphtalia, would she have ended up like these women?

"Raphtalia, it's not like you just accept everything I say, right? If I ever lose my mind, and I'm clearly in the wrong, and I start running wild . . . I expect that you'll be the one to stop me."

". . . I'll do my best."

I'd like to think that if one, if just one, of his women had told him he was wrong—had stopped him before it all got out of control—then he wouldn't have died the way he did.

"He was always kind to us, but he was very serious about his pursuit of power and authority. I cannot disagree with you on that."

". . ."

He was a weird one alright.

Especially his constant, insatiable need for power. In that respect he reminded me of the other three holy heroes. He was just like them. Whenever he met someone more powerful than he was, he'd call it cheating. When things didn't go his way, he'd throw a fit.

Back when I played online games, I'd seen people's jealousy. I had some weapons and items that were limited on the server, and people didn't like that I had them. They'd go on anonymous boards and post things just like Trash #2.

Yeah, I'd seen that sort of thing before.

People want to be special, want to be chosen, and want to be better than everyone else. I knew how it felt, too. People probably played online games to savor that very feeling—that feeling of being the protagonist. They wanted to be in the center of the action.

But Trash #2 wasn't from a modern society like I was. And yet, he seemed so easy to predict.

"Excuse me, but . . . Could you tell me a little more about why he wanted to kill me?" Raphtalia asked.

It was still a mystery. He had been obsessed with hunting her down.

"The vassal weapon chose a new master. I'm sure there are plenty examples in the past of assassination attempts on people that were chosen for important roles."

"Sure."

I knew all about that—firsthand.

The Shield Hero had been inconvenient for the religious institutions in Melromarc, so they'd tried to dispose of me.

"But then again, I'm not sure if I've heard of trying to assassinate someone out of simple jealousy."

There were still things I didn't understand.

The katana of the vassal weapons was like a holy sword. It was stuck in a rock, and only those that could remove it would be able to wield it. I could picture him standing up in a crowd and complaining that King Arthur wasn't supposed to have Excalibur—that was supposed to be his sword. It was a pretty low-class thing to do.

The master had already been chosen, but he still insisted that it was supposed to be him? It didn't even make sense.

"We were open to negotiations, you know. It's not like we want war. Didn't Glass say that she wanted to end this peacefully?"

"But it didn't work out that way did it. If it was going to end this way, then I wish she never had been chosen to wield the vassal weapon."

I guess it went back to that, didn't it—that was the reason their beloved Trash #2 was dead.

"Why was he so obsessed with it? Don't you know?"

"I don't. I've been with him since I was very young, but often there were times when I couldn't understand what he was thinking."

The more I heard about him, the more mysterious Trash #2 became.

"He seems like the sort of guy that was always chasing women. At least you and your friends made it look that way."

All of the women nodded along with me.

"He was always meddling in our relationships. Always trying to *help!* I told him to watch himself time and time again, but he never listened! He was always up to something!"

Uh-oh. I was playing with fire. The complaints were coming quickly now.

So he liked the ladies, was an alchemist that was always working on revolutionary inventions, and was pretty good with a sword.

I guess that's why they called him a genius.

Wasn't that enough? If the vassal weapon had chosen him, he'd have to fight in the waves. He should have counted his blessings.

"He used to drive me crazy!"

"Are you going to stop complaining soon?"

I guess their relationship was always on edge.

"But I loved him. There was no one else like him!"

Good thing too. One was more than enough.

Yomogi and Kizuna came walking over.

"So? How does it feel to be used for Kyo's assassination plans?"

Yomogi shot me an irritated glance.

"I . . . I have to hear the truth from him myself. To that end, I will cooperate with you."

"You did promise, after all."

I didn't want to derail the conversation, so I decided to ignore her self-satisfied comment.

"That's true, I did. But I . . . I don't want to believe that Kyo has done these things. So . . . I will believe in the Kyo I thought I knew, and I will share what I know with you."

She was going to cooperate with us then. And in a weird way, she thought it was in service to the Kyo she'd imagined she was working with the whole time, a Kyo that probably never existed.

"I have heard that Kyo journeyed to another world and caused a great disaster there. Is that a true story?"

"Yeah. That's the only reason we're here."

Yomogi and Tsugumi's weapons had been powered by an energy I was able to absorb with my shield. In all likelihood, it was the energy he stole from the Spirit Tortoise.

I was probably only able to stop those energy attacks because I had the Spirit Tortoise Heart Shield.

"He took control over one of our world's protective beasts, and used it to kill countless people. Heroes aren't normally permitted to cross between the worlds, but I was given special permission to come here specifically to track him down."

"He laughed as he piloted the Spirit Tortoise, as he trampled people to death. Glass tried to stop him, and he said 'What does it matter? This world will be destroyed anyway!'"

"..."

Yomogi listed silently.

I took the time to compare Yomogi and Tsugumi—they seemed very similar to me. They both believed wholeheartedly in whatever their leader told them.

"Hey Yomogi, what's the Kyo you know like?"

"Hm . . . He's very intelligent. He travels around the lands asking people about their troubles and then invents ways to solve their problems. He is also very skilled with magic. He saved me once, which is when I came to trust him with my life, and then . . ."

Tsugumi listened to Yomogi explain Kyo's qualities, and tilted her head to the side in confusion. I felt the same way, really. After all, she might as well have been describing Trash #2.

"Isn't this great? I think you two will be great friends," I said.

"No! Do not compare Kyo to the likes of this other man! Get a grip on yourself!"

Tsugumi tried to grab Yomogi by the shirt and they started to scuffle.

I wished they'd give it a rest already. Their battle wounds weren't even healed yet.

"And yet, it is strange, isn't it? They seem so similar," Kizuna said to L'Arc and Glass.

"L'Arc, didn't you say that you were a good judge of character?" I asked. He had said something like that back in the Cal Mira islands. He'd been talking about Armor, this guy in Itsuki's party. L'Arc was saying that Armor was going to cause trouble. Still, it had taken him a long time to realize that I was the Shield Hero.

"Yeah, what about it?"

"What did you think when you met Kyo and this other guy?"

"I've met a lot of people over the years, and those guys are like two peas in a pod."

"Right . . ."

L'Arc said he knew, just from talking to me, that I hadn't raped Bitch.

If he said that these guys were like two peas in a pod, then he was probably right.

Their similarities were getting harder to ignore, even for me.

"Anyway, we'll have to find out if he's really working on something that will raise people from the dead. But at the very least, you should realize by now that you can't trust him."

". . ."

They couldn't disagree. Not after he treated them as disposable assassins and left them maimed. Not after he'd treated them like pawns in his game.

"Don't you have zombies and things like that in this world? He probably used technology from the four holy beasts to make it look like he can raise people from the dead."

"Possible. Once someone is gone, they don't come back. Perhaps this is punishment for our reckless decisions."

They seemed resigned to defeat. I guess it was a natural feeling to have if you were saved by the very people you wanted to get revenge on. Whatever. We were just trying to get information out of them.

"Yomogi, how did you end up attacking our house?"

"One day Kyo came home, injured and furious, saying that the girl with the fan of the vassal weapons and her friends attacked him. I said I would never forgive anyone that hurt him, and went to grab the weapon he had been developing."

"Didn't take you long, did it?"

"He always told me not to use it, but only showed me how to put it away and how to take it out.'"

I could picture it clearly. He understood Yomogi's personality, so he got her interested in the sword, and let her watch him take it in and out. He guided her actions indirectly—and he didn't go chasing after her when she left.

If I were Kyo and Raphtalia was Yomogi, I would have stopped her.

No matter how fast she was, I would have stopped her.

And he knew that Yomogi and Trash #2's women had

been captured. He had done and said nothing, as if nothing at all had happened.

"Actually, now that I think about it, the sword was suddenly completed the day that he returned. It hadn't been the same weapon until that day."

"And when was this?"

"A little over three weeks ago."

"That's right around the time that we came to this world."

Yomogi was starting to put it all together. She was starting to see what kind of person Kyo really was.

"Anyway, I have to get the truth from him."

"If what we're saying is true, what are you going to do about it?"

"I'll . . ." she curled her hand into a fist, "I'll make him pay. The Kyo that I know made inventions to bring joy into people's lives. If he is spreading destruction and pain, I cannot forgive him."

"Well that settles that. We came here to do the same thing. To make him pay, and to take back the energy he stole from the Spirit Tortoise."

In truth, we really didn't have the time to sit around talking this all through. But at least we got a glimpse into just how suspicious the inventors are in this world.

"Kizuna, Glass, L'Arc, keep in mind what these inventors have been up to. If they are all the same, then someone else might try to take up the mantle."

"Good point. I'll keep an eye out. We can't have more creepy characters running around and causing trouble in other worlds."

"Yes, that is a good point. We should be careful."

"Yeah. There's a problem with the vassal weapons, they're supposed to protect the world. We better get this mess settled."

"Yes, let's," Raphtalia nodded.

I nodded too. Everyone had agreed to fight.

"Yomogi, Tsugumi, do you know where Kyo is?"

Kizuna unrolled a map on a nearby table.

We could start a war if we wanted to, but there was no telling if Kyo would actually come to the battlefield.

He was probably working from a strategic headquarters somewhere. He could be safe in the capital, commanding troops on the front lines. If we went looking for him aimlessly, there's no telling how long it would take to find him. Alto and some of Kizuna's other friends were out hunting for his whereabouts undercover, but we'd yet to hear any news.

And I didn't come to this world to fight a war.

"Kyo's laboratory . . ."

"It's right there," Yomogi said, pointing to the map.

It was far away from the capital. It looked like it was in a village, deep in forested lands.

"A long time ago, he built his laboratory in a sealed mansion here. It's in a deep forest with fog so thick that anyone who wanders in there gets lost. It's impregnable. You cannot find it unless he's allowed you to."

Sounds like he made his hideout in a pretty good spot.

But lucky for us, we had a way to move through the air.

"Alright! Let's get prepared and get going. We can't let up on the war effort either."

"Right. Let's put an end to all this. It's up to us, the vassal weapon holders, and the holy heroes too, to punish this creep that abuses a vassal weapon."

That was what had to be done.

There was going to be war. But if we could sneak over and get rid of Kyo, we might be able to put an end to the war. It all rested on him.

"Oh hey, Romina was looking for you, Naofumi. She's made a bunch of new stuff."

"Nice."

"Yeah, Kiddo. And I got a bunch of material together for you, so get prepared."

"You're coming too, L'Arc."

"Think I don't know that? Who do you think you're talking to?"

"Boy."

"Ha! You just remembered that now, didn't you? Stop it!"

"It's hard to be serious when Mr. Naofumi is around."

"I'm just trying to be serious about all this."

"But sometimes you're so silly!"

Huh? Had I said something? Whatever. I left Kizuna and L'Arc behind and went to visit Romina.

"Yesterday was pretty crazy, wasn't it?"

"Yeah, we were in a pretty rough spot there."

If that spear had actually exploded, it probably would have taken a good chunk of the castle with it. Honestly, I was a little impressed with myself for containing it all, but I also knew there had been luck involved, and that we had been very close to disaster.

"So? I heard you put some stuff together for me?"

"Yeah—took me a while too," Romina said, rummaging through the back of her store and returning with a suit of armor.

It looked a lot like the barbarian armor that I'd left with her. But the coloring was different, and there were patches of black and white fur stuck onto it in various places. The shoulders were capped with tortoise shells. The collar was lined with red things that looked like feathers.

"That's some impressive looking armor."

"It is. I used some of the material we had from the four holy beasts—no small cost for that, but I think you'll like how it came out. It's a damn tough set of armor. I have to show you this. Take a look at the dragon emperor core stone we're using here," Romina said, pointing to a gem set into the breastplate.

It was quite a bit larger than the stone I'd had previously.

It was shaped like a ying-yang symbol, but the black side of it had grown substantially larger than the white side. It looked like a mix between Chinese and Japanese designs. You know those games about the Romance of the Three Kingdoms? It looked like something a commander from those games might wear.

"I based it off the barbarian armor you brought in last time—the set that had lost all of its functionality."

"It looks excellent."

I was surprised. I didn't think there was anyone out there that could even repair the armor the old man made for me— much less improve upon it.

"It's harder than you think, using materials from the holy beasts, I mean. If you don't do everything just right, the materials can backfire on you."

"Oh?" I was starting to understand why Kizuna was so impressed with Romina's work.

"I'm telling you, working with new materials, using new techniques to replicate your last set . . . I put a lot of work into this. Take that dragon emperor core stone there for instance. I had to work out a way to combine the old one with a core stone that Kizuna got a while ago. It's tough to do even without having the stones interfere with one another, but I pulled it off. The effect is even stronger now."

"Is that why it looks bigger than it used to?"

"Yes. Those stones are very, very rare—so you better take good care of this."

"Sure."

Once I defeated Kyo, I was going back to my world anyway.

What if I couldn't use this armor once I crossed back over? What if crossing over worlds would cause the name to become garbled in my status menu?

"With any luck, you'll be able to use it back in your world too, so take good care of it. It won't be good for my reputation if you treat it like it's disposable."

"Sure, right. So what do you call this armor anyway?"

I remember asking the old man at the weapon shop the same question.

Maybe it hadn't been officially named yet, because it wasn't displaying correctly in my status menu. Maybe I wasn't good at assigning names.

"Kizuna suggested the name, actually. She said the last set was called Barbarian Armor, so maybe this should be called Barbaroi Armor."

"The Barbaroi and the barbarians weren't really the same thing though . . ."

There were differences, but I guess they were related. For a human-supremacist nation like Melromarc, the god of the demi-humans, the Shield Hero, might as well have been a barbarian deity.

The old man had probably named the armor that way on purpose. It was all a joke to him. In hindsight, it was the perfect set of armor for me.

**Barbaroi Armor +2 (cursed)**
**defense up: impact resistance (large): slash resistance (large): fire resistance (large): wind resistance (large): water resistance (large): earth resistance (large): HP recovery (low): magic recovery (weak): SP recovery (weak): magic power up (medium): dragon emperor revolt, four holy beasts power, magic defense processing, automatic self-repair, growth power.**

There were tons of imbued effects. I'd lost shadow resistance, but I'd gained a ton of new resistances.

There were so many that it would take me a while to research them all. What would happen if I equipped it?

There was one other thing that bothered me. Why was there "cursed" after the name?

"It turned into a really specialized piece of equipment, so I don't know if you'll really be able to make good use of it. But I hope so, because if there are problems, I'll have to remake it."

"I'm not sure I want to ask, but what do you mean by 'problems?' Will I be able to take it off once I equip it?"

"Yeah, you shouldn't have that kind of problem, but it does lay a curse on whoever wears it. I had one of my assistants test it out, and it got pretty hairy there for a minute."

"Feh . . ." Rishia whimpered in terror.

She was afraid of literally everything. Raphtalia on the other hand looked at the armor with lust in her eyes. Oh, Raph-chan was doing the same thing. I guess that's what you get when they share the same DNA.

"So shiny . . ." Filo muttered. She had that special look in her eyes—the kind that birds got when they found shiny objects to play with.

"Would you like to try it on?"

"Yeah, at least to test it. What do you mean it curses you?"

"I mean it breaks all of your ribs if you try to try it on."

"That's one evil curse!"

The armor was starting to sound downright vindictive. I didn't want to put it on anymore.

"Should I just dispose of it then?"

But the effects were great. Wasn't there some way we could remove the curse and keep the rest?

"Naofumi, you have really a high defense rating, don't you? I think you'll be able to use it without much trouble.

That's why I kept it for you. You might as well give it a try."

"I didn't realize I was signing up for a human experiment here."

"With any luck, this will save your life in the next battle."

She was right about that. I was pretty sure that the equipment I was currently using wasn't going to be good enough for a showdown with Kyo.

Tsugumi had shattered my Shooting Star Shield barrier without much trouble at all, which made me think that I really needed to address some recent deficiencies in my stats. Improvement was necessary to survive the coming battle.

And this new armor was based on the design of my Barbarian Armor, which, despite some initial misgivings, I'd really grown attached to.

So I . . . Well . . . Hm . . . It was a very shiny set of armor, but it also kind of looked like it was surrounded by a dark aura. It was like . . . like the sort of change that came over me whenever I used the Shield of Wrath. Maybe.

"What if I try it on and it seriously injures me?"

"We'll just have to rush to get you treated. I know a good doctor."

"That isn't what I wanted to hear. Oh well. I guess there's no other choice."

What was it they said? To catch a tiger, you have to go to its lair.

I'd have to rely on my defense rating to get in on, but with it on, I might not be able to unlock new shields.

"If it seems like it's going to be a problem, take it off, alright?" Raphtalia said.

"I know, I know. You're the one that looks all excited about it."

I went to the changing room in the back of the workshop and tried it on.

It seemed fine. . .

But just when I thought there was nothing out of the ordinary, I noticed a flashing icon in my field of view. It said "cursed." It wasn't the same as the clock that appeared when I used the Shield of Wrath.

Aside from that though, there didn't seem to be any other problems. I could tell that the armor was hugging me pretty tight, but with my defense rating, it didn't feel any more dangerous than a tight belt.

"Well?"

"The size is actually perfect. It is squeezing a little tight in spots, but that's about all."

I wouldn't exactly call it comfortable though. I couldn't relax. I felt like the armor was looking for a way to take me down, like it would strike if I showed any weakness.

"My assistant had it on for only thirty seconds, and it broke his ribs. So, if it hasn't hurt you yet, I think you'll be fine."

"I guess you're a good craftsman, but can't you make armor that *isn't* cursed?"

The armor was fine for now, and when I looked at my stats, I was surprised to see just how high my defense rating had risen.

Maybe it was raising my defense rating by percentages or something. Regardless, its effect on my defense stats was far more impressive than any armor I'd seen yet.

It might have worked by multiplying the effect of my shield. Its overall effect was much better than trying to power-up the shields themselves.

"I'd like to see if it increases pressure on the wearer over time. Will you wear it until your departure, so that I can test my theory?"

"Sure."

There she goes again—using me for her experiments.

"I also have that kigurumi."

"Oh yeeeah . . ."

I'd nearly forgotten about Rishia's favorite Filo kigurumi.

I was kind of afraid to see what she'd done with it. But I was surprised when she came back with not one, but two new pieces of equipment.

"I used it to make a new breastplate here. That and . . . well, leftovers, I guess."

She showed us a pink breastplate shaped like Filo.

The first piece was a pink breastplate that must have been made with material from the chest area of the kigurumi, judging from Filo's coloring. It also had golden yellow and blue accents, and looked like a refined, high-quality piece of craftsmanship.

"I was focused on the dual nature of her character when making it. The original materials were very strange, so it was actually harder to make this than it was to make the Barbaroi armor. I had to do all kind of research."

"Wow!"

I was impressed. It looked great.

"What is it called?"

"I haven't decided yet."

"Remember when they made a spectacle of Filo, calling her an angel?"

"Well,. then how about we call it the Angel Breastplate?"

**Angel Breastplate**
**defense up: agility up (high): impact resistance (low): wind resistance (large): shadow resistance (low): HP recovery (low): magic power up (medium): automatic self-repair, towing ability up, carrying capacity up, awakening power.**

It was like she made the breastplate with only the good parts of the Filo kigurumi.

It even looked good.

Judging from what I'd seen of her work so far, I was pretty impressed with Romina's craftsmanship. That is, if I ignored the somewhat murderous intentions of the armor I was wearing.

"So let's see what else we have here," I said, unrolling the left over material from the Filo Kigurumi.

I stared at Romina, and she turned her eyes away from me.

It sure looked like she'd turned the remaining kigurumi materials into Filo pajamas. The head was turned into a hood. So I decided to call it just that, the Filo Pajamas.

**Filo Pajamas**
**defense up: agility up (high): impact resistance (low): wind resistance (large): shadow resistance (low): HP recovery (low): magic power up (medium): automatic self-repair, traction ability up, carrying capacity up, transforming, type change, hidden power, hidden weapon.**

The problems when used in monster form, that the original kigurumi had, were gone completely. What did "hidden power" mean though?

Did the pajamas change size when you put them on?

"You've really outdone yourself with this."

"Usually, this is how things get degraded, passing through the hands of too many craftsmen."

"I wonder if Mel-chan would like it?"

"She probably would," I said. They were really good friends after all.

"Okay, so who is going to equip these things?"

I looked around the room at Raphtalia, Rishia, Filo, and at Raph-chan.

Glass and Kizuna might have been interested too, but they weren't here now.

Maybe even L'Arc—he might like the pajamas. I'd like to have him try them on, just so I could see that awkward look on his face. If I included some gems, Therese might even be interested.

"I'd like the breastplate," Raphtalia said.

"You have that miko outfit."

"And it's wonderful equipment, but . . ."

I imagined her wearing the breastplate, and compared it to how she looked in the miko outfit. There was no question that she would look better in the miko clothes.

L'Arc must have really used some money on it, as the miko outfit came with some wonderful equip effects.

It didn't have a ton of abilities, but it wasn't so lacking that I thought it was worth changing to something else.

She should really stick with the miko outfit—at the very least it was good for my eyes.

"Can't you make some new miko clothes for Raphtalia with all these same effects? Can you make it in time?"

"Mr. Naofumi, you don't need be so particular."

She told me off again! Oh well. I couldn't help it.

"L'Arc already requested clothes be made for Ms. Raphtalia here."

Romina already had a miko outfit ready for her. Would the interior be lined with the White Tiger skin?

"I took some cloth I had made from the White Tiger skin and used it to form a miko outfit."

What now? I couldn't really appraise the item at all—but I could see its name.

**White Tiger Miko Outfit**

The colors had not changed much from the outfit she already had.

L'Arc, I have to say, knew what he was doing.

"So that takes care of your equipment, Raphtalia."

Raphtalia sighed. "I don't know why you think these clothes are so important, but fine."

"Raful!"

Raph-chan leapt across the room and hid inside of the new outfit's sleeve, then poked her cute little face out from the opening.

Aww. She was so cute.

"Raful!"

I patted her on the head.

"So both of these . . ."

Raphtalia and I looked over at Rishia and Filo.

Actually Filo didn't need anything. Looks like we had more than enough.

"Feh . . ."

"What is it?"

Raphtalia and I started whispering.

"Which one do you think Rishia will pick if I ask her to choose?"

"I would assume she'd want the pajamas, no? She said she liked to hide her face, after all."

I nodded.

"Right, okay then Rishia, you . . ."

"I wanna wear one too!" Filo said, raising her hand.

"You hate wearing armor, Filo."

"Huh? But there are leftovers!"

She was right about that. The equipment was too big for Raph-chan, after all.

Or actually, maybe Raph-chan could wear the hood. It would probably look really good on her too. Or maybe I could get her a little teapot outfit, and make her look like Bunbuku Chagama.

Oh! I was getting excited just thinking about it.

On that same line of thought, maybe I could get a Santa hat for Chris. Then he'd look just like Pekkul!

"Mr. Naofumi, are you paying attention?"

"Of course I am."

"You're acting a little strange. Why are you staring at Raph-chan like that?"

Oh no! She caught me in the act. She could always tell what I was thinking.

"Which one do you want to wear, Filo?"

I had to steer the conversation back on course. Otherwise Raphtalia would keep trying to read my mind.

"This one!"

She pointed to the Filo Pajamas.

I looked over at Rishia, "What do you think, Rishia?"

"Feh. . ."

"You want something you can use to hide your face, right? Filo wants the pajamas, but I can tell her no."

"But!"

"Fehhhhh!"

"Are you two arguing?"

Alto came walking over from behind Romina's counter.

So he was here too. I'd totally forgotten about him since he hadn't shown his face yet.

"I think it will look better on Filo. The breastplate will do more good on this lady anyway."

"Oh yeah? For a merchant, you aren't so good at identifying the real problem."

"What's that supposed to mean?!" he shouted.

"Listen up. Rishia is a shy weirdo. She wants the pajamas because she can use the hood to hide her face. We're trying to figure out how to divvy up the equipment, but you have to know that about Rishia to understand why it's complicated."

He was right in some ways. I mean, if we were going to choose by what looked best, then Rishia should definitely go with the breastplate and Filo should take the pajamas. But considering Rishia's particular needs, it would probably be best to give her the pajamas and ask Filo to make do with the breastplate.

"Fehhh?!"

How many times did I have to tell her not to scream like that?

"Can't she make do with the breastplate?"

"I doubt it. Rishia would be so embarrassed that she probably wouldn't be able to focus on the battle at all."

"Is that so? It sort of looked like you were trying to force the pajamas on Rishia, you know?"

"How dare you. I'm just trying to do what's best for her."

"Try all you want, Filo's already wearing the pajamas."

"What?!"

"Ta-da!"

Filo was standing there in human form, proudly wearing the pajamas. She actually sort of looked her age in them.

"I feel so . . . so alive!"

I hesitantly checked on her stats.

What?! Filo's stats had suffered so much when we crossed over to the new world that I hadn't been able to depend on her for anything. But all her stats had shot through the roof! What was going on?!

Then I remembered the list of the kigurumi's effects.

Was this all because of the type change and shield adjustments?

I recalled a similar effect when Rishia wore the thing.

She'd lost all those boosts when we crossed between worlds, so I guess it was safe to assume that we'd gotten those effects back by remaking the kigurumi here.

"All the more reason to give it to Rishia. Filo, take that thing off! Rishia needs it more than you do."

"But!" Filo shouted, and quickly turned into her humming falcon form.

When she did, the pajamas changed along with her and the hood rested on her head as she flew around.

"You idiot! Damn! If it can transform like that, then I should have given it to Raph-chan!"

"Um . . . Excuse me! I will take the breastplate, if that's alright," Rishia said.

"Mr. Naofumi, please calm down!"

"I didn't work very hard on the pajamas, but I suppose I'm glad to see you're fighting over them . . ." Romina sighed, "Maybe it says something about the quality of my work."

"It's tough working with customers from other worlds, isn't it? Remember all the trouble you had with Kizuna?"

"Well she was very particular about her fishing rod."

Romina and Alto reminisced absentmindedly as we bickered in front of them.

They finally agreed that Rishia would take the breastplate and Filo would take the pajamas.

That stupid bird. Eventually I'd get those pajamas from her and give them to Raph-chan.

Filo! You better stay on your guard.

## Chapter Eight: Two Swords

I glared at Filo so she'd know I was serious. Romina and Alto went behind the counter to bring out more weapons.

"Huh? There's more?"

"Yeah, L'Arc had a number of requests, so I did what I could."

"Wow!"

"Alto put a lot of work in too, so you'd better be grateful."

I couldn't help but notice that they didn't bother to prepare any shields for me. I suppose it wasn't worth complaining about though . . .

"So what do you have?"

"Naofumi and Raphtalia can just copy what we've made here, right?"

"Yeah."

"Then try these on for size," Romina said, and brought out two katana. They were both stored in ornate sheathes. You could tell with a single glance that they were fantastic swords made by a master craftsman. With the appraisal ability I had, I could only see their names.

**White Tiger Katana**

## Vermilion Bird Kodachi

"These are . . ."

"I made one of them and sold it a long time ago. We have it back, on loan, for now. You can see that it was made with materials from the four holy beasts, which are exceptionally rare. I was lucky to even get the chance to work on it."

Romina mostly worked on things for Glass, Kizuna, and L'Arc. So, she probably didn't get to work on swords very often.

"She really worked hard on it," Alto said.

Romina picked up the White Tiger Katana and pulled it from its sheath. It slipped out with a sharp sound, and it seemed like something flew out of the blade when it whipped past us.

The blade itself was white, polished like a mirror, and the arc of the blade made it appear wider than it really was. It seemed like it was full of light. In fact, I think that it was.

"I think it's very impressive, but what do you think?"

"I agree."

It was the sort of blade that you'd get as special equipment in an RPG, like a Muramasa or a Masamune sword. They were normally some of the best weapons in the game.

And these had been made from materials from the four holy beasts!

Were they even able to do that back in the last world?

"The materials are really quite difficult to work with, honestly. It took a while for me to really understand how to use them."

"How so?"

"Well, I used the skin and bones of the White Tiger. If you add some of the bone to the metal, it will add some effects. The strength of the blade ends up becoming so powerful that you can hurt yourself just swinging it, so there were all sorts of problems."

"Wow . . ."

"This was the first sword I had managed to craft from it. I still had some materials, so I worked on weapons for Glass and the others, too."

Did that mean that Glass's weapons were made out of materials from the four holy beasts? They hadn't seemed that way to me before but . . .

"They're still very difficult to work with. I think that Glass first learned how to use Reverse Snow Moon Flower when she equipped the fan made with White Tiger materials."

That was why she was so strong—her equipment had been better than ours.

"I think she's using the Demon Dragon Fan these days. She says it's simpler to use in actual battle situations."

"Do you have any of those materials?"

"Unfortunately not. I made it from the dragon emperor materials that Kizuna got after defeating him. Only certain blacksmiths are even permitted to work with the stuff," Romina said, then pointed at my armor, "Kizuna's fishing rod is made out of material one level down on the quality scale."

That sounded like a pretty convenient material to work with.

So far all the equipment she was giving us was the same color, a dark shade of black. I was starting to wonder why, but I guess it's because they were all made out of the same stuff.

"I used it when I made that armor for you too, Naofumi. The Azure Dragon has yet to appear and its location is unknown, so I had to make that part out of the demon dragon materials. And the dragon emperor core stone too."

"So you didn't make a shield?"

"I would have made one if I had the time. I didn't have much material to work with either."

I wasn't going to complain, considering how much time and effort she had put into making all these things for us. I was just grateful that I had such a talented blacksmith working for me at all.

I'd have to get a shield some other way. I didn't want to rely on the Shield of Wrath.

"Of course the katana should go to Raphtalia."

"Yes," Romina said, sliding the White Tiger Katana back

into its sheath and passing it to Raphtalia.

There was a crackle when she touched it, like static electricity shocking her fingertip, but she gripped the sword tightly and nodded to Romina. Then she changed her vassal weapon katana into the White Tiger Katana.

That was how the weapon copy system worked. Instead of building a new weapon from materials you gathered, we could copy weapons we found in shops just by touching them.

I could do it with my shield, and now Raphtalia could do it because her katana was a vassal weapon.

"So this is the White Tiger Katana. It's remarkable. I am just leveled enough to unlock it," she said as she drew the blade. Her hand was shaking.

The blade must have been very heavy. Beads of sweat stood out on her forehead with the effort required to wield it.

"How is it?"

"I've unlocked the ability to use it, but I don't think I'm strong enough to wield it well."

I hadn't really worried about it too much, but I had shields that were like that too.

Sometimes the skills you needed to unlock something weren't the same skills you needed to use it well. I had never given too much thought to it—that gap between the ability to equip something and the ability to use it well.

Glass had mentioned a similar problem too. It was an

issue you ran into more often when you got better weapons.

"I guess we'll just have to level up a bit on the way."

"What kind of skills does it have?"

"Hmm . . . The abilities, right? It has Double Sword."

That was one of the better abilities.

Raphtalia released her grip on the blade, and another blade appeared floating in the air before her.

She couldn't hold them both up at the same time, so she held them at her sides and the tips of the blades sliced easily into the ground.

"Hey, don't go slicing up my workshop."

"I'm sorry, but they are very heavy."

"Can't you switch to a different weapon, at least for now?"

"Um . . ." Raphtalia concentrated. The sword in her hand transformed into something else. Only the sword in her right hand changed to something lighter. Her left hand still held the White Tiger Katana.

Hey, hey! That was an awesome ability!

"Raphtalia, sheathe the sword in your left hand."

"Alright," she said, sliding the blade into its sheath. She still held the lighter blade in her right hand.

She could use two weapons at once now. Even though she didn't always have to have both of them out, she could keep two different swords equipped and switch them out on the fly. Furthermore, she could have one sword out while the

other sword charged up for a haikuikku attack in the sheath. It was heavy, and hard to wield, but it was going to make a huge difference once she learned how to use it.

"What should I do with this katana?"

So she wouldn't accidently cut anyone down, she switched one of them into a bamboo trainer sword. But she was worried about what to do with the blade in her right hand.

"I guess I better make another sheath for that one."

She'd have to rush and make it quickly, but it would be worth it.

"Ok, next up is the Vermilion Bird Kodachi," Romina said, handing the next sword to Raphtalia, who quickly used weapon copy on it.

"Man, vassal weapons sure are convenient. You can get a new weapon for yourself just by touching it."

"Yeah. If you could actually produce the weapon instead of just changing it, you could reproduce weapons endlessly."

"Right? I've thought about that too!" Alto said.

Romina looked concerned, "And that would be the end of my business."

Hm? Oh right, that was actually a good point. I sure wouldn't like it if someone found a way to make unlimited potions and medicines. Then again, even if the price dropped, I'd be sure to sell more. So maybe it wouldn't have that much of an impact on my business.

If it was an ability of mine that allowed it, it would actually make my job easier.

"It wouldn't bother me. With more products come more sales."

"I thought you might say that. You really might be better at this than Alto."

"And what makes you think that?"

"Um . . . I don't seem to be able to use this one yet."

Hm . . . It must have been a really impressive weapon.

"At least you have it though. Just switch to something you can use for now."

"Oh well. Regardless, it seems like I'll have to do some leveling to make use of these."

"Maybe, but don't forget, we're heading back to our world once we accomplish what we came here to do. Levels we gain here won't be much use in the long term."

They would disappear.

"That's true. But do you think that I'll be able to bring this with me?"

". . ."

I really didn't know.

If she couldn't let go of the vassal weapon, after we went back to the previous world, if a wave happened in this world, she might disappear before my eyes. I didn't want that to happen.

"Um . . . Mr. Naofumi?"

"Don't worry about it. We'll talk to Therese and Glass and make sure we figure out a way for you to get rid of it."

My shield worked the same way—it was like a curse.

It was great that she had this wonderful equipment, but we needed to think about what that meant in the long term.

"It's so shiny!" Filo shouted. She tended to get excited by shiny objects.

"We're just borrowing it, so I guess I can't give it to Rishia for the battle?"

"Sorry, but I don't think I can allow that," Alto apologized.

I didn't care. Maybe we could steal it and get away with it.

But if Raphtalia couldn't even use it, and couldn't even switch to it yet, then what chance would Rishia have of making use of it? Besides, I didn't know anyone else that fought with a sword.

"Because we've already chosen who will use it," Alto said.

"What? Who?"

"A friend of Kizuna's will use it for the coming battle."

I guess we couldn't steal it then. Oh well.

But would this friend of Kizuna's even be able to use it?

It was pretty confusing. If you couldn't power-up the way that holders of the vassal weapons did, the weapon wouldn't be as powerful.

"As for materials, come check these out," Romina said. She took out a collection of materials everyone had collected over time, and I absorbed them into my shield.

And it unlocked a few shields, one of which was from the White Tiger material. The collection of materials wasn't complete, so for now, all I had was stuff like the White Tiger Pelt Shield.

If only we had the blood and flesh too.

By the way, the stats were excellent.

**White Tiger Pelt Shield conditions met!**
**White Tiger Fang Shield conditions met!**
**White Tiger Bone Shield conditions met!**
**Etc . . .**

**White Tiger Pelt Shield**
**abilities locked: equip bonus: Awareness Boost (medium)**
 **special effects: agility up (strong), impact absorption (medium), parry (medium), support nullification, Wind Pressure.**

 **White Tiger Fang Shield**
 **abilities locked: equip bonus SP 30**
 **special effects: agility up (strong), parry (medium), support nullification, wind pressure, White Tiger Fang.**

I didn't like the support nullification effect; it could really affect my role in battle.

As for wind pressure, it was an effect that triggered when I changed shields. It formed a wall of wind. If that wall was powerful enough to block magic and attacks, then I might have been a bit more excited—but it wasn't. It was just a mild breeze, not good for much. On top of that, it was really loud from where I stood, and it sort of hurt my ears.

The abilities were—if I'm remembering correctly—a bit better than the Soul Eater Shield.

But that support nullification! That was a problem.

Still, after trying it out I have to say that the agility boost was very impressive, and the parry effect was excellent when I pulled it off properly. The shields had great effects too, but they were going to be tough to use.

The Fang Shield had a counter attack. I always liked shields with counter attacks.

But both shields had that support nullification issue.

After those shields, I also received some shields in the Vermilion Bird and Black Tortoise series. But I wasn't strong enough to unlock a lot of them.

Was my level not high enough? This wasn't a game, but did I need to level up before the boss?

"And this is just some of the material . . ." Romina said, passing me some black scales and bones and a piece of dragon core that I'd seen before.

I tried putting them into the shield. But the shield sparked and crackled. What was going on? That had never happened before.

**Locked.**

"It just says that it's locked, but . . ."

Then I realized, I hadn't tried to use dragon-type shields since I'd arrived in this world. At first, I'd thought, I couldn't access them because of my level, but now I wasn't sure what was going on.

"It's not working?"

"I guess not."

Raphtalia absorbed the same materials into her weapon, and she was able to change her katana into a dark, black blade—similar to the weapons that Glass and the others were using.

"Wow! This is incredible! It seems so easy to use, and it doesn't require a very high level."

Why? I was getting jealous!

What was the reason for this? Why can't I do the same thing?

Hm . . . I guess I did have an idea.

My shield wasn't a weapon from this world. So, it unlocked and produced different things than it would if it were from this world. Considering that, it wasn't too surprising that there were shields I wouldn't be able to unlock.

Still, I'd been able to use all sorts of shields, so why was it now suddenly locking anything related to dragons? I had no idea.

Suddenly I felt a pulse run through my shield and armor. "What?"

My shield crackled and shook in my hand. And then . . .

**Demon Dragon Shield conditions met!**

A single shield unlocked.

**Demon Dragon Shield**
**abilities locked: equip bonus: skill: "Attack Support"**
**special effect: Dragon Scale (large), C Demon Bullet, all resistances (medium), magic power consumption reduction (weak), SP consumption reduction (weak).**

The stats were excellent, and it didn't have any weird conditions to deal with. It would be easy to use.

And it had these reductions and increased all resistances too. Taken all together, it was probably the most well-rounded shield yet. I could switch to it whenever I was in trouble.

And it didn't require a high level to use either. This shield was awesome!

"Erm . . ."

"What is it, Filo?"

Filo muttered to herself. She was staring at the shield. Raph-chan cocked her head in confusion, not understanding why Filo was acting the way that she was.

"I dunno, but . . . I feel kind of sick."

"You probably have heartburn from eating like a pig all this time."

I wondered what Attack Support was.

I said, "attack support," and a small, pointed object appeared in my hand.

I held it and looked at it carefully.

It looked like a tiny dart—there was a triangular arrowhead at its tip. It looked like might be made for throwing.

Then it vanished. Is that what this skill did? Make a small mystery dart that vanished in a few seconds? The cool down time was a little long, taking about thirty seconds.

I had no idea what it was used for, but I'd have to try it out later.

"Looks like everyone's weapons share a sort of unity."

"Looks that way."

"Thank you for putting all this together."

"Oh it's fine. Besides, you're out there fighting for me and everyone else. Consider it my thanks for finding and freeing Kizuna," Romina said, smiling,

Alto added, "If you hadn't found her, Kizuna would probably have been lost forever. Thank you again. I'm sure that Glass and L'Arc feel more gratitude to you than they can express."

"Well it just sort of happened by chance."

I had fallen into the enemy's trap and just happened to end up in the same place as Kizuna. I didn't really deserve all this gratitude for it. Though, I guess I did help get her out of that place.

"Anyway, aren't you about to head into a really tough battle? Leave the weapons up to me! You get out there and do what you came here to do!"

That's right. It was nearly time for our battle with Kyo.

There was a war going on. We had find Kyo, where he hid in the shadows of the enemy nation, and make him pay for what he'd done.

We were finished with our preparations, and it was time to depart.

The next day, we were making our way to the castle, and found Kizuna and her friends, Ethnobalt, and Yomogi waiting for us.

Tsugumi was supposed to stay behind and rest, but she was there too—standing with crutches.

"Alright, let's get going."

"Are we taking the boat vassal weapon as far as we can?"

"Yes. Let's board."

"We need to talk strategy. Keep in mind that the vassal weapon holders and the holy heroes are battling together now."

Yomogi's hand curled into a fist when she heard that. Considering the circumstances, it was now very clear that Kyo was the true enemy, but a part of her still wanted to believe in him. Kizuna said, "After we find Kyo, maybe we can talk to him, get some answers . . . but then again, that might not work out so well. But, if he's defeated, Naofumi will take the protective beast's energy back, then we can put an end to this war."

"You make it sound so simple. Is that all we need to do?"

Something bothered me.

Kyo was a coward. He was the sort to set a bunch of traps and avoid battle for as long as he could. I'm not saying that I'm like him, but I felt like I could imagine what he would do if I thought about it.

I looked over at Glass.

I couldn't help but get the feeling that we were missing something—something we needed to defeat him.

I remembered when Rishia threw her sword and it had sunk deep into him—that hadn't been enough to finish him off. He was a monster.

Even if we used Glass and L'Arc's best attacks, would that be enough to take care of him?

Another thing: whenever I thought of Kyo, Trash #2 popped into my mind. They were so similar. I remembered him screaming and calling for our deaths, even after we had told him that he'd die if he moved. Why did he do that?

And why were none of Trash #2's gaggle of women spirits, like Glass?

Huh? Did I just notice something?

There weren't any Spirits in the group.

Why not? I think there were some the first time we fought, but now they were gone.

"Kizuna, can we just identify all of the attackers from the last fight for minute?"

"Uh . . . Sure."

I turned to look at Trash #2's group of women.

"You all liked this guy, right? Why aren't there any Spirits in the group?"

"There were, before, but they went missing. We looked for them, but we never found them."

Hm. I felt like a piece of the puzzle had just fallen into place.

"Glass."

"Yes?"

"Spirits aren't ghosts, right? They're not souls, are they?"

"No. There are some similarities, but we are different."

"Kizuna, there are ghosts in this world, right?"

"Yes. I told you about our fight with the ghost ship, didn't I?"

Who knows what to make of ghosts and souls? Regardless, it was clear they existed in this world too. If Kyo was the sort of person that I thought he was, he would definitely research them.

"Question: Glass, can Spirits like you see ghosts and souls?"

"Yes, certainly more easily than normal people can, but you can see them too if you use your shikigami."

"What are you getting at?" one of the women in Trash #2's group asked.

Glass looked just as confused as they did.

"I was thinking that, when your beloved man died, what if the Spirits that were with you went chasing after his soul?"

"Yes, well . . . there are certainly many Spirits that don't believe life ends with the death of the body."

I was right. I had to be right, but there was still something off.

"Can I ask what Kyo does with the people he captures? This world has its own special crimes, doesn't it?"

"Yes. There would certainly be problems if the people you killed came back as undead zombies, or as ghosts . . ."

Glass suddenly realized what I was saying. Yomogi and Tsugumi did too.

"I think you may be correct. And there's a good chance that Kyo got rid of the guy you loved, so you'd better prepare yourselves for that."

Tears came into the women's eyes, and they turned away from me.

"But if you are so heartbroken that you don't care if you live or die, you are just creating a nuisance for everyone. I'm not saying he'll be an undead zombie. But if I'm right, then . . ." I explained what sort of research I thought Kyo was carrying out.

"I heard a similar idea once, a long time ago. But could it really be?"

"I think so. And I played an action game like that before. If you don't know when you're going to die, it makes sense to have a line of defense ready," Kizuna said.

"Aren't you taking this all a bit far? You're talking about fairytales now!" L'Arc said.

"You've been chosen to wield a vassal weapon, and you're worried about fairytales? Besides, half of the stuff that happens in this world is straight out of a fairytale."

None of this stuff could happen back in the Japan I knew, but I was in a fantasy world now.

L'Arc wasn't convinced, but I was.

Now, we just had to break into Kyo's laboratory to get the proof.

We had to prepare for the siege.

We boarded Ethnobalt's boat and took off.

For the first part of the journey, we rode on the mysterious lines that linked the dragon hourglasses. Along the way we ran into occasional groups of flying monsters, and even some enemy soldiers. Thanks to the new accessories I gave to Glass and L'Arc, we were able to defeat them all easily.

The journey was so easy it almost made me worry.

We traveled like that for three days when we found it.

"That's Kyo's laboratory over there," Yomogi said, pointing to the sky above an area of foggy, misty forest.

"Where? Maybe I just can't see it through all the mist, but it just looks like forest to me."

"You can't see it from the outside."

"We can't take the boat much deeper into the fog. It's too dangerous," Ethnobalt said.

"The mist confuses all who enter. We would certainly become lost within it, if it were not for this bell," Yomogi said, showing us a small bell.

I hadn't heard of this special bell yet, but it sounded really important.

Then again, he had been using Yomogi this whole time—maybe her bell wouldn't work either.

"With this bell, we should be able to see the laboratory

shortly after entering the fog."

"Then I guess we better get going."

"Very well," Ethnobalt said.

Yomogi rang the bell.

The boat lurched forward into the fog and mist.

". . . ?"

Raphtalia looked concerned, but we kept pressing forward. Yomogi continued to ring the bell, and it chimed through the mist.

But then the mist cleared for a moment, and we discovered that we had returned to the place where we originally entered it.

"Weren't we just here?"

"No, it can't be! We must have made a mistake. Let's just try it again," Yomogi said.

Ethnobalt turned the boat back into the fog.

Once again, a few moments later, the fog cleared and we were right back where we started.

If I were Kyo, I would have done the same thing. I said, "I guess that bell of yours doesn't work anymore."

"But I . . . Kyo . . ."

We were stuck. Stuck right before the enemy's hideout. He really did have a good place set up for himself. Even if they lost the war, he'd be safe in there, safe to go infect some other country for his purposes.

"Isn't there something we can do to get rid of all this fog?"

"Sure there is," I said, showing a bioplant seed to Kizuna.

"Naofumi, you can't be serious . . ." she said, her face pale.

"I am. We set the stats to make it reproduce quickly, then seed the whole forest. The bioplants will take over in a couple of days. Then what good will this forest do him?"

"But you'll throw the whole ecosystem off balance. What if it spreads over the whole continent?"

That was something to worry about. But we had to find some way to get to Kyo.

We needed to try something, and this was my best idea. Once we took care of Kyo, we could try using it on the war front too.

"There is a chance that it could pollute the continent, but if it looks like it's going to be a problem, we'll just have to use magic to burn them all up. We have weed killer too, if we need it."

Besides, when the bioplants spread, they always had a central tree that controlled the rest of them. If we took care of the master tree, we could get rid of them all in one blow. When I chose the bioplant stats, I could program a weakness into it that we could exploit later on.

"I don't know. I really don't think we should use that."

"There you go, moralizing again. So what's your plan? I mean, if you know something I don't, then by all means, tell us how to fix this."

"But what about the environment?"

Kizuna and I were really snapping at each other now. Behind us Raphtalia and Raph-chan raised their hands.

"Excuse me. Can we try something?"

"You have an idea?"

"Yes. Ethnobalt, please proceed as I tell you."

"Rafuuu!"

"Very well."

Our flying ship turned, and once again entered the mist.

After we had flown a little way in . . .

"To the right—now to the left! Yes! Now just keep going straight," Raphtalia explained.

Ethnobalt listened to Raphtalia and Raph-chan's instructions, and kept the boat on the course they indicated.

"Angle it to the right. Yes, and now backwards."

"Backwards?"

"Very well."

He did as Raphtalia indicated and angled the ship so it would go backwards.

We slipped out of the fog again, but now we found ourselves somewhere new. The wall of fog stood imposing before us, but there was something new jutting out of it: an imposing building. We'd made it.

"Whoa! We did it!"

"The mist reminded me of the illusion magic I've been

practicing. I suspected there might be a particular path through it, and I was able to find it," Raphtalia told us.

So it was a maze . . .

It was sending us back to the start every time we hit one of its invisible walls.

Raphtalia and Raph-chan could find a way through because they were good with illusion magic. A lost woods gimmick wasn't going to work with them on our side!

"Alright, we found the lab, thanks to Raphtalia! Let's go finish this!"

"Yeah!" everyone shouted in unison.

Ethnobalt piloted the boat into the building's courtyard, and we found ourselves facing the entrance to Kyo's secret laboratory.

## Chapter Nine: Kyo's Laboratory

"So this is Kyo's laboratory . . ."

It looked like an old, very Western-style mansion, which was weird, because this whole country looked Japanese otherwise.

From the look of it, I expected to find his hideout down in a hidden basement chamber.

"This way," Yomogi said, taking the lead. She had spent a lot of time there, but . . .

"I don't see any of the rest of Trash #2's women. If we run into them, I have a lot of questions I'll want answered."

"They probably know that we're here."

I looked around the courtyard, then agreed.

"They might have been sent out on a mission too. Or maybe they evacuated."

There was another possibility, but I didn't want to think about it.

Could he have sacrificed the women for his experiments? No . . .

"Those with a taste for blood might have been sent out to the war front. But he didn't bring everyone here to begin with."

"No?"

"Kyo only brings people he really trusts here. He helps all

sorts of people, but he doesn't like it when people go poking around in his business."

Of course he doesn't; he has a lot to hide. He was like the best student in school, but lived a double life.

"So only Kyo's most trusted companions know about this place. At least, that's what I thought," Yomogi said bitterly. She'd thought she was special.

So we weren't going to be able to use the women as hostages, they were all in this together. Kyo must have brainwashed them, just like he had Tsugumi and Yomogi.

"Whatever. As long as Kyo is here, we can carry out our plan. If he isn't, we raid his laboratory for what we can use in the war, then destroy it."

After all, he might have run away if he knew we were coming.

"Grrr . . ."

"Don't you forget, you are helping an enemy nation. You're not operating on your own, you're a soldier for us now."

Yomogi curled her hand into a fist, "That's cowardly!"

"You don't think it's cowardly to try and take control over another country?"

There were people like that, people that believed you could do anything, as long as you thought you were right. It was a convenient, opportunistic way to live. It reminded me of Itsuki.

"Kiddo. Give it a rest, will you? We'll know the truth once

we get in there and find it."

"Good point."

I had barely finished my sentence when the roar of a beast echoed through the courtyard.

I quickly turned to the source of the roar, and found myself looking at the same White Tiger copies that Trash #2 had been researching. There was also a red bird, which I'm guessing was a vermilion bird, and a black tortoise with a snake for a tail.

"Gahhhh!"

Then there were people, people that looked like they had been merged with beasts and were on the verge of insanity. The beast side of their bodies was much larger than the human side, and it had nearly taken them over completely. Their eyes were fierce and wild, and saliva dangled from their gaping mouths.

"There's the truth for you right there. Kyo isn't trying to hide it. Looks like we are too late for some of them. Kizuna, can you help them?"

"I don't know, but I can try."

Yomogi frowned, "Kyo, how could you do something like this?" She drew the katana that Kizuna had given her.

We were going to support her in battle.

"Let's go!"

"Gahhhh!"

The beasts roared like a gong initiating battle, and they rushed us. We met them head on, and the battle began in earnest.

"Damn. The beast side had taken over too much. My weapon doesn't see them as human anymore."

Kizuna had tried to slice off the beast half of the enemy, bur the holy weapon no longer distinguished between their human and beast parts. That meant that Kizuna was now the strongest attacker in the group.

I'd seen her abilities before, when we were traveling together. She was so strong that it was like being able to fire off Reverse Snow Moon Flower at no cost and with minimal cool down at any time. As long as she wasn't fighting other humans, she was a real monster on the battlefield.

She flew through the crowd, slicing them down. When they fell, they looked like they were saying something.

Kizuna, Glass, and Raphtalia had tears in their eyes.

"What is it?"

"They . . . Before they die, they thank me."

"Dammit! They're really making this hard!" L'Arc shouted. As understanding dawned on him, he hesitated to fight.

I blocked an attack with my shield and nodded.

"Don't sympathize or you'll end up dead. There's nothing we can do for them now."

We had a choice between people we could save and people we couldn't. I wish we were strong enough to save everyone, but we weren't.

"Kizuna, you know what's going on here, don't you? Back

in the world I was summoned to, the Spirit Tortoise familiars infected people like parasites. We couldn't save them. Some of that might have been the Spirit Tortoise's doing, but the other half . . ."

She nodded.

"I had really only understood half of your story until now."

"Kiddo's world took a really hard beating. You're right. We weren't ready."

"If you still want to try and save them, try to knock them out of the battle, at least."

Actually they regenerated very quickly, so unless we sliced all their limbs off, they regenerated and came back after us.

There weren't any good options.

"Uh . . ." Filo muttered. She looked unnerved. She never was very good with this kind of thing.

I knew how she felt, but we didn't have a choice.

"Ha!" Raphtalia swung her sword, then slid it back into its sheath. Then she drew her other sword and dashed through the crowd of encroaching monsters. "Mr. Naofumi is right! We cannot forgive the monster that did this! We must press forward!"

The monsters around her fell to the ground.

She was right. If we hesitated, we'd be done for. And if we didn't make it, there would be no one left to stop Kyo.

L'Arc sighed, "The path forward is covered in blood, but if

it means the people's happiness then we have no choice but to wade through it. I didn't think the day would come when I'd be learning something from you, Kiddo."

"Don't confuse it for wisdom. I just do what I have to, and when someone tries to kill me, I take them out first."

If I didn't, that would be the end.

I'd done it plenty of times. The Church of the Three Heroes tried to assassinate me. L'Arc and his friends tried to assassinate me. The Spirit Tortoise tried to kill everyone to make a magic barrier.

I had to defeat them all, otherwise there would be no future for me.

I'm not saying that I didn't have regrets.

But if we didn't keep moving forward, we'd never repay the debt we had to all those who had already lost their lives.

"The reason for Ost's death is right here. We've come to repay that. The enemy might make it hard on us, but there is no going back."

"That's just like you, Kiddo. I like it." L'Arc readied his scythe.

"Agreed. I like it too," Ethnobalt said, turning his vassal weapon into a much smaller boat.

What was he going to do?

"I may not be the strongest fighter here, but I'll do what I can to support the rest of you."

He turned the boat's cannons on the encroaching enemy.

"All Cannons Fire!"

There was a deafening blast, and everything went white.

I'd heard that Ethnobalt's abilities were very weak, that his attacks were basically useless. And after all the cannons fired, the results supported all that I'd heard.

The monsters and transformed humans turned and smacked the cannonballs down, as if they were nothing but mosquitoes. Ethnobalt rose higher into the air on his boat and waved to us.

"I'll keep them distracted! Please, hurry on!"

"But . . ." Kizuna stretched out her arm to him, but he was too far away to touch.

The vermilion bird copies could fly, and the white tiger copies were jumping on ledges and trees and swiping at the boat from below. The black tortoise copies were wresting boulders from the ground and throwing them at the flying boat.

I didn't want to leave him there. It was like leaving a rabbit surrounded by wild beasts.

"I'll be alright. I have a vassal weapon, don't I? Let me do this! I'll do my best!"

"Ethnobalt!"

"Pen!" Chris bounded forward and leaped onto a white tiger copy, and then a vermilion bird copy, then jumped up onto the stern of the boat.

"Chris."

"Pen!" he waved down to Kizuna, as if to say, "Leave this to me."

"Naofumi, please. Protect Kizuna for me."

"Fine."

"Feh . . . Are we really leaving him?"

"Yes. Kizuna—let's go!"

"But!"

"We don't have the time to sit around entertaining these monsters! Kyo could get away!"

Ethnobalt made up his mind to help us. I had to respect his resolve. And he had Chris with him. If things went south, I hoped he'd be able to escape.

"Now's our chance. Let's go! Let Ethnobalt do what he wants!"

We all ran toward the mansion.

Looking back, I saw Ethnobalt luring the monsters out toward the woods. He was waving to us.

Inside the mansion, it smelled like someone had been there recently. It looked that way too, like someone had set up and been living there for a while.

"You said he only brings his most trusted companions here, right?"

Yomogi nodded, "Yes, and there are deeper chambers of the mansion. He's more selective about who gets to go in there."

"He sounds like a typical wizard or alchemist. He must get obsessed with his research."

"You're absolutely correct—that's exactly how he was. I'm confused by why a hero from another world knows so much about Kyo."

"It's just a guess."

I had my sources. I often read about these crazy scientist type characters in manga, or ran into them in games. But Kyo didn't match up with those characters exactly. There were still things about him I didn't understand.

It was like he really thought that his ideas were amazing, and he wanted nothing more than to make sure they became reality.

"Damn. It's locked."

"Where's the key?"

"Right here," Yomogi said, pulling a key from her pocket and inserting it into the keyhole.

As expected, it didn't work.

"Were you and Kyo friends or what?"

"What? This key always opened the door!"

She hadn't been right about anything yet.

I'd seen this kind of thing before. Yomogi was the only one in that relationship that thought they were friends—for Kyo it had all been an act.

"Calm down. You know what to do in a situation like this, don't you L'Arc? Kizuna?"

"Right on!" L'Arc smiled. He knew what I was hinting at.

"Puzzle solving!" Kizuna chirped.

Unfortunately for her, in this case she was wrong.

"Kizuna, you can go hang out in a game world if that's what you want. And don't bother coming back."

"Hey!" she scowled.

I snapped my fingers, and L'Arc swung his scythe hard, splintering the door.

At least someone understood what I was saying.

"This thing is tougher than I thought."

"Let's grab it on our way out. We can probably make a decent weapon out of it."

"Kiddo, that's not what I was trying to say . . ."

"Ah . . ."

"Oh come on already . . ." Glass sighed, clearly annoyed.

Raphtalia was confused by everyone's behavior, "Shall I slice up the remains of the door a little more cleanly, so they can be easily collected on our way out?"

"Raphtalia?!" Kizuna jumped, surprised by Raphtalia's response.

Raphtalia could be very matter-of-fact about these things.

"Did I say something strange?"

"We don't have time for that. Let's just knock this place down!" L'Arc shouted.

He clearly understood the situation.

And he was right. We didn't have time to go snooping around collecting things.

"You want to solve puzzles, but that would imply that there are puzzles to solve. You think he left behind keys for us to find? I doubt it!"

Who would do something like that? He'd have to be crazy to leave clues for invaders to come find him.

No—we were going to break down all the doors, find Kyo, and make him pay.

That's why Chris and Ethnobalt had stayed behind—to draw the enemy's attention.

We just had to smoke him out.

"Actually, knocking down this mansion isn't such a bad idea. But Yomogi still wants to believe in him, so we snuck in. Let's just keep moving."

Yomogi didn't like that we'd destroyed the door. She muttered, "If Kyo is innocent, you better pay for that."

"Sure."

If there was any grey area left in how Yomogi saw Kyo, it must have been damn near close to black.

The time had come.

"I'm good with this kind of thing."

"I bet you are. You like to break things."

"Kiddo, if you think that's my only talent, you're very wrong."

"What else are you good at? You're not going to pretend to be a strategist now, are you?"

"Well, now that you mention it, I am pretty good . . ."

He was getting harder and harder to take seriously.

"I like adventures, you know?"

"Oh . . . do you now?"

What was I supposed to say? Should I say I'm good at cooking? Did that matter?

Besides, he didn't say he was talented—he just said he liked it. I don't get it.

"Hey Therese, don't I always say that I want to go hunting for ruins?"

"You do! But isn't it better to make new treasures, rather than hunting down old ones?"

"I guess," he said, looking at me enviously.

"I guess you get your pick of whatever you want, huh? Why do you always get what you want?"

"Oh, that's just the way it is."

I didn't understand their relationship at all, but I could tell that they cared for each other.

Anyway, we went through the mansion, breaking down any locked doors that stood in our way.

We ran into some holy beast copies along the way, but they weren't the enemy we were concerned with, and honestly, they didn't put up much of a fight.

With Kizuna on our side, they never stood a chance. She cut them down the moment they appeared. With her tuna knife in hand, she could cut straight through their bones and slice them in half.

"But why are there so many monsters in here?"

We were finding monsters in nearly every room. It was like we were stuck in an action RPG or something.

"Yomogi, where's Kyo's laboratory?"

"That way," she said, pointing.

Along the way there were some pitfalls and traps, but they were all easy to avoid, and simple enough that they wouldn't be much trouble, even if we did get caught in them.

I led the way, so any traps that triggered darts or arrows could be blocked with Shooting Star Shield. And if we came across a pitfall, we could use Air Strike Shield to cross it.

There were rolling balls of iron, and guillotine-like blades too. We avoided or blocked them all with ease. He'd made a real fun house for us, but it just wasn't good enough.

"This will lead us underground soon, and that is where you'll find his laboratory. But the underground area is far more subdivided and complicated than the areas above ground. There are many rooms that I do not know," Yomogi said, looking sick.

I guess I couldn't blame her. She believed in Kyo, and now she saw that he was crazy, using copies of the holy beasts to nefarious ends. Furthermore, we were finding plenty of proof that he was behind the twisted beast-human hybrids we'd battled.

I guess I had to hand it to her—she must have been a loyal friend not to give up hope for him, even after he'd sent her on a suicide mission.

She reminded me of Motoyasu in that sense—she picked the wrong person to believe in.

"You . . . You made it this far!?!"

We entered the underground laboratory and surprised a group of half-human-half-beast hybrids. They seemed to still be aware of who they were. Were they Yomogi's friends?

I looked over at Yomogi, but she shook her head.

Then they must have been from Tsugumi's group. I didn't recognize them.

I looked around at Raphtalia, Glass, and L'Arc, but they were just as confused as I was.

"Wait! We didn't come here to fight you! You're being used! We've come to punish the same person that makes a mockery of your lives!"

"Silence! If we don't stop you, Mr. Albert will be killed!"

Who? Wait a second. Who the hell was that?

I'd never even heard the name. I had no idea.

"Hey Glass, do you know who they're talking about? Do you think he kidnapped some completely unrelated person just to use them as a hostage to motivate these people?"

I guess he didn't really need to limit himself to people involved with us directly.

He could make anyone into his slaves if he had the mind to do it.

"Albert . . . I'm pretty sure that's the name of the person who wields the mirror of the vassal weapons."

Ah, right—the guy that Kyo took control of while Trash #2 was chasing Raphtalia and Glass around the countryside. Hadn't they said he was on bad terms with Glass and the others?

"Al is still alive! We cannot give up while he still lives! We must defeat you!" they shouted. I was only half-listening, as I couldn't keep my eyes off the strange parasitic weapons in their hands—the very same ones that Yomogi and Tsugumi had held.

They attacked!

"Yikes!"

I immediately used Shooting Star Shield to block the attack. It slammed against it with a loud clang.

Yes, the barrier held. It must have been due to the Demon Dragon Shield and the Barbaroi Armor.

"Those weapons are dangerous! You have to put them down!"

"I wonder if he would make the weapons explode here?"

What would happen if they blew up in this confined, underground space?

If the weapons were at risk of explosion, then it was safe to assume Kyo didn't consider this place very important.

Hey wait—didn't they say that the wielder of the mirror of the vassal weapons was dead? Had that been a lie? There was no way to know . . . yet.

"Kizuna, do your thing on them. I want to see if their weapons will explode."

"What are you thinking, Kiddo?"

"If the weapons are set up to explode, and if those explosions are as big as the other weapons, then we can infer that Kyo isn't too concerned with this area."

"Right—because he wouldn't want to destroy his own place."

"Exactly. If Kyo is the kind of person I think he is, then those weapons won't explode here."

He wasn't the sort of person that would try to kill us no matter the cost. No—he would try to be smart about it. He'd try to get all he could out of the situation.

"What do you want to do about the weapons?"

"You guys should be strong enough to destroy them, no?"

I concentrated and cast Zweite Aura on all of them in order.

The enemies' weapons hadn't been powerful enough to break through the Shooting Star Shield barrier. And we were all powered up now, so we'd have a good chance of breaking them.

"Got it. Let's do this!"

Kizuna stepped forward and lined up with Glass, who had just taken a sip of soul-healing water. They readied their weapons and dashed forward.

The fight was over in a flash.

Kizuna sliced through their beast halves, and Glass destroyed their weapons.

Battle fans were . . . well, I've read that they were historically made out of iron, and used specifically to break enemy weapons.

They were sword breakers.

Yomogi was a skilled fighter, so she'd been able to parry Glass's attacks. But, these people weren't nearly as skilled, and they couldn't stop her.

And as for Kizuna, even if she couldn't attack people, she could certainly manage to break their weapons. That is, as long as she didn't have to break a vassal or holy weapon.

Still, their weapons were tough enough to give her some trouble.

"Gah?!"

"Ugh?!"

Their weapons shattered, and the women took severe damage.

The broken weapons fell to the floor. Then disgusting, wiggling tentacles extended from them, reaching out to the women that had held them.

The fallen halves of the weapons reached out to each other, trying to link back up when . . .

"I don't think so!"

"Hya!"

"Sorry, but I don't want you using those things. Naofumi, keep the weapons away from them!"

L'Arc and Raphtalia, followed by Yomogi, rushed forward to deal follow-up attacks, and kicked a weapon at me.

The weapon flew at me and then, as if trying to avoid me, turned in mid-flight before disappearing in a puff of smoke. All that was left behind was the Spirit Tortoise energy.

The weapons must have been made by imbuing monster elements with Spirit Tortoise energy.

When Kizuna and L'Arc killed the monster part of one of them, the remaining part tried to regenerate the lost half, but we blocked it. Then, the Spirit Tortoise Heart Shield sucked up the energy that animated it, leaving only a pile of dust.

"Hey, if you throw them to me they disappear!"

"What?!"

"Are you implying there is nothing we can do?"

"We won't give up!"

The mirror of the vassal weapons holder's group of women howled and ran to attack again.

"I don't think so!"

"Yes, I know that this is not your fault, and that you are not bad people. But you must give up this fight."

Filo and Therese cast spells at them.

"Forgive me. I know that you are fighting to protect someone you love, but we cannot afford to be delayed any longer. Circle Dance Attack Formation: Flower Wind!"

Glass rushed forward with a final attack that incapacitated them.

"That's what I thought. Kyo must be here."

"Agreed. Otherwise all these weapons would have exploded."

That settled it. He was probably whining and wringing his hands right about now.

"I'm surprised he even thinks he can hold us off for this long. He's lucky—I'll give him that much."

Think about it, we're talking about two powered-up holy heroes, and three wielders of vassal weapons. Furthermore, Ethnobalt was still holding them off outside. All together that made for six heroes at once.

Unless he had some genius back-up plan, he'd probably be thinking of how to escape with his life. And yet, he'd filled the mansion with traps, sent copies of the four holy beasts to meet us, and left behind these human-beast hybrids with their special weapons. What was I supposed to make of that?

"Hey! You better not go in that room!" one of the women in the group shouted.

I was about to say that I would do the opposite of whatever they said, but I decided to keep my mouth shut.

I opened the door, then went through a few more doors and found myself standing at the entrance to Kyo's laboratory.

"Wh . . . What is this?"

"I could see this coming. You could too, couldn't you, Glass?"

Everyone gasped.

The walls of the hallway were lined with glass tanks filled with a liquid.

Something floated in the tanks, and it was just what I'd expected.

They looked like humans, but they weren't . . . not exactly. They were the dream of these alchemist-types—homunculus.

"Homunculus . . ." Rishia whimpered, scared by what she saw. The concept of homunculus must have existed in this world too.

The tanks were filled with men that looked just like Trash #2.

There were some other people too, but they all looked mostly the same.

"This is . . ."

One of the tanks held a Trash #2 that had been sliced cleanly in half. Was it the same one that we'd fought and killed?

"Look . . ." Glass said, pointing to a larger tank at the end of the hall. It seemed more important than the others, like it was a special display.

The attractive man inside had long black hair, and he clutched a mirror at his chest. He looked like he might be Japanese, and in his mid-twenties.

"That's the holder of the mirror vassal weapon!"

"Looks like he's being held hostage."

I barely had time to finish my sentence when all the homunculi and the real vassal weapon holder opened their eyes and stared at us.

"Are they capable of reason? Maybe we can talk to them."

The tanks shattered, and the homunculi stepped out. I could hardly believe my eyes—real homunculi.

Then again, I'd seen copies of the four holy beasts, so I expected it.

Maybe they could speak, but had been brainwashed. Or . . .

"Gahhhhhhhh!"

They roared, twisted and strained, and . . . turned into the four holy beasts.

They appeared far more powerful than the hybrid beasts we fought up until now.

But Trash #2 and the holder of the mirror vassal weapon—I guess his name was Albert—hadn't changed at all. They looked like they were ready for a fight.

Trash #2 lurched forward and stumbled toward us like a zombie. His eyes were completely white, and locked on us.

It was kind of gross.

"Do you think they can talk?"

"Ugh . . . Uehhh."

It didn't look like they could to me. He just growled and slobbered like a zombie.

But, as if to show how ready he was to fight, Albert held up his mirror and flashed it at us.

"What's tha . . ."

"What?!"

Raphtalia and Kizuna both gasped and looked down at their weapons.

"What is it?"

"Mr. Naofumi, the vassal weapon is asking for help. That person holding it has lost more than half of his soul. He's tied to the weapon by force."

I didn't really care that he'd lost half of his soul—I was more concerned with how he'd been tied to the weapon. What did that mean?

"He can continue to fight with the vassal weapon, even though they are supposed to leave their holder upon death," Kizuna explained. She didn't have to explain that to me, but I guess she wanted to make sure everyone else understood.

"These are certain to be Kyo's most powerful servants."

I didn't like the look of this one bit. Kyo had another one of the vassal weapons under his control. I guess if they didn't share what they knew about powering up, then the threat . . .

"Moon . . . Verse!"

The mirror flashed, and a shining, moon-like disc of light shot across the hall at us, shattering my Shooting Star Shield barrier easily.

Damn it. Never mind powering up, it looked like he might have been charged or imbued with Spirit Tortoise energy . . . or something.

"Well, well, well. I didn't think you'd actually come all this way . . ." a voice echoed. I didn't like the sound of it.

Behind Albert, the floor shattered and Kyo appeared, standing on a floating platform of light.

He was surrounded by Spirit Tortoise Familiars (neo-guardian type).

He'd been waiting for us . . . with an army.

## Chapter Ten: When Trust is Lost

"You break into my lab and mess with my things! You're like snakes."

"That means a lot coming from you."

"Ha! You're a persistent fool, aren't you? Very annoying."

"Again, you take the words right out of my mouth."

He was annoyed? *I* was annoyed. I didn't want to waste any more of my life on this guy!

"You don't seem to understand how much trouble you've made. I've come to make sure that you do!"

"Ha! You and your pals are all from a world that is going to be destroyed regardless! I just made good use of it before the inevitable. You should be grateful!"

"No. I won't let anyone destroy Naofumi's world, not while I'm around. Give back what you've stolen," Kizuna said, stepping forward.

"Well, well. If it isn't the grand entrance of our long-missing holy hero!"

"Yeah, Glass and— Well, wouldn't we all be in trouble if we lost the holy heroes, or the vassal weapons? Who would protect our world from the waves? If you really think that you're fighting for our world, then you won't hurt us."

If everyone's theories were correct, then the world couldn't afford to lose its heroes. That doesn't mean that he couldn't hurt us though.

"There will still be three holy heroes left after I get rid of you. We should be fine. Just think of all the research I've done on behalf of this world. Once you understand the waves, they aren't so bad. It's just an update—an update!"

What the hell was this guy talking about?! I'd always heard that we couldn't let any of the heroes die. The heroes in Kizuna's world worked the same way, or so I'd been told. Were we wrong?

"Kyo!" Yomogi shouted and stepped forward. "Is it true that you took control of another world's protective beast and used it to destroy?"

"Huh?!" Kyo barked, glaring at Yomogi.

"And did you steal that beast's energy and come back here? Did you do *this* to the vassal weapon holder? Did you turn his friends into monsters?!"

"Oh enough already! Give it a rest, will you?"

"Kyo!?"

"Don't try and instruct me! I always said that you never knew when to shut up, didn't I? Do you think you're my mother? Just because we've known each other for a while doesn't mean you're my wife!" Kyo shouted at Yomogi, like a dam had burst.

The color drained from her face as she listened to him berate her.

"You're always so damn annoying! I thought giving you that exploding weapon and sending you on an assassination mission would finally be enough, but now you've brought these people right into my lab! You're such a bitch!"

"You . . . but . . . so these women, these friends of the man with the vassal weapon . . . or of that scientist from another land . . . why did you turn them into monsters? Why did . . ."

"What am I supposed to do with another guy's used goods? Sure, if some of them wanted to come over to my side, I could have looked the other way."

Used goods? I could hardly believe my ears. He couldn't like a woman that had been with someone else?

"It's good to see your face again though, Yomogi, don't worry. When they kill you, I'll be sure to exact revenge! Everything will be fine!"

Yomogi shook with rage. She'd believed in him for so long, hearing him say these things must have been devastating.

"It seems I was mistaken about you. I should never have trusted you."

"Huh? You're going to kill me know, just because I didn't say what you wanted to hear? You're sick! I'm nothing like what you want me to be!"

The more he spoke, the more I hated him. He really knew how to get you in a bad mood.

Yomogi had truly cared for him, worried about him, tried

to correct his path when he went off course—and now he was calling her a bitch?

If she was a bitch, then this guy was seriously screwed up.

He was trash, below trash—the scum of the earth. He was the male version of my arch-nemesis, Bitch.

This piece of crap had snuffed out Ost and her mission. I was so filled with rage I could hardly think straight.

Yomogi drew her katana and pointed it at Kyo.

"You think you stand chance against me? Really? I'm a genius!"

"It's not about winning or losing. I must make up for being misled, for believing a lie and doubting the truth. I must do it for myself. I must see you punished!" Yomogi turned back to face the rest of us. "Kizuna and your friends, and those of you from another world, please, lend me your strength. We must stop Kyo!"

"You don't have to ask me twice! That's why we came," Kizuna said.

"Exactly. Enough talk! Let's get this over with. A victory tinged with regret for our past missteps—what better way to take this jerk out?"

Sure, there were people like him in the world—people that grated on you every time they opened their mouths. Anytime you gave them the opportunity to speak, you'd regret it. In a way, he reminded me of the other three heroes. Why did my enemies all share these traits? It was still a mystery to me.

But I knew one thing: there was no reason to let this jerk mouth off anymore. There was only one thing left for us to do. Make him pay!

"What? Well, you'll see for yourself soon enough. This is the end of you all!" Kyo held out his hand, and all the homunculi, along with Albert and Trash #2, rushed to attack us. At the same time, the book in his hand slapped open, and its pages flapped out and flew around the room.

"Aim for the one in the back!" Kyo shouted, jabbing a finger at Rishia.

"More and more, every time you speak, I lose more patience. I cannot tolerate you any longer!" Rishia shouted.

What now? It was like something snapped in her. Her voice boomed over the chaotic room, like the hero of a story, if there ever was one. I'm going to start calling her "protagonist."

If only she could figure out how to act like this all the time.

When Rishia got excited like this, she was actually pretty useful in battle. I mean, she didn't have a vassal weapon, but she had really impressed me during the last battle with Kyo.

"Shooting Star Shield!"

"Is that your only skill?" Kyo laughed viciously.

"It's a pretty good one."

"That flimsy thing won't do you much good. Hope you have a better plan than that!"

"How's this?"

Albert, Trash #2, and the homunculi shattered the barrier, but its pieces remained floating in the air.

"Raphtalia!"

"Yes!" she shouted, drawing her katana.

"Oh! You might be fast, but how far do you think you can make it?"

"What makes you think she needs to go anywhere?"

Raphtalia understood what I meant without having to hear it. When the haikuikku activated, she immediately used the speed to cast a spell.

That's right—she could use the speed for things besides sword attacks.

"Drifa Light!" she shouted, casting the spell on the floating barrier chards.

"Raful!"

Oh Raph-chan cast a spell too, and she got the timing just right.

The light flashed over the barrier shards that everyone was focused on, and it was so bright that Trash #2, Albert, and the homunculi were blinded.

"Heh. Is that it?"

"Just wait."

The shining fragments spun around the room as I raised my shield.

It left the perfect opening for my team.

They say the beginning of a battle is the most important part, don't they?

Kizuna and Glass were the first ones to make use of the opening Raphtalia and I made.

"Double Lure Hook!"

Kizuna hit Albert with her skill that doubled future damage, and Glass took a sip of soul-healing water before using her own skill. She used a powerful, fire-based attack.

"Circle Dance Empty Formation: Moon Break!"

Her fan split in two, and she held a half in each hand. Bringing them together over her head she traced out the shape of a full moon, then forcefully brought the fans down.

"Moon . . . Verse!" Albert shouted, as if not wanting to be outdone.

But Glass was much faster.

Her attack met his, tore through it, and kept on going. It slammed into Albert, nearly tearing his shoulder clean off.

"Careful, there! I still have plans for this guy!"

Some pages flew from Kyo's book and fluttered over to Albert, where they attached to his shoulder and pulled it up and back onto his torso. Reconnected, he was bathed in a green light.

It must have been some sort of healing spell.

"I'm not going to get outdone by Kiddo and Kizuna! Therese, let's go!"

"Okay!"

L'Arc's scythe flashed and turned into pure energy, while Therese cast and activated a support spell.

"Shining Stones! Exploding Thunder Rain!"

It was one of her best spells.

What? Rishia held up her short sword and filled it with magic.

"Combo Skill! Electric Disc!"

"Hyaaaa!"

Resonating with L'Arc, Rishia quickly slashed her sword horizontally and neatly slipped it into its sheath.

Enormous discs of electric energy shot from L'Arc's energy scythe, and Rishia's attack followed behind, absorbing the trailing energy and . . . no, it fed the trailing energy back into the rotating disk as it slammed into the crowd of homunculi crowded before Kyo.

The attack was so powerful that it blasted their limbs off.

"My turn!" Filo shouted.

"Wait—you're on magic support duty. Use your humming fairy songs to back us up. Do you have a song that can speed up magic cast time?"

"Um . . . I'll try a song I know!" she said, turning into her humming falcon form and flying over to rest on my shoulder.

I thought Kyo would have a snarky comment for us, but instead he realized that Filo was up to something, and he glared at us spitefully.

I was casting Zweite Aura over and over.

I felt like it was getting easier to cast the spell without thinking too hard.

I don't know how to explain it in game terms, but it felt like my throat was more open and clear, like the incantation just slipped from it easily and activated the spell.

"Gahhh!"

Raphtalia sliced through the crowd of monstrous homunculi. And whenever Kizuna or Glass left an opening for follow-up attacks, Yomogi rushed in to take advantage.

I was impressed by their coordination.

"You idiots all have to work together, huh? Cause you're too weak to do anything on your own!"

"You like to pick fights because you have no friends to work together with."

"Shut your mouth!"

"You first! If I hurt your feelings, why not call for some of your monster women?"

We were like children fighting. Oh well, that's the sort of thing that happened in fights like these. Then again, we were fighting for our lives—this wasn't playground fisticuffs.

"Oh that's right. You didn't want to bring the women over because you were afraid they'd turn on you once they figured out what you were really like. Just like Yomogi."

"Shut up!"

Still, I was glad the women weren't here. They would just make more trouble and more casualties—both of which I'd rather avoid.

We had a lot to worry about. If the enemy's numbers were too large, and if they acted with a lot of coordination, they might be able to attack in ways we wouldn't be able to handle. Then again, the women might figure things out and turn on Kyo mid-battle, which is probably why he didn't involve them in this.

Maybe they just weren't powerful enough to be much use to him—though with those crazy weapons, they might have been a threat.

Maybe he was trying to keep them from getting hurt, and he was really a feminist like Motoyasu.

Doubtful, considering that he called them used goods just because they'd been with someone else. I guess he only cared about his own women.

"Okay, so how about I show you some of those same attacks you saw back in the Spirit Tortoise's core chamber? Or, actually, a lot has happened since then, so I'll have some new variations to show off. Let's see how long you can survive!"

"Survive? Ha! How stupid are you? Did you forget that we already beat you once?!"

Kyo opened his book and began to cast a spell. A mandala-like pattern appeared on the ground around him.

Suddenly, I felt an enormous, invisible pressure, forcing us to the ground.

I'd seen this before, the last time we fought Kyo—his obstruction attack.

"You don't have many ways to get around this, do you?!"

He was right about that. Having crossed between worlds, we were a little weaker than the last time. Enduring this gravity attack took all the strength I had. I don't think the Demon Dragon Shield was powerful enough.

"That same attack, again? We were weak when we met in the last world, but you know that we are back at full power now, right?"

"It's a little heavy, but not near enough to stop me from moving. Did you really think that would be enough to stop us?" Kizuna said.

Glass and Kizuna kept approaching Kyo, attacking whatever was in their way. Of course, Kizuna was just supporting attacks.

When they got near a homunculus, she'd hit it with Double Lure Hook. Then Glass would slice the monster in two.

I was impressed. Kyo's spell really didn't seem to affect them the way that it had back in the battle inside the Spirit Tortoise. It had been devastating then, but I guess it was because Glass and the others were weakened after crossing over to our world.

Still, past victory didn't ensure that we would come out on top this time.

"I knew you'd say that!"

Liar! Did he think I wouldn't notice how surprised he looked?

The pattern on the floor around him grew larger and brighter.

Hm . . . I could feel the power in the room, like it was filling with the Spirit Tortoise's energy.

"Ugh . . ."

I cast Shooting Star Shield, and the barrier broke immediately. The shattered pieces flew at Kyo, but they fell to the floor before reaching him.

Just how strong was this gravity field of his? Was it going to crush us to death?

Now Glass and Kizuna were forced to take a knee.

"Aha! This world's heroes and vassal weapon holders, I'd forgotten all about you. You're all so weak, I can't tell you apart."

Everyone on our side of the battle was forced to the ground. We put both hands flat on the floor and were straining to climb to our feet.

"Ughhh!"

Even Filo fell from my shoulder and struggled to stand against the gravity field.

The homunculi didn't seem to have any trouble at all, which made me think Kyo was able to control who was affected by his spell. What could be worse?

"Ugh . . . I can't move."

Kyo turned to focus on Kizuna and Glass.

"Looks like this is going to be over even faster than I thought. Are you really going to lose right now?! To my very first attack? Ha!"

If there was any time to cast a spell, this was it. I could use a skill or two during the incantation.

"Air Strike, Second, Dritte Shield!"

I quickly called for shields to materialize and protect us from the wild attacks of the homunculi, Albert, and Trash #2.

Under the weight of the gravity attack, they weren't going to stay in place for very long. Their defense was higher than Shooting Star Shield's barrier, so they were holding—at least for a little while.

"Your struggles are worthless!"

"You sure about that? Change Shield!"

The shields were already taking a battering, so there was only one thing left for me to do. I'd change them to the shield I had equipped—the Demon Dragon Shield. It had an equip effect called C Demon Bullet.

C was short for "counter attack," so I assumed it meant that the shield would fire a magical bullet whenever it was attacked.

The shields instantly transformed, were hit by attacks, and began to fire magical demon bullets at the enemy.

"?!"

The bullets were made of magic, so the gravity field didn't affect them.

They flew in every direction, slamming into the enemies and into the mandala pattern on the ground.

The mandala flickered, and its effect on the gravity field in the room weakened—that was our chance!

"Heh, I'm impressed. I'll have to make a note of that one."

"Don't get too haughty! Chain Shield!"

Chains shot from the shield, linking all the shields together. Then they spun around the room, entangling Trash #2 and the homunculi.

"Now!"

"Yes!"

Raphtalia drew her charged katana, activating the haikuikku state and using it for a skill.

"Double Lure Hook!"

Kizuna didn't let the opportunity slip by—she hit the enemy with Double Lure Hook, which would double the damage from the next attack.

"Nice work, Kiddo! Let's go, Therese!"

"Yes!"

Lightning struck his scythe again.

"Combo Skill! Electric Disc!"

L'Arc and Therese teamed up and used a combo skill to follow Kizuna's attack.

The disk shot over the battlefield, and Raphtalia dashed to follow it. Just before the disk collided with the enemy, she shouted a skill name.

"Instant Blade! Mist!"

It was Raphtalia's most powerful attack, the same one that had killed Trash #2 the first time.

L'Arc's electric flying disk crackled with energy—it was their strongest combo skill.

"Gahhh!"

Trash #2 and the homunculi were sliced to pieces and electrocuted at the same time.

Had they just been cut apart they might have been able to regenerate, but with the electricity, it should be enough to end it.

"That's not all! Ruby Flame!"

Rushing to finish the job, Therese summoned burning balls of magic flame from the accessory I made her and sent them careening into the monster corpses.

"Naofumi! Protect the others!"

"I know! Shooting Star Shield!"

Just as the barrier appeared to envelop us, Glass slapped open her fan and began to dance. She was holding Kizuna's hand—they were dancing together.

"Circle Dance Zero Formation: Reverse Snow Moon Flower!"

A breeze lifted cherry blossoms and blew them at the enemy. Therese's magic set them ablaze. They burned and sliced up the fallen enemies.

Snow Moon Flower was an area of effect attack, but she could keep it from hurting her allies by holding hands with them.

After all the attacks cleared, there was no trace of the enemies they'd hit.

"Not bad," Kyo muttered.

Kyo remained, along with his neo-guardians and Albert, the man with the mirror of the vassal weapons. Everyone else was gone.

Glass was facing Albert, ready to take him on. She could probably handle him on her own. Kizuna couldn't attack humans anyway, so she was stuck supporting Glass for now.

"Looks like we took care of your little experimental homunculi army, eh? What are you going to do now?"

"Experimental? Ha! I didn't make these things. I suppose I made some improvements to them, but you just killed the person who made them."

He must have stolen them from Trash #2.

"He was doing his own research, you know. The things that I make are far more impressive."

"I bet," I sighed. I didn't want meet any more inventions.

But isn't it strange that all three of them were researching homunculus? What was going on? There were too many coincidences.

"You must be proud of yourself for surviving my gravity attack, ha! You are so clueless—you'll see!"

"Kyo! Give it up! You're finished!" Yomogi shouted.

"Shut up! I'll kill you along with the others! My research is nearly complete—and you're all getting in the way!" Kyo snapped, stepping forward and raising his book.

How were we supposed to fight Kyo if he commanded all the Spirit Tortoise's energy?

We were weaker than the last time we fought Kyo, but on the other hand, Glass and L'Arc were stronger. We had a chance. We could do it.

"I'll make it quick and finish you all off at once. Behold my skills!"

Pages flew from his book and filled the room, fluttering and flapping around our heads before they turned into shining sheets of energy itself.

"You losers can't cast combo skills without the cooperation of your allies? Pathetic!"

This guy couldn't say anything without turning it into some kind of boast.

I was really getting tired of him.

Trash #2 had been the same way. These people were enough to drive me crazy.

"Behold!" Kyo shouted, pointing a finger at Kizuna. "Flame Formation: Magic Explosion!"

Kizuna quickly dropped to a defensive posture. A split second later, I realized why.

Flames appeared around Kizuna and . . . no—the flames were pouring out of her.

"Arrghh! My magic!?" Kizuna shouted. She was on her knees, staring at her hands. She looked like she was about to collapse. Glass ran over to support her, lifting her to her feet.

"It's shaving away my soul power, too?!"

"Ahahaha! This is my first time using it on a holy hero, but I'm impressed with how well it works!"

I was about to cast a healing spell on Kizuna when Kyo pointed his finger at me and howled, "Don't bother with that! Rot Formation: Magic Explosion!"

"Ugh . . . ah . . ."

Spiraling wind whipped up all around me, dark and thick with magic power. I could feel it draining my magic away.

But . . . But that was all it did.

"Damn. You're the type with no offensive magic to begin with. You're an irritating little bastard!"

"Yeah . . ." I moaned. I took a bottle of magic water out of my shield and drank it, then immediately cast Zweite Heal on Kizuna to heal her wounds.

I had given Kizuna a bottle of magic water before the

battle, and she drank it, realizing it would replenish what she'd lost to Kyo's attack.

"Ah, I see. Your skill steals the opponent's magic power, then uses it to produce a spell that hurts its owner," I announced. It was clever—and hard to counter. The stronger your magic power, the more the skill would hurt you.

It had a weakness though. It wouldn't work very well on people without offensive magic to begin with. That was why it didn't actually hurt me at all.

"What do you think? There's more where that came from! Let's see what it does to that foolish spirit who's been sipping soul-healing water!"

"Glass!"

Kizuna ran to protect Glass.

"Kizuna! Ahhhhh!"

Kizuna was caught right in the path of the attack. She was sliced all over her body. She took heavy damage. Worse than that was she hadn't been able to protect Glass from the full brunt of the attack, and Glass took damage too. The attack must have had an effect over an area.

Luckily, Glass didn't take so much damage that she was knocked out of the fight, but that attack of Kyo's was going to become a problem if we didn't figure out how to deal with it.

It appeared to have a very short cool down time. If he used it in quick succession on us, we'd end up taking a lot of damage.

It was close cousins with the defense rating attacks I'd dealt with before. Only that this was for magic.

"Think we'll just sit back and take this? Ha! Kiddo, let's do this!"

"Wait, L'Arc! He's already hit us with magic power and SP attacks! He could have . . ."

"Strength Form Explosion!"

Magic blades of light burst from L'Arc and spun around him, slashing at him ruthlessly. Knicks and cuts and gashes appeared all over his body. Blood spurt from his wounds.

"Gahhhhhh!"

"L . . .L'Arc!"

"I'm alright! Ain't nothing I can't handle—ARGH!" he shouted, swinging his scythe.

The tip swished by Kyo's face, missing him by a hair.

"Oh look at you! Not good enough!" Kyo jumped back and sent a stream of pages flying at L'Arc. They slammed into him and sent him soaring backwards, but Therese ran over and caught him before he fell to the ground.

"Whooeee—The Spirit Tortoise energy is great stuff. I can do anything with it! I can use your own strengths against you!"

All he had to do was point at us.

And based on how quickly he'd been using it, it must not have needed much from him.

The very strengths we needed to beat him powered his attack. He could use them against us!

Luckily, the attack didn't seem fatal—yet.

Its attack power must have been based on some kind of calculation that was different from simply taking the target's attack power as is.

The sort of person that would be most affected by an attack like this would have a special attack power that ignored defense all together. There was no one in our party like that.

I was probably the closest, actually.

The worst part was that Kyo's attack actually used whatever trait it was targeting. Not only would the target take damage, but it would also lose the ability of whatever trait had been targeted. It was a really bad combination for us.

If he hit me with it and took advantage of my defense rating, it would leave me unable to defend for a while.

"That's enough experimenting for now." he said. Pages from his book curled up and turned towards us.

He wasn't going to send out all those attacks at once, was he?

"Take this!"

I felt an impact jolt through my stomach, followed by a sharp pain that ran through my insides. I heard myself moan in pain. I could hardly stay on my feet. I quickly checked my stats.

It was as I feared. I'd taken heavy damage. But worse than that, I was left without any defense.

The Shooting Star Shield barrier had absorbed a lot of the

direct damage from the attack. Had it not been there, I might have been killed. But, considering my defense rating, the barrier shouldn't have been enough to keep me alive. The damage must have been calculated some other way, or I must have been blocking it with some other ability . . . like maybe something I'd gained through support magic, or one of my equipment's effects.

It wasn't an attack that any of us could use, so it was difficult to pin down exactly how it worked. My guess was that the skill was really intended as a debuff, and this attack ability was some kind of side effect.

"Ouch! Owwie!"

Filo and Raphtalia had taken heavy damage. Filo was rolling on the ground in pain.

I'd been able to protect Raph-chan, so she was okay.

There was only one person who managed to stay on her feet. Someone whose stats were so low to begin with that Kyo's attack hadn't managed to do anything to them.

The better your stats were the more damage the attack did. But, it wasn't able to deal any fatal damage, and that was its weakness. But it had another weakness—it was no good against people with low stats, against someone whose true power wasn't reflected in the numbers.

"Ri . . . shia . . ."

Rishia didn't look like she'd been hurt at all.

Judging from that, the attack must have only worked on base stats, which are raised or lowered to hurt the target.

It didn't work on support effects, or on other, more specialized types of power.

At first glance, it looked like it was invincible, but it had weaknesses—and now we knew them.

As for the weapons, I hadn't figured out what it did to them. It was a bit different from the defense rating and defense ignoring attacks that Glass ad L'Arc used. Glass's stats went up when her energy increased, which is why Kyo's attack might have been able to kill her. Kizuna had been there to take the brunt of the attack.

Rishia stepped out ahead of Raphtalia, Filo, and I, and glared at Kyo. She was going to protect us.

"You! How can you still be on your feet?"

"Because your attacks are worthless against me."

"I guess that means you're the weakest of the bunch! Ha!" Kyo burst out laughing while Albert raised his mirror, preparing to finish her with a final attack.

And the only person that was left to stand against them was . . . Rishia?

"Does it feel that good? Paralyzing your enemies so you can laugh at them? Does that make you feel powerful?" Rishia barked, glaring at Kyo. She drew her sword and leveled it at him. She moved so easily it was like she was completely unaffected by the gravitational field.

"Exploiting the enemy's weakness and making the kill, it's sort of the first rule of battle. Don't you know that much?"

"That is not a battle. That is called trampling on the weak."

"God, you're insufferable! Die already!"

Pages shot from his book and folded themselves into the shape of a flaming bird.

"Do not think you can take our lives so easily."

Moving like a ninja, Rishia dashed left and right, slashing through the flying birds of flame with her short sword. The birds fell to pieces and fluttered to the ground.

"What the hell? You're really getting on my nerves!"

Yes! It was like this was the very moment that Rishia had been waiting for—the role she'd been born to play. She'd been relegated to assisting the rest of us for so long, but now she was the best fighter in the party.

"You're so annoying! I can't stand it! Barking on about justice, you're just as bad as Yomogi!" Kyo shouted like a spoiled child.

Ha! What a brat!

I climbed to my feet and cast a healing spell.

"I'm not mature yet. I can't do all that I should, and I always need help. But . . . but I . . ."

She griped the hilt of her short sword and held it out in front of her. She was moving exactly how Eclair did when she used her skills.

She hadn't studied and she hadn't trained extensively. She was just trying to copy what she'd seen.

"If there's such a thing as destiny, then I believe it is mine to put a stop to your ambitions!" she yelled, rushing forward, the top of her blade glinting in the light.

I cast a support skill just in time to help her.

Then I saw that Kizuna had the same idea, and her skill landed at the same time as mine.

"Attack Support!"

"Double Lure Hook!"

The skills flew at Kyo, they would connect just before her blade hit him. I hoped that my skill hit before the Double Lure Hook skill. If it didn't, Rishia's attack would only be strong enough to annoy him.

"Ugh!"

Kyo quickly grabbed Albert and shoved him between himself and Rishia's blade.

My skill hit him, followed by Kizuna's Double Lure Hook. Finally Rishia's thrust followed, and her blade slammed into Albert's mirror.

I felt the force of the impact from across the room.

The vassal weapons, like the holy weapons, were impossible to destroy. If he used the mirror like a shield, he'd probably be able to fend off her attack. But if her attack was strong enough, it would pierce right through the mirror itself and impale Albert.

Glass had done that once to me, when she used Moon Break after drinking soul-healing water.

"Ugh . . . ga . . . gagagaga . . ."

Her blade stabbed through his mirror and slipped deep into his chest.

"Ah . . ."

Rishia was stunned at the sight of blood, and stepped back a few feet, speechless.

Blood sprayed from Albert's chest, splattering both Rishia and Kyo.

Albert's eyes rolled back in his head, and he collapsed.

A glowing ball of light rose from his corpse and then slowly circled the room. Then it looked as though something split off from it before the ball of light floated through the wall and left the building.

Was that . . . was that the mirror vassal weapon?

It was like it checked to make sure that the person who held it was really dead before it left for good.

"Unbelievable! I'm supposed to believe that this weak little girl just killed a holder of a vassal weapon?!" Kyo snapped, glaring at Rishia. He shot a glance over at Kizuna and me.

I wonder if the Support Attack skill I used was . . .

"It looks like you can use a skill just like Double Lure Hook, Naofumi," Kizuna said.

"I guess so. And if we can use both of those skills, then we can do some serious damage."

That's right. If it worked the way it seemed, then we could use two multiplying skills at the same time, essentially quadrupling the amount of damage we could do. Pretty damn impressive.

When Rishia was in this awakened state, her attacks were pretty strong to begin with.

"Rishia, I know there are still these neo-guardians around, but focus your attacks on Kyo."

Kizuna and I waited for the cool down time on our multiplying skills to run out, then prepared to use them again.

Kyo was speechless, like he truly couldn't believe what he'd just seen. He glared at us with bloodshot eyes. He looked furious.

Oh man, I'd been waiting so long to see that look on his face! Ha!

"This isn't over! Not yet! You'll see what I have up my sleeve!"

Again, pages flew from his book and filled the room. The mandala appeared on the floor around him again, and the gravity in the room began to grow stronger and stronger.

But Kyo was breathing heavily, and it showed. He was trying really hard. Things weren't so easy for him anymore.

I became aware of energy flowing around the room. He was gathering more and more Spirit Tortoise energy around himself.

But a lot of the energy flowed into my shield. An icon appeared in my field of view.

"Sorry to say it, but I don't think that's going to work," I shouted at Kyo.

I held my hand against my shield and imagined the shield I wanted to switch to.

I hadn't met the conditions to unlock it, but I had to believe that it had been waiting for this exact time to reappear.

Kyo was glaring at me—staring at the shield in my hands.

He's seen it before. That's right—it was the very same shield I'd used to defeat him in the last world!

The Spirit Tortoise Heart Shield.

It was the shield I'd received from the same being he tortured and controlled, the being whose energy he stole—The Spirit Tortoise. Ost.

Let's see if he recognizes it—the real difference in our power!

**Spirit Tortoise Heart Shield (awakened) 80/80 AT**
**abilities unlocked: equip bonus: dragon vein protection**
**equip effect: gravity field, C soul recovery, C magic snatch, C gravity shot, life force up, magic defense (large), lighting resistance, SP drain nullification, magic support, spell support.**
**special effect: 20%; mastery level 100**

Any trace of exhaustion I'd had disappeared in an instant.

"Looks like changing weapons will take care of Kyo's status nullification attack."

"Ahhh. That's really good to hear," Kizuna nodded, pleased with my new discovery. She switched to a new weapon.

If we kept on top of the healing magic, we'd be able to avoid losing the battle due to that.

But there was a bigger problem.

It didn't look like I could use Energy Blast. Twenty percent was not a very big number.

I wasn't sure what I needed to do to raise that number, but it seemed pretty clear that I couldn't use the attack if it was only twenty percent charged.

But there was yet another, bigger problem.

I was concerned about the gravity field listed under its equip effects.

When I focused, I could see a gravity icon in my field of view. It indicated that the current gravity level was very high. I thought hard about lowering the level, and suddenly, all the people that had lost the ability to move climbed to their feet.

"I feel so light!"

"What's going on? Did you do this, Kiddo?"

"Yeah. Looks like I can control gravity with this shield."

"Wow! That's pretty convenient!"

It was. That would take care of one of Kyo's most irritating attacks—the one he'd clearly stolen from the Spirit Tortoise.

"See? What do you think? You better keep on generating that gravity field if you want to keep us down."

"You fool! Don't condescend to me!" Kyo screamed, his eyes burning with rage. "How long do I have to entertain you weaklings?!"

"Oh, calm down. You're like a little kid that screams when they don't get their way."

He was happy as a clam when everything went according to plan—when he had control over everyone. Otherwise, he threw a temper tantrum. How old was this guy?

Kyo tried to use his ability stat-based skill again. But I found that it was relatively easy to dodge. A quickly deployed Air Strike Shield was all it took to block it.

I'd found a way to deal with both of his worst attacks, so unless he came up with something more impressive, it looked like victory was becoming more and more likely.

I didn't want to overplay my hand here, but I felt like it was time for a taunt or two. "Alright then, do you want to hear about all the ways I'm going to make you pay for your misdeeds?"

I used Attack Support to summon the little dart into my hand, and turned to face Kyo.

"Kizuna and I will hit you with these attack multipliers. Once we confirm that they've both hit you, the rest is easy. It doesn't matter who actually delivers the attack—whoever hits you next and . . . boom! That's it. Maybe it will be Glass or L'Arc. That would be ideal. They could use a stat-based attack just like you!"

For example, we could deal enough damage that he'd need to use a lot of magic to heal it, but then, we could make it so that the magic itself would kill him.

"It's really kind of elegant, the way it punishes you for accumulating all this power."

"You . . . you bastard!"

"Kyo! If you surrender . . ."

It was Yomogi. What was she going on about now? I didn't want him to surrender!

Did she think I'd let him live if he did? If that's what she thought, I'd have Kizuna remove her from the battle all together.

"I'll make your death easy."

I nearly fell over. I liked where she went with it, but she really was like a wild boar.

Comparing her with Glass and Tsugumi, she really stood out—she was different from the rest.

Kyo went on trying to hit Rishia with his special ability and stat-based attack, but it wasn't going well.

Pages from his book flew at her, but she was slicing them all out of the air before they could connect with her, even when they approached from behind.

It was like she'd gained abilities specifically for destroying Kyo.

Her abilities and his weaknesses fit together so perfectly that it was hard to not see an element of fate in it.

"You think you're so special! You're nothing but a pissant!"

"Then you're getting your ass kicked by a pissant!" I shouted.

Kyo stamped his feet in in anger, "Silence! I'll kill you! How dare you talk back to me like that!"

This whole time I'd thought that he had grown extremely powerful because of the Spirit Tortoise's energy, but maybe the strength he'd had last time was a temporary thing. Still, I couldn't help but feel like he was still holding back.

"I'm not finished with you yet!" he shrieked, grabbing a strange, creepy looking object from where it hung at his waist. It looked like a bookmark. The moment his fingers touched it, he smiled.

"You're so proud of yourself because you found a little accessory that made you stronger. That's not real strength! I'll show you what real power is!"

He stuck the bookmark into the book of the vassal weapons. The second it slipped between the pages, I felt a great weight fall over the battlefield.

Damn it. I should be able to control the gravity field with the Spirit Tortoise Heart Shield, but . . .

"Not so fast!" Kyo barked, and hundreds of book pages plastered themselves all over the surface of my shield.

That's all that happened, but immediately a floating "X" appeared over the gravity field adjustment icon. He locked it!?

Worse yet, I could feel the pages draining energy out of the shield.

Damn it! At this rate I was going to be forced to switch to another shield.

"Eat this!"

"Feh! Not so fast!" Rishia shouted. Her movement was clearly slowed by the increased gravity field. Kyo dodged her attacks and the followed up with a barrage of fluttering book pages that sent her flying.

"Dammit! This creep has so many tricks up his sleeve!"

He seemed to have an endless variety of ways to defend himself.

"Ahaha! Weren't you going to hit me with your little multiplier skill? I'm over here!" Kyo laughed.

I wanted to throw the attack support dart at him, but I couldn't even raise my arm.

"Well, you heroes with your holy weapons, and you creeps with your vassal weapons, have been a bit more trouble than I expected. Time to take care of that!" Kyo laughed, pulling another bookmark from his pocket and thrusting it into his book. "I thought something like this might happen, so it's a good thing I went ahead and messed with your dragon hourglass in advance."

"What are you talking about?!"

He had already done something to the dragon hourglass? How could that be?

"I wasn't able to destroy the dragon vein defense barrier, but the effect works outside of this building. How did you think I was able to see what was going on over there?"

He was watching through the dragon hourglass? How many secret technologies did he have?!

"Unfortunately when I use it, you'll all get a bit of a power boost too. But if I don't use it, I can't steal your power—so I guess I have no choice!"

What was he blathering on about? What was going on?

A liquid-filled tank rose up from the floor behind Kyo.

What was it? What was he doing?

His lips moved quickly, he was whispering some kind of incantation to himself.

What was happening? I had a really bad feeling about this.

The incantation itself was very short. He reached out and brushed the tank with his fingertips, and in response the liquid in the tank swirled and vanished, as if he were absorbing it.

Was it magic water? Or could it be . . . soul-healing water?

It looked like the skill was pretty expensive.

"Different world, different reason. Shatter the barrier walls,

and summon the great phenomenon!"

"Waves of Destruction! Dimension Wave!"

Crash!

Immediately after Kyo finished the incantation a terrible sound rang out.

"Wh . . . A skill that causes dimension waves?! What?!"

"How could . . ."

"It can't be! What are you thinking?!"

"Kyo! You're the one behind the . . ."

Before she could finish shouting in surprise, Kizuna and the others vanished from the room.

## Chapter Eleven: Sacrifice Aura

Raphtalia, Filo, Rishia, Raph-chan, and I were the only ones left.

Yomogi had been registered to Kizuna's party, so had been summoned to the wave along with Kizuna.

Dammit! He'd planned to split us up the whole time!

A thudding sound echoed in the recesses of my mind—which made me think that this wave was occurring back in the previous world.

"I hope you're pleased—I used this book to keep your shield from sucking you off to the wave. Hm? The holder of the katana of vassal weapons has nothing to say? I guess it is tied to an idiot from another world, after all."

So he could even stop the automatic teleport that had tied me to the waves since I found myself in Melromarc.

At least I still had my party members: Filo, Raphtalia, Rishia, and Raph-chan. That was better than nothing.

Kizuna and the others must have found themselves facing down the wave right about now.

"Ahaha! Now I have the stupid Shield Hero to play with! This should be fun!" Kyo giggled. He was acting like everything was going his way, but the gravity field in the room had grown noticeably weaker.

Stats slowly filled my field of view.

Lv 76 + 75?

L'Arc had said something once about gaining the total levels from both worlds.

Was that the reason I was able to stay on my feet in Kyo's gravity field?

Unfortunately, the effect seemed to work on Kyo as well. And he had those stat-based attacks. They had the weakness of not being able to deal a killing blow, but they were still a serious threat.

And we didn't have Kizuna around to help.

We had no choice but to continue the battle under these new conditions, but I didn't like the look of things.

At least I could use all the shields I'd gained in both of the worlds.

But, I still had the Spirit Tortoise Heart Shield equipped, with pages from Kyo's book plastered all over it, so I wasn't able to switch it out for anything else.

Judging from what he'd said, I think I was the target of his new plan. Maybe he had set this up so that he could block any of my skills that made use of the Spirit Tortoise's energy. Then, when I lost, he'd have one hundred percent of the Spirit Tortoise's energy at his disposal.

He'd artificially summoned a wave so that he could get his hands on the remaining Spirit Tortoise energy.

What was I supposed to do? How could I fight in circumstances like these?

I couldn't use Portal Shield either—the copies of the four holy beasts roaming the grounds made that skill inaccessible.

We'd have to find some way to defeat him on our own.

"Ahahaha! Look how well it suits me!"

The room was brimming with Spirit Tortoise energy. It spiraled around and into Kyo.

"Ha! Take this!"

Spirit Tortoise familiars (neo-guardian type) rose to their feet and came after us. They were holding weapons that looked just like the holy weapons held by the other three heroes back in the previous world.

This fight was starting to look a lot like the last one, when we'd met in the Spirit Tortoise's core chamber.

. . . Except that there were less people on my side now.

"Raphtalia, are you ready?"

"Yes."

"I'm ready too, master!"

I hadn't addressed her, but Filo was in human form now, on her feet, and ready for battle.

She was dressed in pajamas, but I could see the Karma Dog Claws sticking out from the feet. I guess that was the hidden weapon effect.

At least I wasn't alone. Time to see what we could do.

The pages stuck all over my shield were draining me of energy somehow. It felt awful. I couldn't keep using the Spirit Tortoise Heart Shield for much longer.

"Uh-oh! Have you started to figure it out? That's right, I'll take whatever energy you've got in that obnoxious shield of yours! To get the very last drop of it, I'll have to kill you first! It's a protective thing, you know, that's why I needed the wave to break through."

So this had all been part of Kyo's plan. To get at the energy I still had stored in my shield. To get at it he had to summon a wave. If the four holy heroes existed to protect the world from the waves, then he must have found a way to break the rules by intentionally summoning a wave. The heroes were part of the protection, just like the beasts. He'd found a way around it, and now his plan was in motion.

With the wave occurring in the other world, the energy in my shield might be summoned back to the site of the wave, and that was his chance to take it.

That was some plan. How did he even think of it?

The strongest powered-up shield I had at the moment was the Demon Dragon Shield. The world I was in wouldn't affect that.

But I had to fight with what I had.

"If you think we're less capable of battle then you are, you'll come to regret it!" Raphtalia shouted, switching her katana to the White Tiger Katana.

Exactly. Now we could use weapons that our levels and stats had prevented us from using before.

I didn't know what kind of effect to expect from it, but the White Tiger Katana was made from better material than the Demon Dragon Shield, so it was probably a force to be reckoned with. Raphtalia could barely raise it before, but things were different now!

"Here I gooooo!" Filo shouted. She started to gather magic power about her, humming and singing the whole time.

Now that we were connected back to our old world, Filo should be able to use more of her filolial powers. That meant she now had access to an ideal combination of attacks and support abilities.

We'd lost Kizuna and the others, and Kyo was blocking my use of the Spirit Tortoise energy, but we weren't going to lose that easily.

"Heh. You idiots! Aren't you forgetting something?" Kyo shouted, pointing at us.

He was probably going to use his stat-based attack to try and deal some serious damage.

He's been powered up just like the rest of us, so it was easy to imagine him having some more deadly tricks up his sleeve.

Once he lowered my defenses, he'd hit me with a special attack I wouldn't be able to block . . . . or so I thought. He glanced over at Rishia.

"I guess I'll deal with the stupid Shield Hero later. I'll take care of this justice-obsessed wench first!" he said jabbing his finger at Rishia.

But before he could do anything, before he could mutter an incantation, Rishia flew across the room as if she was using haikuikku. She somersaulted and took down a neo-guardian with one hit.

"?!"

"Why are you so surprised? You seem to think me a fool, and pester me with your little taunts! Now you'll see how wrong you are!"

Did she know what had happened?

I quickly checked her stats and could hardly believe my eyes.

I expected to find them higher than before, maybe up closer to mine.

I expected to find her abilities improved a bit, but all her stats had risen dramatically—surpassing even Filo's! They were higher than Filo's, even when accounting for the growth adjustments from my shield!

If this was what an awakened Rishia looked like, she was a force to be reckoned with!

"What was that? These neo-guardians have the power of both worlds! How did you defeat him so easily?! You fool!"

"Who's the fool here?"

Rishia was so powerful now she could probably defeat a hero.

They say that great talents take great time.

Maybe Rishia was the type that grew unbelievably powerful after crossing a certain line. I mean, of course, that's what I'd expected this whole time. That's why I'd spent so much time and energy on her.

Once she hit that line, she was something new, something completely unlike what she'd been.

The world I'd been summoned to had a cap at level 100. Apparently, there were similar limitations in place in Kizuna's world. If Rishia's power boost came after level 100, then her talents would remain forever inaccessible.

The old hengen muso lady said she had talent, and this must be what she meant. Glass had said the same thing when she saw Rishia in the last battle with Kyo.

But what would Rishia be like when she was fully boosted—when she could use all of her latent talents?

Kyo's attacks were at least as powerful as they had ever been, but now she was more than powerful, more that fast enough, to avoid them.

"ARRGHGH! You're so annoying! Annoying! Annoying!!!" Kyo wailed, pulling at his hair.

When he summoned the wave, we'd lost half of our allies, but it was starting to look like we were actually better off as things were now. That's not to say that victory was guaranteed, but his trick with the wave might have been a miscalculation.

"You're starting to really bother me!"

"You're the one that did this, so what are you whining about? Now we just need to finish you off."

"Yes," Raphtalia said, sliding the sword into its sheath and storing its power.

I didn't know how the sword would react to Raphtalia's new level, but the gemstone I'd set in the sheath was charging up for a haikuikku very quickly.

"Me toooo!" Filo shouted. She was all charged and ready.

Raph-chan sat on my shoulder, chirping for battle.

"That's enough. I was going to play with you bit, but I've had enough. There's no point in playing games with the likes of you," Kyo sighed, running his fingers through his hair. "Yeah, yeah, you're all leveled up and all—great. But you keep forgetting this one thing, so I guess I'll have to tell you myself."

"Yeah? What's that?"

"The holy weapons and the vassal weapons in this world can be powered up in the same ways. You spent all that time with what's-her-face, so you should know that."

". . . True."

I had already figured out what he was getting at, and I'll be honest, I was worried. I felt cold sweat prickle my forehead.

Kizuna and the others had figured out various ways to

power up their vassal and holy weapons, so of course they'd shared all that information. It was an obvious thing to do. I'd even had a meeting with the other three heroes back in my old world to share what we knew about powering up.

But until Raphtalia was chosen to wield the katana, the others had been more powerful than she was.

"To tell you the truth, I've been pretty cautious about those stat-based attacks, so of course, I have ways to deal with them. But what about you?!"

For a long time, I'd thought that only L'Arc and the others would come at me with a defense rating attack, so I hadn't been on my toes. The White Tiger Shield had a parry attack that would mitigate some of the risk. Switching to it would be a good idea.

But I didn't want to lose my support effects. There must have been a reason he hadn't used those attacks against Raphtalia and the others too.

"So here's the real issue. I pay careful attention to information, you know? So, did you think I didn't know the power-up methods you and your vassal weapon friends have used? Who do you think defeated Albert, the mirror vassal weapon holder, right from the start?" he said, flipping open his book and showing me a page from it.

"I only learned about the Hunting Hero's methods relatively recently. I'll have to add it to the list."

I knew what he was trying to say.

Kyo knew the power-up methods used by Kizuna, Glass, L'Arc, Ethnobalt, and Raphtalia. He knew how they'd improved their weapons. He had a vassal weapon himself, and he knew how Albert's had worked too.

Glass had said that power-ups worked best on holy weapons.

The vassal weapons didn't respond quite as well, but still, if he had combined knowledge of the holy weapons and the six vassal weapons' power-up methods, I couldn't even guess how much power he would wield.

But then how had we managed to corner him like this?

The only thing I could think of was, and it was just a guess, but based on the how Glass and the others had reacted . . .

"Quit bluffing. The vassal weapons despise you. You think you can command their power?" I shouted, jabbing my finger at him.

He gritted his teeth and said, "Think what you want! Come try me!"

I was right—I knew it. The book of the vassal weapons despised the man that held it.

I didn't know how he managed to maintain control of it given the circumstances, but it didn't look like he had perfect control over all of its power. Now he was trying to make us think that he'd been holding back this whole time. So how was he supposed to suddenly get stronger? He'd have to find some way to boost his powers with some kind of external input. And if that was his plan, he'd try to fill himself with the Spirit Tortoise energy.

"Rishia,"

"Yes! What is it?!"

She was still a bit nervous, but she was filled with a burning need for justice and ready to fight.

"Can you pull off the attack that the old lady taught you?"

The old lady could use defense-rating attacks without breaking a sweat. I had a feeling it would do wonders.

"I'll do my best!"

"Raphtalia, how are you doing?"

"Ready to use a skill!"

"What about meee?" Filo chirped.

"Get ready to attack. You're more than strong enough."

"Okaaaay!" Filo shouted. She went on humming a song that raised all of our abilities. Now that she was both a filolial and a humming fairy, she was serving mostly as battle support.

We had plenty of surprises up our sleeves, too.

I couldn't use the Spirit Tortoise Heart Shield at the moment, and our movement was impeded a bit with the gravity field that Kyo was using. But, we'd received a big level boost, so we could at least move a bit. Now we had to find a way to defeat Kyo, who was high on Spirit Tortoise energy and knew about every power-up method we'd ever used.

We were out of time.

"Die!"

"Air Strike Shield!"

Kyo lashed out with a stat-based attack, but I blocked it with Air Strike Shield. The shield shattered under the weight of the attack, but it stopped it. At least the shields were strong enough to stop an attack.

"Damn! A decent block. You impudent fool!"

"Here I go!"

"Yes!"

Raphtalia drew both her swords at once.

The haikuikku move that activated was twice as powerful as usual, and she dashed around the room at a blinding speed. Pages from Kyo's book flapped about the room to block her attacks, but Raphtalia slipped between them easily and dashed forward for her own attack.

"Attack Support!"

I knew that I wasn't going to make it in time, but I threw the dart as fast as I could anyway. Rishia dashed off after it, tearing through any pages that got in her way with rating-based attacks.

"Haikuikku!"

Filo shot off behind Rishia.

"Pathetic! Weak!" Kyo thrust his hands out before him, and the pages of his book flapped furiously.

What was he doing?!

"You've already fallen into my trap! Libraria!" he shouted and the room turned black and white, and the sound of a book slamming shut echoed in my ears. "Ahahaha! See how you like this space compression restraint skill!"

Kyo vanished from before our eyes.

But something was strange about it.

We had been in his underground laboratory this whole time, but now we appeared to be in a white room.

Kyo's skill had produced attacks that swirled all around us. Birds made of flame and lightning, tornadoes, massive boulders, and a huge particle beam like the Spirit Tortoise had used.

"Ahaha! Take that! Can you block them all at once? Any one of them will kill you! Better dodge what you can!"

Damn it. His skill trapped us in a confined space and bombarded us with attacks. What were we supposed to do?

"Shooting Star Shield!"

The barrier stopped some of the attacks, then shattered, but its jagged pieces remained floating in the air.

The target, I guess, was the whole room.

While waiting for the barrier fragments to shoot off, I blocked attacks with my shield, dodging whenever I could.

It was very difficult to do in such a confined space, but it wasn't anything I couldn't handle.

I took the bioplant out of my shield and forced it to germinate.

It grew unbelievably quickly, and soon it would break the space itself.

"Like I'd let that happen?!" Kyo sent a skill hurdling at the bioplant, destroying it instantly. "You know I wondered how you managed to get out of the labyrinth. Now I know. Thanks."

Damn it. If I didn't find a way out we'd be pummeled to death by Kyo's attacks.

"Hya!"

"Ho!"

"Rafuuu!"

Rishia, Filo, and Raph-chan all tried attacking the walls, but they were only able to make small cracks, which repaired themselves instantly.

Skills and attacks rained down on us the whole time.

I continued to use the sequence of Air Strike Shield, Second Shield, Dritte Shield, Shield Prison, and Shooting Star Shield. It was working, but I couldn't keep it up forever.

There must be a limit on how much the space itself can endure. If we could just break through it, we could escape.

The problem was that Kyo continued to reform the walls and send a barrage of attacks at us the whole time. It seemed to me the book pages were producing the attacks, and the walls of the room must have been equivalent to Kyo's field of view.

"Raph-chan! Cover that wall with a curtain of smoke!"

"Rafuuu!"

She knew what I meant, and she used her illusion magic to cover the room in smoke. Then she also snuck a hallucination into the center of the wall of smoke.

"You think you can hide? Think again!"

A howling wind blew through the room and took all of the smoke away with it, but the hallucination she snuck into the smoke remained, and for a moment, all the skills rained down on the wrong place.

"Damn! But I'm not done yet," pretending to be hurt, I signaled to Raphtalia and Rishia with my hand.

I clapped a hand over Filo's mouth to keep her quiet.

I pointed to my shield, and then I wrote "wrath" in the air with my finger.

Raphtalia's eyes grew wide. Rishia was so surprised she audibly gasped.

I was going to burn this whole place down with Dark Curse Burning S, the strongest attack I had, one that left a curse behind to make recovery difficult.

I had to try it.

Raphtalia was shaking her head—she knew how dangerous it was. But I had survived it a few times before.

If I encased everyone in Shield Prison, I was hoping we could all survive. Just to account for the worst possible outcome,

I could probably have a protection skill cast on Raphtalia too.

Realizing that I had made up my mind, Raphtalia gave up and signaled to Filo, Rishia, and Raph-chan to follow her and get as much distance as possible from me.

What was the big deal? I'd done this plenty of times. Just like every other time, I just needed to survive my own attack.

". . ."

How many times had I let myself use this attack?

It was a cursed shield that I was forced to rely on in my lowest moments—and I was about to rely on its power again.

I wrapped my fingers tightly around the shield grip, closed my eyes, steadied my breathing and changed shields.

Due to the increased amount of dragon core stone, the shield had become more powerful!

**Shield of Wrath IV (awakened) +7 50/70 SR**
**abilities locked: equip bonus: skill Change Shield (attack),**
**Iron Maiden, Blood Sacrifice, Megiddo Burst,**
**special effect: Dark Curse Burning S, Strength Up, Dragon Rage, Roar, Vassal Berserk, Magic Power Share, Robe of Rage (large), Demon Dragon magic power.**
**Mastery level 0**

I'd had a vague feeling of dread about using this shield, but

I hadn't expected it to become so powerful!

The appearance of the shield had changed too, growing somehow even more ominous and brutal. It was so large that it was nearly impossible to support with one arm. I think shields like this were called tower shields.

My heart was filled with powerful rage and hate, far more furious than before. And yet my relationships with my friends, my trust in them, my desire to protect them from harm . . . those emotions had grown stronger too. They were strong enough to keep me from losing control over myself.

I didn't know what the last two special effects were about, but I was sure they referenced some type of power I'd yet to see—something that might also be more dangerous than anything I'd yet to see.

As for Megiddo Burst, I didn't even want to try it out. I wasn't sure I'd survive a single use.

"Ugh . . ." Filo moaned. Her arms and legs were engulfed in roaring black flames. She was doing all she could to keep control over herself.

But the hatred swirling inside of me was too strong. It was so strong I was going to lose consciousness!

"Rafuuu!"

Raph-chan jumped up on Filo's head and started nibbling at her cowlick. Just then, black flames burst from her puffy tail.

"Me too!" Raphtalia placed her hands on Raph-chan and

Filo, and closed her eyes in concentration.

I felt the weight of the hatred and rage lessen just a little. They were accepting some of my burden. Just when I'd thought the flames would consume me, they doused water on my heart.

It felt amazing. Like crystal clear water seeping into a parched throat.

Yes, I could go on.

"Let's go! Shield Prison!"

A cage of shields appeared in the air around Raphtalia and the others, protecting them from Kyo's rain of skills.

The shield suddenly weighed on me heavily, like it had doubled in size. A warped, twisted light emanated from its surface.

"Arrrhhhhhh!"

"What?!"

Cursed flames roared and leapt from the shield, burning everything in sight and instantly destroying the space that Kyo had trapped us in. There was a burst and a hiss and we found ourselves back in the underground laboratory.

I turned and was happy to see that the Shield Prison had survived unscathed.

"You broke through my skill. I'm impressed."

"Of course you are. We tricked you."

We had time to pull off the attack because he'd been tricked into attacking the hallucination that Raph-chan made.

"You haven't come close to seeing the attacks I'm capable of!"

Should I use Blood Sacrifice on him?

No. If I failed in the casting, it would all be for nothing.

It wasn't time for that. No, not yet.

Kyo unleashed another attack and the Shield Prison shattered. Raphtalia and the others leapt free and brandished their weapons at Kyo, dashing forward to attack.

"Brave Blade! Mist!"

Using both of her swords she traced a cross in the air and it shot across the room, tearing through the swirling book pages that Kyo sent to stop it.

"Ha!"

Rishia was furiously unleashing the defense-rating attacks that she'd learned from the old lady.

"Ha!" Filo barked, darting across the room with a spiral kick.

"That old attack? Again?! You never learn, do you? Constriction: Composition Four!"

Kyo's book snapped open and a cage emerged from its pages that enclosed Raphtalia and the others.

He could use his skills so quickly!

"Continuation! False Ceiling!"

Needles grew from the ceiling of their cage and rained down on everyone inside.

"Not so fast! Air Strike Shield! Second Shield! Dritte Shield!"

Three shields materialized in the air over their heads to protect them from the rain of needles.

"Haaa!" Raphtalia shouted, quickly drawing her sword and slicing through the cage that enclosed her. She leapt free again and ran for Kyo.

That's right. We were stronger than we had been.

We can defeat Kyo. Even without Kizuna!

"You think that will work? You telegraph your moves so far in advance!"

Kyo had boosted his abilities too, and Raphtalia wasn't quite fast enough to hit him before he could evade her attack.

We just weren't fast enough. The words "attacks don't matter if they don't connect" kept running through my mind.

If my friends could charge up their speed attacks, we could probably catch up to him. But, if they did that, while they charged, he'd have time to encase us in that confined space again.

Of course, if he did, I might be able to get us out by using the cursed flames again, but that wasn't the sort of plan that would work forever. Just to make things even more annoying, we'd occasionally have to fend off a rogue holy beast copy. And, the neo-guardians that we defeated were regenerating and getting back on their feet.

"Take this! Composition Eight: Divine Punishment!"

The pages of his book flapped wildly when he called the skill's name. Then lightning erupted from them and fired straight at us.

It chased us when we tried to evade it! It was homing lightning! It looked like an attack that could be pulled off with magic, which made me think, was there some other aspect to it we hadn't seen yet?

"Air Strike Shield!"

"Hah!"

The lightning quickly changed course and avoided the shield that materialized in front of it.

Damn it! What was I supposed to do about an attack I couldn't block?

"Shooting Star Shield!"

Raphtalia and the others were doing all they could to avoid the lightning attack. So I quickly deployed Shooting Star Shield to protect them and stop the crackling bolts. Because Wrath Shield IV was so powerful, the barrier was able to stop the attack without shattering.

It didn't shatter, but it crackled, and started to glow with heat.

What . . . What was going on?

The barrier itself suddenly shot out glowing orbs of dark flame. They slammed into the fluttering pages from Kyo's book, burning them to ash instantaneously.

I was very happy to see Kyo's attacks fail one by one.

The orbs were bouncing around, burning everything they touched. The bodies of the fallen holy beast copies, the homunculi, the bodies of Trash #2 and Albert, were all reduced to piles of ash.

"You're so obnoxious! I've had enough! Take this!"

He flipped through his book and something appeared in the air before us. Something that looked just like the head of the Spirit Tortoise.

"Too bad it takes so much time! But you better be grateful! Not many people get to see this attack!"

He was playing it up—it must have been a special finishing move.

Could I block it and survive? I honestly didn't know.

"I don't think so!" Raphtalia shouted.

She dashed at Kyo with Filo and Raph-chan at her side, but he quickly deployed layers upon layers of barriers to protect himself.

Rishia and Raphtalia's defense-rating attacks shattered the barriers very quickly, but it wasn't enough to break all the way through.

And that gravity field was still slowing us down. How did we solve this problem the last time, when Ost was with us?

Could I do it? Could I pull it off?

There was no reason for me to stand there like a stick in the mud. I had time to try. I had to use it.

Sure, I was alone. And sure, I didn't really know how to use it, but I forcefully called out the Way of the Dragon Vein incantation.

I concentrated as well as I could, and tried to recall what it had felt like.

Therese had shown me how to guide my power, so I tried to do that the best I could. The shield was the medium and the power was mine. I called for the energy of the Spirit Tortoise, in the air all about us, to help me.

. . . But it wasn't working.

I felt the shield respond, ever so slightly. I could feel the Spirit Tortoise energy in the room gathering in it.

Maybe there wasn't enough power, but I had to try. I called to mind the incantation for All Liberation Aura.

Before I spoke the words, I felt a strong jolt surge up my spine—something I had never felt before. It was like the voice I sometimes heard when using the Shield of Wrath, only different. I couldn't tell what it was. But I knew there was something deep inside of me—something terrifying.

—You are trying to cast the ancient magic, are you not?

—Your death here would greatly inconvenience me. I suppose I must assist you.

The voice wrapped around my heart, suffocating and powerful. I couldn't resist it. Then suddenly the same puzzle that Ost had shown me appeared before my eyes, and began to assemble itself.

—That should be sufficient.

—But the use of my power comes with a heavy price. Be prepared to pay it.

—Do you understand that which you ask?

I had no idea who was speaking to me, but I could hear the voice clearly.

I didn't know what the price was and I didn't know what fate awaited me, but I knew what I came here to do and I wasn't backing down. Kyo had to pay for his crimes!

I didn't hesitate. I was ready to activate the spell.

But before I starting chanting, icons appeared in order to select the target.

What? That normally didn't happen until after the spell was cast.

There were three icons, so I could only select three targets.

It was set to cast on myself.

I was going to use All Liberation Aura.

Who would benefit the most from increased stats and abilities?

I could count on Raphtalia, but Rishia also needed an ability boost.

I quickly set the spell to focus on Rishia. Suddenly, my field of view toggled red.

I was getting a bad feeling about this. A feeling that I shouldn't use the spell after all.

What if I wasn't the one to pay the price? What if we all had to pay?

—Tsk, Tsk. Do you think victory comes to cowards?

—The Hunting Hero knew the risks and came anyway.

Damn it! Even if that were true, I couldn't ask Raphtalia and the others to suffer.

"Master! I'll do it! I'll make up for the turtle lady! I'll help you and big sis and everyone!"

Filo?

Could she hear what I was hearing? How did she know what was happening?

I guess it wasn't that surprising. She'd always been influenced by the Shield of Wrath.

She was right. If I held back, then we might lose a fight we could have won.

I changed the spell to focus on Filo instead of Rishia.

And nothing happened—no red flashing.

It was like . . . like something deep inside me had warned me not to set Rishia as the target. Like my heart had pumped the breaks.

It was time!

"I, the Shield Hero, borrow the strength of the Demon Dragon and the power of wrath to command the heavens, command the earth, defy all reason, join, and spit up blood. Oh great strength of the dragons, join the power of the heroes with magic, life force, and sacrifice. The source of power that is the Shield Hero commands you. Read and comprehend all that is under the sun, and show your power to me! I command you—give them everything!"

"All Sacrifice Aura!"

## Chapter Twelve: A Heavy Price to Pay

What?! Sacrifice? No! I was trying to cast "Liberation!"

There was no stopping it now. Terrifying black flames burst from the shield and engulfed Raphtalia, Filo, and I.

"Ugh . . ."

I felt my whole body burning, and I could see my HP, my life force, begin to drain away.

Strange black and red particles covered the three of us completely, producing a power from the energy it drained from us.

"What the?! But I . . ."

"It hurts! But I feel really strong now!"

All three of us felt a rush of power.

"Ha! Powder Snow!"

Raphtalia leapt forward, her blade slicing through Kyo's defensive barriers like butter. It was so easy. She didn't need a follow-up attack—only one slice.

Filo was right behind her, her claws flashing. In an instant, his barriers were all gone. He was exposed.

Then Rishia was on him. She flew at the opening and delivered a solid hit.

"What?!"

Taken off guard, he quickly threw up an arm to block her attack. He stopped the attack, but blood gushed out. His arm was broken.

"Arrgh! That really hurt! Dammit! Damn you!"

He pulled a page from the book and tried to use it to cover his open wound, thinking he could use the Spirit Tortoise energy to heal it. As if I would let him.

I ran forward, charging with my shield, bashing through the barriers he'd deployed. He'd used a skill that had taken on the form of the Spirit Tortoise's head. At contact, black flames poured from my shield, burning the head and destroying it.

Then I grabbed Kyo by the collar and used skills with my right hand.

"Attack Support! Raphtalia! Rishia! Filo!"

"Yes! Misty Moon!"

Raphtalia lowered her sword then quickly sliced upwards. The blade flashed, and a darkened, ghostly moon-like disc appeared, spinning and slicing at Kyo's torso.

Then . . .

"Hyaaa!"

Rishia dashed forward in a perfect emulation of Eclair's thrust, her short sword shining.

The sword plunged deep into Kyo's chest.

"Hey book-guy! You made the Spirit Tortoise lady cry! Book-guy, say goodbye!"

Filo swiped her claws right through Kyo's throat.

"A . . . Ah . . . ARGH?!"

Kyo was unable to speak, but it wasn't over yet!

Spirit Tortoise energy was running from the cuts and wounds all over his body. I used my shield to absorb it all.

"Not done yet!"

"That's right! Brave Blade: Mist!"

"Haikuikku!"

"I'm not finished! So many great people have died because of you! I will not forgive you!"

I still had a grip on Kyo's collar, so everyone was able to make an additional attack.

"Rafuuu!"

Poor Raph-chan. She wasn't strong enough to join in.

But she wasn't content to sit back and watch. She jumped up on my outstretched arm and started punching him in the face.

Yes! I finally had enough power to switch back to the Spirit Tortoise Shield. But it wasn't time for that. Kyo was already beaten to a bloody pulp.

"You . . . You think you can . . . I'll . . ."

"What do I care? You killed my friend Ost! You killed so many! My anger . . . *Our* anger will wipe you from existence!"

I leaned all my weight forward and threw him against the wall.

"Shield Prison! Change Shield (attack)! Iron Maiden!"

The cage of shields appeared around him and spikes appeared on the inside of the cage closing around him. Finally he was enclosed in a giant iron maiden, piercing him through in all directions.

The problem with Iron Maiden was that it used all of my SP, but with any luck it would be enough to finish him off. Truthfully, All Sacrifice Aura had basically made a drawn-out battle impossible.

". . . ?!"

Kyo's screams echoed throughout the laboratory.

Finally, the iron maiden opened and disappeared. Kyo had been stabbed all over. He tottered, and fell forward.

Ugh . . . I was in so much pain I could hardly see straight. But I couldn't fall. I couldn't let myself fall—not while the battle was still on!

"D . . . Damn . . . Not . . . over."

The punk was still alive!

He clumsily tried to heal his wounds, glaring at us as he did.

All the energy draining from him continued to stream into my shield.

Raphtalia and the others were all exhausted and out of breath.

"It's over! You haven't seen anything yet! The forbidden composition . . ."

Kyo held his book aloft—the cover had changed dramatically. It was ominous and frightful.

It must have been his equivalent of the curse series.

Damn it! If he had a stronger attack up his sleeve, we were out of options.

I had already used my strongest support magic—and the Shield of Wrath too!

I didn't know what to do—then Ost passed through my mind.

. . . That's right. She . . . she would want to finish him.

I changed to the Spirit Tortoise Heart Shield.

The indicator that only twenty percent of the necessary energy had charged up suddenly flashed and, as if it knew exactly what was going on, changed to read one hundred percent.

"My strongest attack will kill you all! Revelation!"

"Energy Blast!"

A pedestal formed from magic appeared before me. I set my shield on it and readied myself to destroy everything in my path. I fired Energy Blast!

At the same time, Kyo's book opened and creepy white feathers flew from it. They turned and danced in the air. They almost looked black depending on the angle.

Then I knew why. Every feather started firing burning, black lasers around the room.

Then many of the feathers clumped together in one spot, and all their laser beams converged to form a giant black beam that slammed into my Energy Blast beam, stopping it in midair.

Other feathers flew back to Kyo and encircled him, healing his wounds.

The skill was offensive and defensive at the same time?! It was healing his wounds and attacking us at the same time!

But judging from the way Kyo had avoided using it, and the things he'd said, I was guessing there was some risk involved on his side.

"Ahahaha! What do you think? You're greatest move is nothing compared to mine! Ahaha!"

"Damn."

Slowly, inch by inch, my Energy Blast beam was losing ground.

I focused and gave it all the power, emotion, and determination that I had—but it was still losing to Kyo's skill.

If his attack broke through Energy Blast, how was I supposed to protect Raphtalia and the others? I wasn't sure if my shield could take a direct hit from that black beam of his.

If I lost, if the beam broke through, we would all die. Rishia, Raphtalia, Raph-chan, Filo—they'd all die.

That single thought ran through my mind, and I couldn't tell how much time was passing. I was filled with a sense of inevitable loss, of losing things you can't get back.

Time slowed to a crawl, but my heart was pounding quickly in my chest.

I felt myself slipping into solitude and despair, but then I heard voices calling for me.

"Mr. Naofumi!"

"Master!"

"Naofumi-san!"

"Rafuuu!"

Everyone called for me, rushing forward to support me and keep me on my feet.

That's right. I wasn't fighting this battle alone.

And I . . . I wasn't about to lose. Not here!

There was a reason I was here, a reason I'd made it this far.

For Ost, for all those that had been sacrificed to this man's insanity . . .

And that's not all.

It was for those I couldn't save, the enemies I defeated, and the friends that fought with me.

I carried all their wishes, all their hopes with me. I had to make sure justice was served.

Just then, a light came flying though the wall and flew into my shield.

Was it the mirror vassal weapon?

Many mirrors appeared in the air around me, concentrating the Energy Blast beam.

"The mirror vassal weapon?!"

"Everyone and everything hates you! It isn't hard to see why!"

A pulse like a heartbeat thumped inside my shield. The gemstone set in its center filled with energy and began to glow.

63% . . . 61% . . . 58% . . . 62% . . . 65%.

The energy was slowly depleted before it stopped and began to rise again.

It was almost like it was reacting to my willpower.

"W . . . What?!"

98% . . . 105% . . . 110% . . . 120% . . . 130%.

As the energy level surpassed one hundred percent, the beam grew stronger and thicker, moving in pulsing waves until it began to push back Kyo's attack.

"HA! Not yet! That's not enough to beat me!"

He produced another bookmark and slid it into his book. The number of feathers dancing in the air increased, but it wasn't enough to keep up with the rapidly strengthening Energy Blast coming from my shield.

"Haaaaaaaa!"

The pedestal of light was formed of magic, so I quickly sent that energy flowing directly into the attack. Finally, the beam was powerful enough to blast through Kyo's attack.

"This is it! It's over!" I shouted, bracing my back foot and pressing the shield forward.

Raphtalia and the others stood behind me, their hands on my back, pressing me forward, supporting my weight.

"Mr. Naofumi! We're almost there!"

"You can do it!"

"This is it! We can do it! For Ost-san!" Rishia steadied her footing and launched her short sword at Kyo.

The shining blade flew beside the Energy Blast beam, absorbing its light. The blade was unharmed. In fact, it seemed imbued with new and furious power.

The shining blade sliced through the remaining black light from Kyo's attack before plunging deep into his chest.

The whole sequence reminded me of the battle we'd already fought with Kyo—the one in the Spirit Tortoise Core chamber.

But there was one important difference.

That time, Rishia had thrown her sword to save another hero. This time, she threw it to defeat Kyo.

"Cough! Ugh! You bitch!"

I didn't have time to see how the blade had hit him, how it had hurt him, because at that same moment the energy blast completely overpowered his attack and burst through.

He was engulfed in crackling light. It burned and scorched.

"Gyaaaaa!"

His skill was washed away in a torrent of light. Our attack—and Ost's too—pierced through his heart.

The beam blasted a hole through the wall that led outside.

Kyo stood before it. Clutching his stomach, he fell to the ground, battered and beaten.

He was a stubborn bastard. I wished the Energy Blast had just vaporized him.

"If he tries so heal himself, what are we supposed to do?"

Rishia stalked over to him and used the handle of her sword to roll him over.

"Ugh . . . you . . . Kill you all . . ."

It didn't look like he'd be getting up anytime soon.

Still, I was shocked he was still alive after taking a hit like that.

But he was haggard, and seemed to be hanging on by a thread. He coughed up blood, and his breath was heavy and weak.

He'd die soon.

"Time to repent. Any last words?"

"Who's . . . dying? It's just . . . because . . ."

He didn't finish his sentence before he died.

Suddenly the gravity field grew lighter.

It left a bad taste in my mouth—watching someone die.

But knowing justice had been served helped lessen my feelings of guilt.

"I suppose this means we've won."

"I suppose so."

But the energy he stole from the Spirit Tortoise hadn't returned yet.

Had we wasted it? Had it been used up in the battle?

I looked at the book of the vassal weapons.

It rose softly into the air. I thought it would fly off, but it didn't.

Instead it shot over to the area where Kyo had originally appeared.

"Rafuu! Rafuuuuuu!" Raph-chan was barking and pointing desperately at the book, trying to indicate its destination.

"Filo, turn back into your filolial form and stomp that whole area flat!"

"Okay!" she shouted, transforming in to her filolial form and dashing forward to cut off the book.

I chased after them both. That's when I figured out what all the fuss was about soon enough.

There was a tank jutting from the floor, and inside it was . . . Kyo's body.

There was no way to tell if we'd been fighting a homunculus this whole time, or if that person had been real and this person in the tank was a homunculus.

But one thing was certain: it was being used for experiments to turn the body into a vessel for the power of the Spirit Tortoise.

"Well, well . . ." I switched to the Shield of Wrath, summoned a blaze of black flames, and snatched the book out of the air. "Look at that. Who knows if this is the real Kyo, or if we just defeated the real Kyo. But I know one thing for sure: I don't plan on sticking around to see if this thing reanimates and starts that whole battle all over again."

Raph-chan was barking and pointing, like she could see Kyo's soul.

"Rafu," she chirped, jumping up onto my shoulder and placing her paw on my head.

I could see something. Whatever remnant of his soul that was stored in the book was floating out from its pages and toward the body in the tank. It looked like a ghostly thread floating on the air.

It slowly changed to resemble a person, but it didn't look anything like Kyo. It looked like a skinny man in his thirties. Is that what his soul looked like?

"Ahaha! You think I'd be defeated so easily? Just you wait! This body is filled with the power of the Spirit Tortoise, and once I join with it, you're all as good as dead! I'm invincible!"

It sure sounded like Kyo.

The soul is a mirror for the heart—I guess.

"Rishia!"

"Y . . . Yes!"

"Throw an ofuda at that thing, the one you got from Kizuna!" I shouted, pointing at the tank with Kyo's body inside. The soul was just before it, reaching out its ghostly hand desperately to touch it.

"Kyo! I won't let you forget what you did to Tsugumi and the other women, what you did to Albert. Have you forgotten?"

Kyo turned around and his face was pale.

He had figured out what I was planning.

"W . . . Wait! I swear! I'll let you live if you help me! Let's talk this over!"

"It's too late for that. I'm tired of dealing with you. Here's what you would say in my shoes, 'You idiot! Why would you believe that? Everyone lies when they are begging for their lives!'"

"Ha!" Rishia threw the ofuda and activated it.

It was a control ofuda, and we'd already imbued it with a monster. Back in the previous world we called it a Soul Eater.

In this world, they called it a Soul Devourer.

It was the natural enemy of spirits—a monster that fed on souls.

When I thought of Trash #2's behavior, the concept of homunculi, and that an alchemist could invent spare bodies to be killed, I prepared the ofuda. I had thought, I bet Kyo would make things like that. And I was right!

"Are you kidding me? A dumb monster like that? You think that thing can defeat me?"

The evil spirit—Kyo's ghost—flew to attack us.

I could see it clearly now. He was nothing but a monster.

"Raphtalia, I don't know if the vassal weapon will be much use against an enemy with no body."

"Excellent point. Then I will use a skill, along with the katana I gained from the Soul Eater materials."

Kyo floated to attack, but he was too slow. I grabbed him, and a pale light flashed from the katana in Raphtalia's hand.

"Spirit Blade: Soul Slice!"

Sacrifice Aura was still affecting her.

A ghost attack was nothing to worry about. He was just another weakling.

"Cough! I . . . I'll return. Reborn! Stronger than . . ."

He fell to pieces before he could finish his threat, and the Soul Eaters that Rishia had summoned rushed in for their meal.

The sounds of their chewing and crunching echoed through the room, before they dispersed, satisfied, and floated around us.

He died talking about reincarnation. What a joke.

"Now to take care of this soulless body. If we destroy it, the Spirit Tortoise energy should return to us. "

"Let's do it!"

"You can do it!"

"Feh . . ."

Uh-oh. Now that the battle was over Rishia sounded just like her old self again.

I was exhausted, and I knew I couldn't continue to use the Shield of Wrath IV. I needed to get my strength back, so I switched to the Spirit Tortoise Heart Shield and shouted: "Raphtalia! Filo! Destroy everything!"

They nodded, reared back, and ran around breaking everything they could.

His research was gone. No one would be able to recreate it now.

"Ost. I kept my promise," I whispered, remembering her.

## Epilogue: Kizuna Between Worlds

When we killed Kyo and destroyed the body in the tank that was housing the Spirit Tortoise's energy, the energy burst free and went into my shield. It took a while for all the energy to make its way into the shield, but it did eventually.

In the meantime, it looked like Kizuna and the others must have finished the battle with the wave, because our levels returned to the way they were before.

The crystal in the center of the shield was now glowing so brightly that it was blinding.

**Duty fulfilled. Spirit Tortoise energy recovered.**
**Time remaining for special processing to complete repatriation . . . 71:55.**

The words appeared before my eyes.

I guess it really was over.

Now that the Spirit Tortoise energy had been recovered, we could only remain in this world for three more days.

When the time ran out, I guess it meant we would be sent back to the previous world automatically.

"Alright then, we'd better get going."

"Right."

"I'm tiiiired!"

Everyone seemed to grow even more exhausted at the thought of all the effort it would take to get back to the castle.

"Everyone, what happened?"

"It's the curse. You'd better not touch us."

Maybe I was being a little over-dramatic, but using Sacrifice Aura really had lowered all our stats significantly.

Luckily for me, the curse didn't touch my defense rating—but all my other stats had fallen. Judging from the numbers, they seem to have fallen to about thirty percent.

Had it only affected me, it would have been the same as Blood Sacrifice, but this time it had affected Raphtalia and Filo too. With how things were, I didn't think we could survive another fight.

"There're monsters on the way home, aren't there?"

"Yeah . . . there are."

And I didn't want to meet them. What if we came all this way, only to die on the way home?

Maybe it would be better to stay where we were until we felt better.

I didn't have time to worry about that though, because I suddenly found the book and mirror vassal weapons floating in the air near us. It looked like . . . well, it almost looked like they were thanking us.

They'd either fly off to find new masters, or stick themselves somewhere and wait for someone worthy to appear, like Excalibur had done.

They floated softly out of the room, stopping and turning to us, as if they were trying to show us the way. Sometimes they would float in front of a doorway and block us from passing through it—but why?

Luckily, we didn't run into any of Kyo's holy beast copies.

We slowly made our way up from the basement and back down the path we'd used to enter the laboratory.

"Can you use Portal Shield?"

I tried to use it, but it was still being blocked by something.

Wandering around and drawing attention to ourselves wasn't smart, so we took our time, moving cautiously. Probably two hours or so had passed when we entered a room with a mirror on the wall. The mirror vassal weapon floated into it and disappeared.

A second later . . .

"N . . . Naofumi!"

Kizuna and the others all stepped out of the mirror.

What had just happened? Had it flown to where they were and brought them to us?

"This mirror just appeared in front of us and . . . Is that Kyo's laboratory? What happened to Kyo?!"

"If we'd lost, you'd probably be fighting him now, no?"

"I guess that's a good point. Are you okay? You all look exhausted."

"We used the forbidden technique, and the price we paid wiped us out. Don't make me explain it all."

"Are you alright?"

"Not really. Our stats have plummeted. It's kind of serious. We were just thinking of sticking around and recuperating. Without your help, I'm not sure we can do much else."

L'Arc reached out and slipped an arm under my shoulder, supporting me.

Therese and Glass were helping Raphtalia.

Filo was a bit shorter, so Kizuna and Ethnobalt helped her stay on her feet.

"You did good, Kiddo. You beat Kyo without our help."

"The freak had tons of tricks up his sleeve. It was a pain."

Yomogi spoke up next, softly, "What about Kyo?"

"He's back in that room, dead. We killed his soul too—the guy had a backup body prepared."

"Is that so? I wish it had been by my hand, but thank you."

The book of the vassal weapons flew around the perimeter of the room once, then slipped through the wall and disappeared.

"It looks like the book and the mirror of the vassal weapons protected you until we were able to meet up."

Glass nodded. I couldn't argue with that. We hadn't met any monsters and the mirror had brought our friends directly to us.

"Yeah, I guess they did. We didn't run into any of the holy beast copies—or fall into any of Kyo's stupid booby traps."

"That mist that barred our entry seems to have dissipated as well. That's why we were able to get here so quickly."

The vassal weapons had been a huge help. I guess it was them showing us their thanks for releasing them from Kyo's control. Those vassal weapons sure knew how to treat a guy right, unlike a certain shield I knew of.

"Let's head home. I'm guessing you still have some time in our world, since you completed your mission?"

"Yeah. About three days."

"Three days, huh? Guess we'll have to say our goodbyes pretty soon, eh Kiddo?"

"I guess so."

"I'm not sure this is the best place to have this conversation. Why don't we board my ship and leave this place?" Ethnobalt said, tapping his staff on the floor.

I guess the guy had managed to stay alive. Even after pulling one of those "don't worry about me! Go on without me!" stunts.

It's better that he didn't die, right? Whatever. I wasn't about to disagree with getting back to the castle as soon as possible.

All I wanted to do was get some rest.

It had been one fight after another for so long now.

I didn't even know where to start counting the battles I'd

been in since we crossed over to this world.

We quickly climbed into Ethnobalt's ship and returned to safety.

Once we landed, the mirror of the vassal weapons took off, flying away.

Was it looking for a new master? Or would it stick itself in a boulder like Excalibur, awaiting someone worthy?

As for the country that Kyo had manipulated into war, Yomogi went back to meet with their leaders that very same day and exposed all of Kyo's misdeeds. As proof she brought Tsugumi and the other women with her. On top of that, the book of the vassal weapons itself appeared in the capital and played back recordings of all the words Kyo had exchanged with us.

Furthermore, when they lost Kyo, they lost a great deal of their technology too. Apparently, the main force of their army was Kyo's holy beast copies. They all went crazy when Kyo died. The war was essentially over at that point. They were at a disadvantage. But when Kyo's most trusted follower, Yomogi, showed up and started telling them all the evil things he'd done, there wasn't much left for them to say.

The rest of this is hearsay, but when the country lost their puppet leader, the remaining officials all thought it was their chance to seize leadership, and the whole place fell into chaos.

The three countries that had once owned the book, mirror,

and katana vassal weapons were all in disarray. But it if I knew Kizuna and her friends, it wasn't hard to picture those countries eventually joining with L'Arc's in a healing alliance.

But enough about all that trouble—what about our curse?

L'Arc summoned a specialized doctor to have a look at us, and here's what he said:

"That's a pretty bad curse."

I think someone had said the same thing about me after I used Blood Sacrifice.

When I got back to our world, I'd have to go to some medicinal baths as soon as . . .

"The only thing that will cure it is time. I estimate it will take at least two or three months."

"What? Hold on there! Isn't there a hot spring for this kind of thing? Or some medicine I can use?"

The doctor simply shook his head.

"This is a rather particular sort of curse. Furthermore, if it were to be applied again before you fully recovered, I'm not sure that you would survive the ordeal."

WHAT?!

That wasn't the sort of souvenir I wanted to take home after all this!

To make matters worse, this time it wasn't just me: Raphtalia and Filo were cursed too, and they were very sluggish.

In hindsight, I'm glad I didn't use it on Rishia. I didn't want to think about what would have happened to her.

She probably would have died! Whatever made me stop before using it on her, I was impressed.

"Oh no! I guess there's nothing we can do about it now, but what a pain," Kizuna said, like she wasn't actually worried.

Ha! This all should have been HER responsibility in the first place!

Oh well. I knew the risks when I used it.

"This is the result of availing yourself of the cursed weapon—and to think that you took this burden on yourself for the sake of our world. I cannot begin to express my gratitude," Glass said.

"You can start by not letting this happen again. There are still three protective beasts in our world. The last thing I want is another Kyo showing up and causing trouble."

"Naturally, Kizuna and I will fight to make sure this never happens again."

"Definitely. But you know, Kiddo, I'm sure things will settle down for a while once you return the Spirit Tortoise energy to your world."

"You think?"

L'Arc nodded.

"Yeah, at least that's how it was for us. When the first protective beast fell, there was a while where no waves came."

"Things won't go so smoothly if vassal weapon holders invade our world before I get back."

Why did there always have to be something to worry about?

"Relax. No waves means no visitors from other worlds, so you'll have a lot less to worry about."

There were still plenty of things to worry about, but at least I could count on the people back in Melromarc to be on the lookout.

The queen of Melromarc would have spread the word about the Spirit Tortoise's possession while I was occupied with Kyo in this world.

"So the Spirit Tortoise is done. I'm just guessing, but that leaves the Phoenix, Qilin, and Dragon. I guess we won't have any problems until those seals are broken too."

"Probably. Not that I'm an authority on how your world works, Kiddo."

That was a good point. Why did I bother asking them anything about our world?

"I guess I'll just keep hoping that another Kyo doesn't show up."

I had no idea how long the Spirit Tortoise energy would keep the waves at bay.

But there were a lot of preparations that we needed to get under way while we could.

We'd have to collect the world's armies and find new allies.

I learned a lot of new tactics to counter the threat of the waves during my time in Glass's world.

I would have to make sure they were put to good use.

Fitoria was doing all she could to handle the waves that we couldn't cover on our own, but if we wanted to survive what was coming, we'd have to find some way to get the world to cooperate.

Just thinking about everything we had to do was depressing.

And worse—we might run into more people like Glass during the wave.

I couldn't wait to get back to my original world once all this was over—that much would never change.

The world to which I was summoned was trash, a pile of filth. I couldn't wait to leave it—that is, once I remade it so that Raphtalia could live there in peace.

"Sounds good to me, Kiddo! Time for a victory party!" L'Arc said, throwing his hands in the air like a little kid.

"This guy . . ." I sighed.

"What? What's the problem? Didn't we just win a battle? Didn't we just win a war? What's not to celebrate?"

"Rafuuu!" Raph-chan jumped up on her hind legs and tried to look cute.

I couldn't argue with that.

"Fine, fine. You'll do what you want anyway, so I won't complain. I'm going to get some rest."

"Yeah! The soldiers are in the mood for a party too. It's going to be wild!" L'Arc howled and left.

Whew.

We spent the rest of our time with Kizuna and her friends, drinking the sweet liquor of victory. Actually that's just an expression—I've never been drunk.

It was nearly time to return to our world.

We made our preparations down in the castle courtyard, and Kizuna, Glass, L'Arc and Therese, Ethnobalt, Alto, Romina, and everyone else came to see us off.

Kizuna threw her hand in the air and came walking over.

"I guess a lot has happened since we met."

"It's only been a month or so."

"Is that all? I guess it was pretty short."

"I guess so."

A holy hero from another world was someone I never should have been able to meet, because of the limitations imposed by our weapons. In a way, it was kind of miracle that we'd met at all.

"I know we live in separate worlds, but I hope we can keep fighting on the same side. I wish we could form an alliance between our worlds."

"Yeah, yeah. Don't spend all your time fishing, okay? As for your alliance, consider it a verbal agreement. I don't have any reason to break it."

All I could do was protect people, after all.

The things we'd learned in this world shook the mystery of the waves to the very core.

What was I supposed to make of all we'd heard? About one world extending its lifespan by destroying another world?

"And you open up a little, okay? You can trust people you know."

"Oh shut up!"

"Raphtalia, please take good care of Naofumi. Just like Glass and I, I hope you'll keep him close."

"Yes, I intend to."

"Filo, Rishia. I wish you both the best."

"Yup! I learned a bunch of songs here, so Imma keep singing them when we get back home!"

"Yes, I learned a great deal."

Kizuna shook their hands and stepped away.

Glass came next.

"First we were enemies, then we became friends. Life can be so mysterious."

"Sure."

Glass looked at me very seriously, then bowed.

"Thank you very much for finding Kizuna. I do not know what awaits us in the future, but I will do what I can to return the favor."

"If you have to fight us, next time stop and explain yourself."

"Is that really what you wanted to say?" Raphtalia scolded me.

"Things can change so quickly. Why keep fighting in the face of ignorance? I'm just saying that if we have to fight, I at least want to know what I'm fighting for."

There were so many times that I'd fallen into situations I couldn't believe. L'Arc and Therese came charging into the conversation, the adventurer, Boy, as cheerful as ever.

"Anyway, let's stay friends, eh Kiddo? I can't wait to see you again!"

"I can wait. I hope it never happens."

If it did happen, it would be in the middle of a wave or some other horrible event.

We had to stop the waves. I didn't want L'Arc sitting around looking forward to them.

Therese sighed, "The gemstones you made for me are sad to see you go."

She was all decked out in the accessories I'd made for her, and they were all shining in the sun. She looked ridiculous! It was so bright! Stop flashing those things at me!

"L'Arc . . ."

L'Arc nodded gravely.

"I will. If I don't, Therese is likely to escape to your world the next time a wave comes."

"I don't think she's that cold."

I swear, this guy's girlfriend was really annoying.

Granted, she had helped us out plenty of times.

"Ms. Raphtalia, Filo, Ms. Rishia . . . I wish you all well."

"Likewise. Please stay well," Raphtalia replied.

"That reminds me . . . Boy."

"You still calling me that, Kiddo?"

"You're always talking about Raphtalia and the women as if they are little girls—did you ever notice that?"

"I guess you've got a point there."

Kizuna nodded.

"Alright already! Geez! What can I say, I don't like calling people younger than me by their names, alright? There're so many girls around here that it just makes it easier to call them the same thing! What's the problem with that?"

I kind of did have a problem with it, actually—but it wasn't worth fighting over.

"Besides, you're one to talk, Kiddo! You're always coming up with crazy nicknames for people!"

"So are you."

"Yeah, yeah, well . . ."

"You finally understand, don't you, L'Arc," Ethnobalt said, floating over. "Thank you for everything. For all you did for Kizuna, Glass, L'Arc, and Therese."

I couldn't shake the feeling that he was acting a bit familiar with me. Was it my imagination? No. He was an attractive boy that was actually a giant rabbit. Just like Fitoria, he acted like we'd known each other for a long time.

Filo ran over and clung to me, and Raph-chan hopped up onto my shoulder.

"Muuuu!"

"Don't worry, Ms. Filo. It's nothing like that," Ethnobalt said, smiling softly.

This guy looked like your typical scholar-type.

Maybe he had true powers, like Fitoria, but different, that he'd awaken to soon.

"I won't waste the experience that I earned while fighting with you."

"I hope not. Good luck."

He turned to Rishia next, "Ms. Rishia, I've heard about your amazing deeds in the recent battle. I will work hard to become more like you."

"Feh . . ." she muttered and her face flushed red with embarrassment. She probably wasn't used to getting compliments like that.

"Please take this book I found in the labyrinth library. I pray that it will be of use to you."

"Okay! Thank you!"

If I knew Rishia, she'd figure out how to read it.

"And . . ." he said, reaching out and taking off a small anchor-like accessory that was attached to the ship vassal weapon, passing it to me.

"What's this?"

"This accessory was described in a book I found recently. Please take it with you. I think it will prove . . . useful."

"Oh . . ."

If he was giving it away, there was no reason not to take it.

"If it's being offered, you'll take it, no? You're a merchant, after all."

"Good point. But if I get going on that, you'll never get me to shut up."

"Excuse me. Mr. Naofumi is not a merchant. He is a hero," Raphtalia corrected Romina and Alto.

"Anyway, take this too—a going away present if you will," Romina said handing me a bag. It was heavy, and seemed to have all kinds of different things in it.

I took a peek inside and saw that it contained accessories with this world's special technologies, such as emulated drop item functions and wave-site-teleporting.

There was a bunch of other stuff too.

These things didn't even exist back in our world—they were sure to come in handy.

"I know you threw some other things in there too."

I guess Romina had me all figured out.

As for Alto, if he smiled and gave me something, I would feel weird about it.

"You seem to think I'm some kind of miser—but you're wrong about that."

"Liar."

"Yeah, that's a lie," Kizuna and Glass both chimed in.

But Alto didn't back down.

"I was able to make a pretty profit with all the crazy things you've been up to. This is in thanks for that."

"Ah, so that's what you meant."

He was like the slave-trader back in Melromarc. He'd eventually seen increased profits because of me. Alto had a reputation for being a miserly merchant, and it seemed to me that he'd earned that reputation.

"Ah, that's right. Glass—"

I had a book of recipes written in Japanese. I gave it to Glass.

"What is this?"

"I wrote up a collection of recipes that you should be able to follow with the tools and ingredients you've got in this world. Have Kizuna read it to you."

You see, I hadn't just been wandering around randomly in a world I couldn't understand. A lot of the language in my status menu was garbled when we crossed between worlds, so I'd been taking meticulous notes on what effects had stopped working, and about the differences between the items we collected.

Things that I couldn't make in this world, because the necessary materials didn't exist tended to show up garbled.

But we could use soul-healing water just like normal, and I could read it too.

That meant you could make it with materials from this world.

We were going to face tougher battles in the future. She'd need to drink soul-healing water like normal water. So I wrote down the recipe for it.

"This should do the same thing. Try it out."

"Wow! You're pretty impressive, Naofumi."

"You could be too if you ever did anything besides fishing. But actually, you need fish to make that recipe, so she'll need your help with that."

To make the medicine that worked like soul-healing water from materials available in their world, they'd need a certain type of rare fish.

I'd found it by accident while analyzing a catch that Kizuna had been particularly proud of.

"Thanks! I'll do what I can!"

"Don't let this world's other holy heroes die or anything."

"Oh . . . right. Yeah, we'll do what we can."

We both had problems with our fellow holy heroes, so I knew how she felt. We shook hands.

"And watch out for Alto."

He was sharp alright.

Who was left? Oh— Yomogi, Tsugumi, and the other women.

"Kyo did terrible things. Leave the rest to us."

"Say that to Kizuna too. I made him pay for his crimes and his helper too. I even killed their souls."

"Yeah." Tsugumi said. She looked like she still harbored negative feelings about me, but it wasn't as bad as it had been. "If you all hadn't come, this never would have happened."

"We won't be back—feel free to hate us all you like."

What was with her? Did she come just to whine about us?"

"... Yet, you also saved us all. Thank you for setting———free. Kyo used him even after his death. Thank you."

A wind blew through at just the wrong time, and—once again—I couldn't catch Trash #2's name. I decided to give up on trying to figure out what it was. Tsugumi would probably just get mad if I asked again. And besides, I probably wouldn't catch it. I decided to just ask Raphtalia about it some other day.

"I wonder if we'll ever know why he was so obsessed with the katana of the vassal weapons."

"Hey that reminds me. Did you say that there were some Spirits in your group that went missing?"

" . . . "

Tsugumi said nothing, but nodded.

Some of their bodies had been found in a basement room of Kyo's mansion.

Apparently Kyo had taken Trash #2's soul from his body and used it to feed soul eaters.

The Spirits that had followed him around learned of the truth and were all killed for it.

So many people had died. Including Albert, the holder of the mirror vassal weapon, who met the same fate as the rest of them.

"The katana was essential to the wellbeing of the country. But there's no way for us to know why he was so confident that it would choose him to wield it."

Raphtalia drew the sword, then held it horizontally out to Kizuna and the others.

"I return this vassal weapon to you."

Right, I guess she didn't have a choice. Even if it had chosen her, we couldn't take this world's vassal weapons with us.

We owed the weapon a lot though. It had helped us when we needed it most.

"It doesn't look like it wants to leave you."

"And for some reason, it didn't summon her when the wave occurred."

Glass and Therese, who was a Jewel, touched the blade and spoke to it, but it didn't respond to them.

Kizuna touched it too, and nothing happened.

"It's no use. It's hard to explain, but it has a sense of duty to her, and it seemed to have complex emotions. It will not answer to us."

"Do you know what it wants? Is its will clear?"

"We only have a vague sense of its intention."

Hmm . . . Did it mean that Raphtalia was going to be able to take it back to the previous world with her?

"Perhaps it feels responsible for Kyo's actions against your world. Perhaps it wants to fight for the sake of your world—at least until this world really needs it," Kizuna said.

The katana shimmered with light in response.

"Looks like Kizuna might be right."

"Hm . . ."

We talked about a lot of things, but we were running out of time.

Soon enough, we'd run out of time all together.

"Alright!" I barked, smiling wickedly. "We'll take the katana vassal weapon with us then! You all can just wish you had it!"

"Aww, Naofumi's pretending to be a bad guy again."

"Kiddo's always doing that."

"He's actually a really good person."

Kizuna and her friends sighed as they analyzed me.

Raphtalia just shook her head. Filo looked confused.

Rishia was looking all around in nervous twitches. Raph-chan jumped up onto my shoulder and waved goodbye to everyone.

"I guess it's really time to say goodbye."

There were only a few more seconds on the timer.

When it ran out, we'd be summoned back to our world automatically.

"Our weapons will probably keep us from seeing you again, but we had an alright time while it lasted. Later."

"Yeah, goodbye. Naofumi, thank you for helping me. If you hadn't shown up, I'd still be trapped in that labyrinth. We'll be in different worlds, but we're heroes on the same side."

We were all waving goodbye now.

"Naofumi!" L'Arc shouted, loud and clear.

They all waved and shouted together in unison: "Thank you!"

Their words echoed in my ears, but before we could answer the counter ran out, and we were transported back to our world.

We passed through a tunnel with a strange light on the way, but it was over in a flash.

—And we were back in the world we came from.

# Character Design:
## Yomogi

ヨモギ

# Character Design: Altorese

アルトレーゼ

The Rising of the Shield Hero Vol. 9
© Aneko Yusagi 2015
First published by KADOKAWA in 2015 in Japan.
English translation rights arranged by One Peace Books
under the license from KADOKAWA CORPORATION, Japan

ISBN: 978-1-944937-25-6

Written by Aneko Yusagi
Character Design Minami Seira
English Edition Published by One Peace Books 2017

Printed in Canada

6 7 8 9 10

One Peace Books
43-32 22nd Street STE 204 Long Island City New York 11101
www.onepeacebooks.com